Books of Merit

UNDERGROUND

A NOVEL

UNDERGROUND

Antanas Sileika

THOMAS ALLEN PUBLISHERS
TORONTO

Library and Archives Canada Cataloguing in Publication

Sileika, Antanas, 1953–
    Underground / Antanas Sileika.

ISBN 978-0-88762-736-1

I. Title.

PS8587.I2656U53 2011   C813'.54   C2010-907342-8

Editor: Janice Zawerbny
Jacket design: Michel Vrána
Jacket photo: Snaige Sileika

Published by Thomas Allen Publishers,
a division of Thomas Allen & Son Limited,
390 Steelcase Road East
Markham, Ontario L3R 1G2 Canada

www.thomasallen.ca

ONTARIO ARTS COUNCIL
CONSEIL DES ARTS DE L'ONTARIO

Canada Council
for the Arts

The publisher gratefully acknowledges the support of
The Ontario Arts Council for its publishing program.

We acknowledge the support of the Canada Council for the Arts, which
last year invested $20.1 million in writing and publishing throughout Canada.

We acknowledge the Government of Ontario through the
Ontario Media Development Corporation's Ontario Book Initiative.

We acknowledge the financial support of the Government of Canada
through the Canada Book Fund for our publishing activities.

1 2 3 4 5   15 14 13 12 11

Printed and Bound in Canada by Transcontinental Printing
Text Printed on a 100% PCW recycled stock.

There was, I knew, blood beneath the verdure and tombs in the deep glades of oak and fir. The fields and forests and rivers had seen war and terror, elation and desperation; death and resurrection; Lithuanian kings and Teutonic knights, partisans and Jews; Nazi Gestapo and Stalinist NKVD. It is a haunted land where greatcoat buttons from six generations of fallen soldiers can be discovered lying amidst the woodland ferns.

— SIMON SCHAMA, *Landscape and Memory*

For the six generations

PART ONE

*A*N ILL-DEFINED BORDERLINE wavers somewhere around the middle of Europe; its precise location has not been stable over the decades. At present, on the far side of this boundary, the Eastern side, lies a zone where beer and hotels are cheaper than they are in the West, and so planeloads of young men travel there to drink, far from the eyes of wives and girlfriends. Indiscretions, transgressions and sometimes even crimes committed on the far side of this line don't really count.

Once, the line was a metaphor called the Iron Curtain, and before that it followed a jagged course along the borders of countries freed from the Hapsburg and Czarist empires. Like the mythical town of Brigadoon, these countries appeared for only a short time between the wars, before they disappeared from memory for fifty years in 1940.

What followed was *such* a confusing war on that side of Europe! The war was much easier to understand in the West, where the forces of more or less good triumphed in May 1945. On the Eastern side, on the other hand, the messy side, the war sputtered on in pockets for another decade, fought by partisans who came out of their secret bunkers by night.

When that fighting finally ended, sullen resistance went more deeply underground, to be nurtured in memory, as well as buried in hidden archives below the earth or left to moulder in the files of the secret police, called the Cheka, where no one was ever likely to look. Aboveground lay a series of police states.

This place was somewhat quaint, yet so much more brutal than the West. It was a place where generations were mown down as soon as they were tall enough to meet the scythe. And yet many lives went on in their own way, even during the worst of the fighting.

On a cold, snowy April evening in 1946, in the Lithuanian provincial capital of Marijampole, an engagement party was taking place on the second storey of a wooden house with four flats, a house not far from the exquisite train station, where railway cars of goods and captives rumbled by eastward with great frequency.

When Lukas walked into the kitchen to get another bottle of vodka late that night, he found Elena with her back to him, leaning over the counter, her curly brown hair loose. He could see the tension in her shoulders, squared and stiff, as if braced for a blow. After a moment she turned and looked at him.

Elena's brown eyes were very large, a little moist from the cigarette smoke in the flat. She wore a dark grey wool suit, her work clothes, with a natural linen blouse beneath the jacket and an amber pendant on a silver chain.

Behind her on the white ceramic counter lay two massive loaves of black bread, one of them almost finished, a large dish of herring and onions, the remains of a cooked goose, a ham and a string of sausages. Elena had worked hard to get her hands on so much food, rare in these postwar years, and the scent of it had helped to bring the seven distinguished guests.

The accordionist in the next room was playing a jaunty dance version of "J'ai Deux Amours," a tune that Elena remembered from before the war. Her mother and father had danced to the recording in their house, the French doors open to the garden. It had been an anniversary or a name day, she couldn't remember which.

It didn't matter. Her mother was dead, her father gone, the house destroyed.

Looking into her eyes, Lukas realized he should comfort Elena, but he was not feeling altogether calm at their engagement party either. He was sweating profusely. He was slim and fair and wore a threadbare two-piece suit with a jacket that was a little too long for him, as well as a sweater vest mended at the collar and a red tie and puff. On reflection, he realized these adornments were a little exaggerated, almost provocative, but there was no way to remove them once the guests had seen them.

Lukas was unaccustomed to being inside a flat with so many people, unaccustomed to the niceties of conversation, of saying one thing and meaning another. He found it hard to keep his feelings buried, and the struggle was showing, but he needed above all to support Elena.

Lukas glanced at the engagement ring on her hand. It was a very thin gold band with a tiny red stone, not much better than a high school girl's first ring, but the best he could do. There wasn't much jewellery around, and those who had it didn't show it.

Elena flinched as he put his hands around her neck and looked into her eyes. "We don't have to go through with this if you can't do it," he said. "Nobody would blame you."

"Not even you?"

"Especially not me."

"It's been a very short engagement, after all," said Elena.

She was joking. A good sign. "A whirlwind romance," he agreed. He left his hands where they were, around her neck. He wanted to kiss her but felt awkward, didn't know if that was permitted now.

Lukas heard the kitchen door open and he pressed into Elena, his middle tight against hers as if they were making love. He kissed her, the pressure of her lips obliterating all other thoughts for a moment.

"I wondered where you two were," a voice said. "There'll be plenty of time for kisses later. Get back in here."

Gedrius was the district chairman, the first to have arrived that
evening and therefore the drunkest of them all. He'd taken off his
jacket and loosened his tie, and his shirttails now hung out at the
back. He had stained his shirt and talked much too much, but he
was affable, almost lovable in his own way, or anyway, better than
the rest. Gedrius and the others came from a different world, one
of documents and rubber stamps, boardrooms and meetings, dust
and sheaves of paper pinned together. Not like Lukas's world at all.

To fortify Lukas's stomach against the drink, Elena had served
him half a glass of cooking oil before the evening began. It had
made him gag at the time, but now he was holding up better against
the vodka than he had expected. Maybe too well. He couldn't feel
the alcohol at all.

Elena shook out her curls and brushed her fingers through her
hair, and then linked hands with Lukas. "Give us a moment and
we'll be right out."

"All right, but don't delay too much. Everyone's dying to spend
a little time with you."

As Gedrius stepped back, Lukas could see briefly into the other
room, where the two beds had been pushed aside to make a small
dance floor beyond the dining table. The others were dancing in the
dimly lit room: Elena's roommate with the director of the Komsomol, and her sister, Stase, with the city chairman. Two candles lit the
dining table because the electricity went off at ten each night. Vinskis
kept wanting to talk to Gedrius about some internal passports stolen
from the office where he worked, and he took the man by the arm as
soon as he stepped out of the kitchen.

"You're a bundle of nerves too," said Elena. "Call it off. We can
cool down for a while and try this again later."

"I wish I could call it off, but I can't. It's too late. Did you see the
look he gave me when he walked into the kitchen?"

"I didn't see anything. What are you talking about?"

"Vinskis suspects me. He must have said something to Gedrius."

"Do you want to get out of here?"

"Vinskis and Gedrius are by the door."

"Say you're going to the toilet."

"They might not let me pass. Do you want to wait in here?"

"No, I promised I'd help you. I'm going with you." Her willingness made him feel warm toward her, but the emotion was brief. He had other things on his mind now.

"Do you have your handbag?" asked Lukas.

"Under the table." Elena reached beneath the table and withdrew her bag. Inside the other room, the accordionist started up another tune. "Be careful of my sister."

Lukas nodded and reached into his pockets. He held the Walther PP in his right hand because it was heavier and had eight rounds. The lighter PPK with seven rounds was in his left. Elena had one in her handbag as well.

When Elena opened the kitchen door for him, Lukas strode out with his arms extended and turned first to face Vinskis and Gedrius because they were standing and their own pistols would be easy to get to, whereas the men sitting at the table would need to rise first. Lukas fired at Vinskis, two shots to the neck, and the man's head rolled onto his chest as he collapsed. Gedrius, for all his drunkenness, had his own pistol halfway out of his pocket when Lukas fired at him. The man went down.

The accordionist stopped playing and stared at them, but Elena's roommate was more cool-headed and leaned forward to blow out one of the candles. The other two men were rising from their chairs.

Lukas fired with his left hand, but his shots went wild. Elena killed them for him. Her roommate opened her mouth to say something, but Lukas did not want to hear it. He fired once at her forehead and she went down too.

"Let's go," said Elena.

"Wait."

Lukas went toward Elena's sister, Stase, who had fallen from her chair and pulled herself to a wall, where she stared at them with terrified eyes. Lukas crouched down to look her in the face.

"I have to do this for your own good," he said. Lukas had to act quickly before Elena intervened.

Stase's lower lip was trembling and her eyes were wild with fear. Lukas stepped back and took aim at her. If he was too close, he might leave powder burns. If he stood too far away, he might miss in either direction.

Stase shut her eyes as Lukas fired, and then she yelped with pain and the blood came down her arm. Lukas turned quickly to face Elena before she could shoot him, which she might do if she misunderstood.

"Stase has to be wounded or the Chekists will say she was part of this all along," said Lukas.

"Why didn't you tell me this before?"

"I couldn't. It was too dangerous."

Elena's face was flushed. The room was filled with blood, splatters up on the wall, pools on the floor among the wreckage of bodies and overturned chairs.

Elena dropped her hand with the pistol in it and crouched down beside Stase. "I'm sorry I couldn't tell you. When the Chekists come, you can honestly say you didn't know anything. They'll let you go."

"You've turned into a monster. I don't even know who you are."

There was no time. As Elena stood up, the accordionist, wounded in the throat by a ricochet, struggled up from his chair and charged out the door with the accordion still on his shoulders. The instrument squawked like a frightened animal all the way down the staircase. The Komsomol director began to stir from where he had fallen beneath the table, tried to rise, and Lukas fired another shot into him.

The neighbours would soon overcome their terror and go to the militia. Lukas and Elena put on their coats, closed the door behind them, and walked down the steps and out onto the street. It was snowing. There was a sleigh for them a few blocks away, near the train station.

The streets were empty and profoundly silent. If a militiaman passed by, he would be sure to ask them for their documents just for something to do. Elena tried to pick up her pace, but Lukas held her back slightly so they would not seem to be rushing.

"We did it!" he whispered. "I couldn't have done it without you."

"It was so easy to kill those two hateful men, but so strange. What must you think of me now?" asked Elena.

"I love you even more."

"I feel light-headed, good in a way, yet it was unbearable. I'll never be the same."

"No, you won't. I wasn't like this either. But we have to strike back, even if it means hardening our hearts."

Elena would need to do that. Her heart was beating wildly at the moment, so hard that she was afraid it would burst in her chest. She was holding Lukas's arm and now she gripped it more tightly.

Lukas enjoyed the pressure of her hand on his arm. They so rarely had the opportunity to touch one another. He had killed many others before this, but never at such close quarters, and never after talking and eating together. It was all horrible, yet the killing had brought Elena to him again.

TWO

LITHUANIA

SUMMER 1944

*T*HE JEWISH PINE FOREST in the county of Rumsiskes did not have many pine trees left. What trees there were stood in twos and threes on the ancient sand dune, which had been mostly taken over by tufts of giant grasses, many taller than a man and so tough that even goats would not eat them. The sand dune drank up whatever liquid was poured onto it, from the urine of boys, to the tears of heartbroken girls, to the blood from battle-inflicted wounds. But where these liquids disappeared to was anyone's guess; the dune was dry as bones.

The nearby village of Rumsiskes consisted of a few hundred houses strung along several streets, with farm fields running right up to the back doors. Death came by this way very often, fording the river Nemunas to kill again and again. It came with the Teutonic Knights in 1381, with the Swedes in the Northern Seven Years' War of 1563, with the Russians in the Great Northern War of 1700, and with Napoleon's army in 1812. Then came a long period of uneasy servitude to the czars until independence in 1918. Death had visited again in recent times, as the town traded hands between the Reds and the Germans.

If there were few pines in the Jewish Pine Forest, there were still fewer Jews. Killed shortly after the German "liberation" by the Nazis and their local helpers, the Jews were buried in a mass grave by the Kaunas road.

In the summer of 1944, it was unclear how long the Germans would hold back yet another assault from the Red Army on the other side of the Nemunas River. If the current chief of police lingered in Rumsiskes too long, the Reds would blame him for collaboration with the Nazis. The police chief before him lay dead in his grave; the locals had accused him of collaboration with the Reds the first time they came, in 1940. The police chief before that, during the independence period, had been beaten and sent off to die in Siberia. The Reds had accused him of collaboration with the independent government.

The town lay in a bend of the river, a very old route for the exportation of lumber or the transit of armies. There were several barrow hills in the county as well, and the ruins of a hill fort, of which nothing remained but the cellar. Thus the hill had a sunken top, like a volcano, where some of the locals had hidden during the current artillery barrage from the Red Army, having fled up the hill like their ancestors from centuries past. One night the cellar suffered a direct hit, and the hilltop blazed like a true volcano, with wounded adults and burning children rushing and tumbling down from the top as far as the places where they died, frozen in their descent like lava that had solidified after an eruption.

The Petronis family farm bordered the sand dune, on the side opposite the town of Rumsiskes, and although crops would grow grudgingly on their property, the earth was not particularly fertile, so the farmer and his wife encouraged their three sons to study and make other lives for themselves. The farm itself could be the dowry of their sister, the youngest. But all their plans were muddled by the war. None of the boys, not even Lukas, the eldest, had finished his studies. He was a lithe optimist who refused to be discouraged by this setback, although it was trying at times to be home again, where his parents expected so much of him and his younger brothers occasionally resented his care. The second son, Vincentas, had also been sent back from the seminary for his own safety, to wait out the passing of the front.

The Petronis family had thought of withdrawing behind the German lines in the summer of 1944, but what would life be like in Germany? They would be refugee foreigners in a land under attack from two sides. Besides, staying might not be all that bad even if the Reds did come back. What did a farmer have to fear? Petronis owned a modest fifty acres of land, and a farmer was only designated an enemy of the people, a "bourgeois," at seventy-five acres. He was safe as long as the category was not enlarged to include him.

He was uneasy about that. The Reds had coined a new term: "debourgeoisation," an excellent bureaucratic word for expropriation. A tailor could not have thought of a better term, because it was like a bolt of cloth that could be cut to fit any size. During the first Red occupation it had been applied to large landowners, policemen, government ministers, deputy ministers, assistant deputy ministers, people with relatives abroad, anti-government activists, school principals, and even the one-legged jazz saxophonist in the Metropolis Café in Kaunas, along with his wife, a hairstylist. One could not be sure the category wouldn't be adjusted again.

It was the end of July and very hot, but the windows were shuttered, an oil lamp on the table casting poor light and adding to the heat. The family was eating lunch at a long table. Above the thatched roof of the wooden farmhouse, German and Russian mortars crossed paths. Occasionally the distant sound of tank rounds was heard, as well as automatic fire. There was nothing to do but wait it out, so Petronis senior dipped his spoon into his bowl of beet greens soup and the others followed.

Then they waited throughout the day, old man Petronis anxious in case the shelling lasted so long it kept him from milking his cows. Late that afternoon, the firing moved west.

About an hour before sunset, the Jewish Pine Forest dune began to move, with wave upon wave of Red Army soldiers coming over the hill. Hundreds of them came on, their faces tired and dirty, their uniforms torn.

They were hungry because the front lines travelled without field kitchens, so the men had to live off the land. Father Petronis sent his daughter inside and the three brothers brought out a table on which they cut up slices of bread and laid out pieces of sausage as well as poured out all the milk they had into jugs. About twenty of the soldiers ate there while others fanned out to neighbouring farms, but they did not stay long because they had to rejoin their units before nightfall.

The first day had ended fairly well. The soldiers were just young men after all, tired and hungry. Maybe they were afraid too. Maybe things would turn out all right.

The German lines stiffened near the East Prussian border, so the lack of Red Army field kitchens became a burden to the local farmers, especially those who lived near the main roads and whose farms were easily accessible. The Red Army rode about in Studebakers, Lend-Lease gifts from the Americans.

Red soldiers believed that food, at the very least, was their due. Declaring themselves liberators and guests, they could show up at any time in groups of four or six. If food was a soldier's due, liquor was his reward, and these same soldiers appeared with farm goods, guns, grenades, saddles and even horses, which they traded happily for buckets of home-distilled *samagonas*. A farmer's joy at a good trade could be marred, though, when another farmer from a few kilometres away recognized his saddle or his horse and demanded its return.

Once drunk, the soldiers reflected on the unfairness of their own poverty and that of their families back on the collective farms, and began to steal from the farmers at night. The barking of the farm dogs did not deter them; the soldiers shot barking dogs. They emptied storerooms of food and took farm implements. The people of the countryside no longer wore wristwatches. It was also dangerous to be thoroughly cleaned out by the thieves, because subsequent thieves became angry if they wasted a walk up a farm lane only to find there was nothing left to take.

More worrisome than theft was the Red Army's hunger for labour and recruits. Trenches needed to be dug in case the German army counterattacked. And the front was a maw that devoured young men who were thrown at it without arms or training. Since Lithuania had been occupied by the Reds before the German occupation, Lithuanians were deemed Soviet citizens, whose duty it was to fight the Germans. Any who chose not to fight were deemed fascists themselves.

And so the Petronis boys, Lukas, Vincentas and Algis, went to their uncle's farm a dozen kilometres away, where the locals did not know them well, and helped to bring in the August rye. The young Petronis men passed for labourers, and whenever Russian cars or press gangs appeared, the women warned them and they hid in the forest or in a pit under the barn floor.

Lukas and Vincentas found out that university students and seminarians were being given draft exemptions, and so they left their younger brother behind and made their way home. They packed bags with food and clothes to go to Kaunas to have their passports stamped with military exemptions so they could continue their studies.

The Lithuanian capital had been moved to Vilnius, so many of the buildings in Kaunas were abandoned and some were in ruins. Even so, the streets were full of soldiers and trucks as well as country folk, often women in head scarves, scavenging for lamp oil or aspirin or any other items that were no longer available in the countryside. The Jewish houses were empty and long since sacked.

Lukas was relieved to be back in Kaunas, relieved to get back to his life. He wanted to *get on* with things now, to live in a city, to read books and talk in cafés, to see movies and listen to the radio. Above all, he was tired of armies and wars, which had already eaten up enough of his twenty-three years. He was slight and quick, and he liked to laugh. He had been an excellent shot as a hunter and a very good explorer of the Jewish Pine Forest as a boy, but he intended to study literature and teach in a high school, or even the university if he was lucky. Vincentas was not that different from him, and they looked something alike, although Vincentas wore glasses. But the younger brother was otherworldly; he adored vestments and incense and had practically taught himself Latin before he even started high school. Only their brother Algis preferred life in the countryside.

Having left Vincentas at the nearby seminary, Lukas went to the main office of the university, which hummed with phone calls, secretaries carrying sheaves of papers, and some of the younger professors, huddled in committees, discussing their various tasks to get the university up and running in some fashion for the fall semester. Kuolys, the long-haired Latin professor who had terrorized Lukas in his first year, now looked up, smiled and came over.

"Just in time," said Kuolys. "Do you have your exemption?"

Lukas held out his hand.

Kuolys took his hand and shook it distractedly. "Put your bag in the corner there and go out to check on the library archive for me, will you? I'm on the housing committee and nobody has a place to stay. But I'm worried about the Latin books I've stored in the stacks. Who else would care?"

"I don't have anyplace to stay either," said Lukas.

"Then come back here after you're done and camp out with the rest of us. Plenty of us are at loose ends. Is everyone in the family all right?"

"Yes."

"Is Vincentas back at the seminary?"

"I just dropped him off there."

"You might tell your brother that I could put him in an advanced Classics class here, if he wants. It might be safer. The new regime doesn't like priests much."

"He always wanted to be a priest. He's like a bird who only knows one song."

"We'll all have to learn to sing new songs now. Get to that archive. I have someone to help you."

Rimantas was a student as well, a year younger than Lukas and a year behind in his studies. Rimantas was reedy and tall and walked with a slight stoop, as if to minimize his height. He had a pale, scholar's face, and the habit of chewing on the inside of his right cheek, which gave him a twisted, comical look.

"I'm glad they're sending us to the archive," said Rimantas.

"Why?"

"We're literature students, aren't we? I haven't read anything decent for months. Maybe we can borrow something. Have you read anything good recently?"

"Who's had time to read? I had to help with the farm work over the summer, and spent my nights hiding from the Reds."

Rimantas nodded skeptically. "True enough. But I can't stand doing nothing with my mind. I waited for two hours for my turn with the officer who stamped our exemption papers. I was dying of boredom. No newspapers in the waiting room. Everyone a stranger. I tried to compose poetry in my head because I didn't have any paper to write on, but I couldn't even settle on a single couplet."

For all the bustle at the university, Rimantas seemed lethargic. Having him around was like dragging a reluctant, talkative donkey. "Poets need to suffer," said Lukas.

"Yes. They say the best always need to suffer. Is that a homespun shirt I see beneath your tie?"

Lukas reddened. Homespun was a sign of country folk, looked down upon by the sophisticates. Lukas had been proud of his homespun shirt, made from flax grown in the family fields, but it would do no good to defend farm values against Rimantas.

Although Lukas had been attracted to the idea of café society in the city, he found Rimantas a little too artistic for his taste. Rimantas had stood out in university by wearing dramatic clothing in his

first year, a long black raincoat, too hot in the fall and too thin for
the winter. For a while he'd even worn a beret. His mother was a
minor opera singer, so Lukas forgave him his pretensions, believing
that a child raised in cafés was bound to be different from one raised
on a farm.

A collapsed arch blocked the entranceway to the courtyard in which
the library archive lay. The front of the building had been either
shelled during an artillery barrage or blown up by the retreating
Germans, although it was unclear what military significance it might
have had. The young men searched through the alleys before they
found another way into the courtyard. Cigarette butts, papers and
tins lay on the cobblestones, and the door to the archive was locked.
But the bars on the window to the right had been torn off and the
glass was broken. Lukas reached inside, opened the window latch,
and the two clambered in.

Someone had been in before them. Hundreds of books lay open
on the floor, some of them burned and some of them ripped. To see
such destruction of expensive books troubled Lukas more than the
sight of the ruined buildings in the streets.

The archive was uncannily quiet. Dust motes rose into the air
and hung there in the shafts of light that came through the small
windows. All of Kaunas was dusty from the earth churned up by
military vehicles, from mortar and stone and soot particles that
rose up after explosions and hung in the air for days and weeks at a
time before settling on the city, ready to be stirred again.

Lukas and Rimantas talked quietly to one another, as if a stern
librarian might appear at any time, and yet they were possessed by
an unexpected sense of adventure, never having had such access to
so many books before. If they had had food, they could have settled
down in those rooms and read until Germany surrendered.

A translation of H.G. Wells's *The Time Machine* lay open on a
table as if someone had been interrupted while reading it. Glancing
at the Wells book, Lukas reflected that the world had been turned

inside out: the Morlocks had come up from the underground to rule, and now the Eloi would need to burrow down to escape their slaughter. Either that or find a little of the Morlock in themselves.

Outside, a sudden roar rose up and a motorcycle rattled the windows before echoing down the narrow street.

When the two students made their way deeper into the stacks, they found a long study table heaped with files. They were the students' records, and among them they found their own files.

"Listen to this," said Rimantas, reading about himself. "'Keeps irregular hours. Missed final Latin exam—claimed to be ill. Has a knack for writing satiric verse.'"

"Sounds about right," said Lukas.

"Yes, but listen to the rest: 'Editor of the second-year student paper. Writes spoofs of Stalin.'" Rimantas looked up at him.

"Well, did you?"

"Of course I did! How can you not make fun of Stalin? That moustache and that pipe! Ridiculous. His clothes are a fright, and yet he's the leader of a country—he could wear anything he wants. What does your file say?"

"'Member of Catholic Youth League in high school.'"

"A death sentence," hissed Rimantas. "This is all subversive activity."

"You're exaggerating."

"But it will do you no good. 'Religion is the opium of the people,' remember? We need to destroy these."

"What if we ever need transcripts? We'll be killing our academic careers if we do that."

"And we'll be killing ourselves if we don't. Nobody is going to ask for your transcripts in prison. We have to save ourselves—that's our first responsibility."

They burned the files in a large fireplace. Once their own sins had been turned to ashes, they regarded the stack of files on the table. Hundreds of other students, their friends, would go to hell if their pasts were uncovered. So they burned everything, though the chimney was partially blocked and smoked terribly, and the soot from their files rose up to join the rest of the dust hanging over the city.

The chaos at the university made going back to school all the more exciting that fall. Some of the lecture and study halls had no electricity, and it was difficult to take notes in them or read on overcast days. Other rooms had no desks, and the students sat on their books and coats like novices in an Asian monastery. Most of the food shops were closed because there were no goods to be had, and the students with farm relatives fed themselves with supplies from home and exchanged homegrown tobacco for rare items such as lighter flints, fountain pens and blank paper upon which to write.

At first the only danger lay with soldiers who resented the sight of able-bodied young men going about ordinary lives. Students were liable to be stopped on the streets for document checks in order to justify their being in the city instead of at the front. Some of the soldiers were not that impressed by university exemptions and needed to be bought off with cigarettes, liquor or food.

Lukas ended up living in a dormitory with bedrooms on the upper two floors and a kitchen and common room on the ground floor. His place was on the third floor, where he was one of five young men assigned to a room with two double beds and two desks. Farm boys were used to sharing beds; better to share a bed than be the last one in at night and consigned to sleeping on the floor.

In addition to Rimantas, Lukas shared the room with Lozorius, Ignacas and a quiet lowlander, the latter a friend of his brother's who had left the seminary when he lost his calling. Some studied history and others literature, and their room became the centre of activity in the dormitory because the engineers, chemists and architects found the humanists entertaining.

Lukas came in one night after dark to find that his roommates had several guests in the common room. Ignacas had received a package of food from his parents in the country, and Lozorius had brought in a couple of litres of home-distilled *samagonas*. The room was full of smoke and laughter, the first such party that Lukas could remember since the arrival of the Reds.

Steadily supplied by his parents with smoked sausages and butter, and somewhat richer than the others as an only child, Ignacas had a ruddy face at the best of times, and now it shone brightly with sweat and alcoholic elation. He was the only fat young man that Lukas knew. As the donor with the most food to contribute to the party, he had been given the most to drink by Lozorius, whose ears turned red when he drank. Ignacas's cheeks were as red as Lozorius's ears, and he was holding forth on the political situation, egged on by the less talkative engineers.

"I predict that the war with the Americans will begin as soon as the two armies meet in Germany," he said. "The Americans will take one look at their so-called allies, the Reds, recognize them for what they are, and push them all the way back to Moscow."

Lukas's smile faded and he looked around the room to make sure he knew everyone there. It was not the kind of subject one raised in public. But none of the students present belonged to the Komsomol and none of their parents, as far as he knew, worked for the Reds.

"Do you think those Soviet soldiers want to be there any more than we do?" said the lowlander. "They're not even real Reds. They're Byelorussians, Mongolians, Ukrainians and who knows what else. The Reds gathered up all the provincials to throw at the Germans first, to wear them out."

"Politics, politics," said Rimantas. "Hasn't anyone read any good poetry lately?"

The others hushed him.

"Don't think the Americans will go to war because they don't like the look of someone's face," said an engineer. "Why should they keep on fighting after the Germans are beaten?"

"Because they signed the Atlantic Charter," said Ignacas. "Roosevelt and Churchill met in Newfoundland before the Americans even entered the war. The charter says we all have the right to self-determination and no territorial changes will be made without the agreement of the people."

"All very sweet," the engineer replied, "but what do the Reds care about this charter?"

"They signed it too," said Ignacas.

The room broke out in laughter.

Ignacas was a good-natured man, so he laughed at himself along with the others. He laughed so hard that he had to wipe tears from his eyes before going on. "Europeans are one big family, and the Americans are just an extension of that. They would no more forget us than they'd forget their children."

"My father forgets me whenever I ask for money," said the engineer, "but he remembers me again when it's time to harvest back at the farm. The Americans are like that too. They'll remember us when they need us."

This statement brought on a note of sobriety, because no one could think of anything the Americans would need the Lithuanians for.

The next day, Lukas was asked to go out with an expedition to dig peat for the coming winter to heat the university buildings. It was already September, too late to dry the peat well for the winter, but the university was desperate. Thus, for a week Lukas spent his time digging up squares of peat and then going back the next day to turn them so they dried more quickly. The expedition had difficulty finding transportation to bring the peat back to Kaunas because farm horses were in short supply due to the war and the harvest season, but eventually they had the damp squares stocked in the sunny library courtyard in the hope that they would dry in time to be used during the winter.

When Lukas finally made it back to his dormitory room at midday a week later, he found Lozorius sitting on the bed. Lozorius had prominent ears and eyes a little more widely spaced than most. He was usually in high spirits, but when Lukas looked at him Lozorius stared back with a stricken face.

"What are you doing here?" asked Lozorius.

"I've come back from the peat expedition. I was just going to clean up and go to my afternoon class."

"I thought they might have taken you. Ignacas was taken away this morning. They've taken your brother too."

"Taken Vincentas? Where?"

"To prison."

"What for?"

"Nobody knows for sure. They took me too, but they let me go."

Lukas's first thought was for his brother, but Lozorius continued to wear an odd look. "What happened to you?" asked Lukas, sitting down beside him.

"They signed me up."

"Who did?"

"The Cheka."

These were the secret police, the interior and exterior troops who called themselves NKVD or KGB or MVD and various other names. But to the people, they were Cheka. To join them, to become a Chekist, was to join the Reds at their worst.

"Why did you agree?"

"Not much choice. No one knows where my father is. He went to visit his brother while the front moved across Lithuania and he never came back. Maybe he's been killed or maybe he went west. But they said his absence makes me suspect. They said they'd have to keep me under lock and key unless I agreed to work for them."

"Doing what?"

"Reporting on what all of you say." Lukas grimaced involuntarily, and Lozorius put his hand on his forearm as if to hold on to their friendship. "I can't stand to be locked up. I need to be free."

"Some freedom."

"I shouldn't be telling you this. But do me a favour. Spread the word about me, will you? I don't want anyone talking politics in my presence."

Lukas drew his arm out from under Lozorius's hand. No matter how much his friend protested the impossible circumstances of his situation, Lukas was slightly disgusted by him. He should have found another way out. More pressing, though, was the matter of Vincentas.

The seminary was a short walk from the university, in a walled compound of a former Bernardine convent. It had been a very beautiful place, with a fine baroque church, but both the German and Red armies had used the seminary, and the walls were broken in places and the roof of one of the stables had caved in. The late summer air made the benches beneath the trees seem attractive at a distance, but the bench that Lukas passed had a turd on it.

The cleric at the reception desk seemed preoccupied, even angry, and could tell Lukas nothing about his brother. Lukas had to search out his brother's roommates, whom he found smoking outside the library. They were not much more forthcoming than the cleric at the reception desk, but Lukas did find out that his brother had been one of three seminarians taken away to prison. No one knew why.

The prison administration would tell him nothing either, whether Vincentas was there or had been shipped out, but a pasted notice in the reception room said packages were accepted for inmates between ten and noon each working day. That night Lukas put together a parcel containing bread, smoked meat from home, a change of clothes, a comb, soap, toothpaste and a toothbrush. The package was accepted the next day. Now, at least Lukas knew where his brother was.

The mood back at the dormitory had changed since Ignacas had been taken away. People spoke far less than they used to, and there was a kind of sullenness in the air. No one threw parties. Lozorius was preoccupied as well, absent most of the time, but silent and furtive when they met.

Three days later, Vincentas appeared at Lukas's classroom door as the students were leaving. Lukas embraced him, relieved that he would not have to write the dreadful letter to his parents. Vincentas looked tired and frightened. His spectacles were crooked and Lukas could see thumbprints on them.

Their parents were religious, and of all the children, Vincentas had taken to religion most. He always seemed to look through the surface of things to something good beyond. But now he seemed to have seen something less than divine.

"Did they beat you?" Lukas asked.

"A little. Not much. Not as badly as some of the others. They just kept questioning me about a paper I was supposed to have been aware of. The cell was very full and it was hot in there."

"What paper?"

"Some sort of subversive document they found in the room next to mine. I was supposed to have known about it."

"Did you?"

"No."

Vincentas broke off and looked at Lukas searchingly. Lukas was not sure what he wanted at first, but divined that Vincentas was seeking some sort of support or direction from his older brother.

"You should go back to the seminary and get some sleep," said Lukas.

"Somebody betrayed me there. I wouldn't feel good. And besides, the authorities released me."

"You weren't guilty."

"No, but the other two were kept behind and I know one of them was beaten badly. If I was released, the others will think I've been let go to spy among them." Vincentas looked down, as if he could not bear to look into his own brother's eyes.

This was not the same Vincentas who had walked to Kaunas with Lukas several weeks earlier. It seemed odd that he should be so

shaken by what had happened. Anyone so shaken after three days
in a cell and lucky enough to have been released would not do well
under greater pressure.

Refusing to do so much as step into a classroom at the seminary,
Vincentas moved in with Lukas, who tried to get leave documents
that would permit them to return home for a few weeks. But the
noose around the necks of men of their generation was tightening.
Travel documents were getting harder to obtain and there was talk
that the humanities department would be closed down altogether.

Vincentas brooded in Lukas's residence room day after day and
week after week, stretched out on one of the beds most of the time.
There was room now: Ignacas and the lowlander were gone, and
Lozorius had disappeared. In an effort to distract Vincentas from
his musing, Lukas made him go with him to some of the classes at
the university. They were returning from just such a class late one
winter afternoon when they ran into Lozorius, walking along the
narrow sidewalk of an empty quarter in the old town.

Lukas's fellow student was utterly transformed from the distracted Cheka recruit of a few short weeks before. He walked with
an easy step that one hardly ever saw on the streets any longer. He
was slightly cocky, his eyes prominent and bright, his shoulders
square. As always, his ears were turned out, making him seem a little funny too.

"Vincentas!" said Lozorius happily. "You got out of prison. Congratulations! Did the Cheka try to recruit you?"

"No," Vincentas said awkwardly, removing his glasses and wiping them distractedly, "they just beat me. A little."

"Consider it a positive sign of your true heart. They knew you
could never betray anyone from the moment they saw you. Believe
me, the Chekists are some of the best psychologists in the country."

Lukas looked around uneasily. One did not have these kinds of
conversations in the street any longer. The Jewish quarter was mostly
empty, many of the windows just gaping holes in the buildings, the

glass and even the frames smashed. But there could be squatters in there somewhere among the abandoned houses and courtyards, people who might be scavengers of information they could sell to the Cheka. Three people talking together on the street would also be suspicious to police or military patrols. The army would want to know why they were not in uniform, and the police would separate them and ask what they had been talking about. Anyone who did not behave as if he were hunted was an affront to the hunters, an insult to their power.

Lukas tugged on Lozorius's sleeve. "Come in here."

They stepped through the broken door of a wooden house, and then went more deeply inside to another room that had no other light but what came in through the doorway. The place smelled of mould and cat piss. When they could go no farther, Lukas turned and looked at Lozorius, whose face beamed unnaturally in the gloom.

"You look well," said Lukas.

"I feel it."

"Did you reconcile yourself to working for the Cheka?"

"The opposite, actually. I decided that I couldn't live like a slave. I needed to be free, so I made myself free in my mind."

Lukas believed in good spirits and a light tone, but the world they were living in was getting darker. They were under their third occupation in six years, and had become like grain in a mill—soon the stones would grind them to dust.

"So what are you doing here?" he asked. "I haven't seen you around for weeks."

"I have to organize the transport of a printing press, no easy matter these days."

"A printing press?"

"I'm with the partisans now."

"Keep your voice down," said Lukas.

Lozorius laughed, his voice echoing slightly in the empty room. "Nothing to fear around here. The place is deserted. Anyway, with the printing press, we make up our own documents. I'm moving around with forged documents myself. I passed through three check-points today without any problem."

Lukas considered the information. Under the Reds, one could not go anywhere without some kind of document. Papers were needed to leave town, to live in town and to undertake any sort of trip at all.

"Our younger brother, Algis, is hiding out at home because he's afraid to be taken by the army," said Lukas.

Lozorius reached into his breast pocket. "No problem. I have some blank military exemptions. Here, take two. The only things you need to be careful about are the official stamps, but if you have any skill at all with carving tools you can make those up yourselves."

"You're not afraid?" Vincentas asked.

"Not anymore. The forests are full of people like me. We rule the whole countryside by night, and some parts by day as well. It's only in cities like this where young men tremble." He looked at his watch, squinting to make out the hour in the gloom of the abandoned house. "I have to get moving. It's a complicated job, because even a small press is heavy. Good luck in your studies. I'll see you around."

Although it had been good to see Lozorius, the street seemed all the more forlorn after he left, the dormitory all the more unwelcoming for his absence. Vincentas lay down on an empty bed and stared at the ceiling as Lukas sat at the desk and tried to read. The university had quickly instituted an obligatory course on Marxism-Leninism, but there were not enough texts and he had to read his own quickly before passing it on. The economic theory was deathly boring and did not hold his interest.

The dormitory was unusually quiet for late afternoon, a time when students should have been returning to their rooms.

In winter the night came early, and soon it became too dark to read. Lukas turned on the overhead lamp and looked over to see if Vincentas was sleeping. He was not. Behind his eyeglasses, his eyes were open and fixed upon the ceiling.

Vincentas sensed Lukas's look. "It's only a matter of time before they come for me," he said.

"Oh, I don't know. The Germans are collapsing. When the war finally ends, they won't care about young men like us anymore. We'll be all right."

"Don't patronize me."

Lukas wondered how it was possible for younger brothers to be both needy and touchy at the same time. Vincentas tested his patience.

"What do you want me to say? That you're doomed? First, I don't believe it, and second, even if it was true, I wouldn't say it."

"Why not?"

"It's unlucky and does you no good. Didn't they teach you anything at the seminary? Isn't despair supposed to be a sin?"

"Yes, it is."

"So how are you supposed to fight it?"

"With prayer."

"Well?"

"I've been praying for weeks, and it doesn't seem to do me much good. I wish we could go home. I miss the open fields and the forest. I feel hemmed in here."

"We could make ourselves some forgeries."

"It would probably take too long."

A door banged downstairs and some muffled voices made themselves heard through the walls and doors. Even at a distance, even muffled, the words sounded harsh and brought no liveliness to the building.

"I want to live like Lozorius," said Vincentas.

"A partisan?"

"They're free."

"Winter's just beginning. What do you think it's going to be like in that season? Shivering in the cold in some barn."

"It's going to be cold here too. There's no coal. We're hungry all the time."

"You were never very good on the farm. You're an intellectual from the first. You'd make a great priest or a teacher or some kind of administrator. The woodland life of a partisan isn't for you."

"You think you know everything, don't you?"

"I've watched you grow up. I was barely out of diapers when I had to take care of you."

"But I finally did grow up—you don't need to take care of me any longer. I'm going to find Lozorius and join the partisans."

"Speak a little more softly, will you?"

"Listen to yourself. You're behaving like a slave already. We're afraid here. I'm sick of being afraid."

"Do you think skulking through the forest is going to be any better?"

"I do."

Lukas studied Vincentas, whose face was flushed with emotion and whose eyeglasses were in danger of fogging up from his passion. His chest was narrow and his manner nervous. There was no way Lukas could permit his brother to go into the forest alone. He would go with Vincentas, just for a while. Lukas's studies would have to wait.

LITHUANIA

DECEMBER 1944

A SAD, SINGLE OIL LAMP burned in the window of a farmhouse where a middle-aged man hunched over a newspaper. Sleepless, he flipped the pages, looking for something to distract him.

His right hand was missing the index and middle fingers, and his right shoulder sagged a bit lower than the left, scars of industrial accidents from his other life in America. His wife and three children lay asleep on benches and beds in the combined farm kitchen and parlour, the warmest room now that the December cold had descended on them.

The locals called him the American. Unlike the others who had disappeared into America to make new lives for themselves, he had returned, a migrating bird that lost its way.

Back in the 1920s, as an immigrant to America, he'd worked hard in the Worcester Spinning and Finishing Mill. In those days he suffered from homesickness. He couldn't get used to the endless noise of the looms, the shouting of foremen and the honking of cars out in the street. The mill was dangerous, taking first one finger and then another. He became slightly deaf and didn't hear a truck backing into him, breaking his right shoulder. He thought then that he was living in hell and dreamt of returning to the fields of his homeland.

Little by little he put money aside, until he could stand America no more and returned to Lithuania in 1931 to buy almost forty acres of land. He married and had children. His hand and his shoulder could not be healed, but the rest of him felt stronger in compensation. His colour became better from working out of doors and eating well. If anything, he worked harder on the farm than he had back in the U.S.A., but he could see the fruits of his labour, and he imagined his dead parents, a landless farmhand and a maid, looking on approvingly from up in heaven at their landowner son.

If there was such a thing as heaven. Over the last few years, as his luck began to turn for the worse, he had started to doubt there was any divine plan at all.

The Red requisitions were stiff enough in 1940, when farmers were forced to sell produce to the state at very low prices, and then the German requisitions were higher still. And now the farmer had a glimpse of the future, and he didn't like what he saw.

The numbers the new regime asked of him were frightening: four hundred kilos of meat, so he had to kill two of his cows and thereby fell behind on his milk requisition; one thousand kilos of wheat, although it had been trampled in the fields by both the German and Red armies; a thousand kilos of potatoes, although there had been no farmhands available to dig them out because all the hired hands, the workers, had been drafted or fled to the forests. And maddeningly, the potatoes and wheat that he did manage to deliver were dumped in a yard and left to get wet and rot because there was no room in the warehouse.

The state policies didn't make sense. He couldn't understand why they wanted to destroy him and his farm. Wouldn't these actions destroy the Reds as well? He wished he could go crazy if only to reconcile himself to living in a madhouse. His neighbour, Javas, the one with the big mouth who couldn't learn to keep his thoughts to himself, was already in jail for failing to meet his quota. Two of the

neighbouring farms were empty, gone to seed, one through deportation of the family and the other because the farmer had fled west.
The farms were going back to wilderness, back to weeds and grass.
Left long enough, they'd go back to the forests they'd been carved
from hundreds of years before.

The new rulers were barbers, who sat you down in the chair and
promised a trim but kept on clipping and clipping all the way down
to the scalp, and when it looked as if there was nothing left to cut,
you saw them eyeing the straight razor and you shuddered to think
what might be coming next.

Regret kept the American awake while his family slept. His mind
kept turning on the mystery of living in the place where he did, a
place where history moved backward.

The farmers would be forced into villages again, as they had been
in the times of the czar. The state paid no wages at all on collective
farms. It was like going back to 1860, before emancipation of the
serfs. And these were the "liberators" who had saved them from the
Germans. He felt as if he was living on the wrong side of a mirror.
Why did the French have all the luck and get the Americans?

This winter night on his farm, he was living in the silence he had
missed while on the shop floor in Worcester, Massachusetts. Sitting
by the oil lamp, he could fill the silence with his thoughts about
how things might have been.

On the edge of the American's property, on the fringe of a forest,
Lukas and Vincentas tried hard not to make noise as they followed
the partisan guide in front of them. With each step forward, the
crust of snow beneath their feet seemed to squeal like a guard
dog whose tail had been stepped on.

The men cut across three kilometres of forest, and then came
upon an open field. Light snow began to fall, covering their footprints. They came to a river and waded through the shallowest part,
managing to get wet no higher than their knees.

At dawn they came to another forest. Their guide paused to draw a pistol from its holster and slip it up the sleeve of his sheepskin coat. He led them straight into a dense mass of pine branches, on the other side of which was a trail.

The guide held up his hand and they stopped. From somewhere a voice said "Ashes" and the guide responded "Dust." They followed the trail, and soon there was a widening of the path and a clearing, at the end of which they could see a large campsite, the first in a series of linked sites, where a few men were moving about.

There were two long tables made of rough-hewn logs, an unlit bonfire was stacked in a deep pit, and the first clearing contained over a dozen lean-tos made of pine boughs with small fires of smokeless oak sticks burning at the ends.

This was the main camp, but as Lukas looked more deeply into the forest he saw that there was a series of clearings and the camp he stood in was only the first of several which ran one after another as far as he could see. At the other camps, some of the men were up and sitting around campfires. There were dozens of men in each of the campsites and therefore hundreds in all. A small army of irregulars was living among the pine trees.

He had never thought the Reds had undone so many. "Why all these camps?" Lukas asked.

"If we let the men stay in one big camp, they start to talk and make jokes and carouse too loudly at night, and the sound carries," said the guide.

Just then Lukas heard a concertina begin to play quietly and some men started to sing.

His guide laughed at Lukas's astonishment. "Some of them sing a little in the mornings during the winter to keep their spirits up. We forbade it in the summer because the shepherds started to bring their flocks around here to listen to the music."

Between the second and third camps there was a crude corral with three cows in it. The Reds were driving cattle out of the defeated part of Germany along abandoned railway lines nearby, and the partisans went shopping for meat along this highway whenever they were short of food.

In the camp where they stood, most of the men were sleeping in twos and threes in their lean-tos. They were dressed and shod. Many had no blankets beyond their wool coats. At their sides lay weapons, an assortment of Russian and German grenades, pistols and automatic rifles as well as light machine guns. A heavy machine gun stood at the edge of the clearing.

The guide left them where they stood and went across the way to speak to a man with a beard.

The air was cleaner here, and the quiet music in the distance was sweet. Most of the partisans in this first camp were still sleeping, as it was after dawn and partisans did their work by night, but three men in a knot where they'd been studying a map on the table looked up, and one of them nodded and saluted them informally by touching the brim of his hat with his finger. Lukas nodded back.

It was going to be all right.

The guide returned and led the brothers to a lean-to of their own and gave them a bundle of rags to wrap their feet in so their socks could dry by the fire as they slept. Neither of the young men had slept outside in the winter before, but they were so tired that they did so easily.

Lukas awoke in the early afternoon to the smell of barley soup. His socks were dry on their sticks by the fire. Vincentas lay beside him on his back, his mouth slightly open. Lukas studied his brother, who had been so tired he had not even taken off his eyeglasses. They lay crookedly on his nose, steaming up slightly with every breath deflected from the scarf that Vincentas had tucked up over his lips.

Since he was otherworldly, Vincentas had required care all his life. Tree roots seemed to search out his feet to trip him, doors swung shut suddenly behind him, clipping his heels, and rabid dogs had a way of finding him, hoping for salvation. Sometimes

Lukas got tired of looking out for him, especially because Vincentas was not particularly grateful. His mind was on loftier matters.

Even though he'd come here for the sake of his brother, Lukas was now happier than he'd been back on the uneasy streets of Kaunas. He did not need to pretend here, to force his feelings underground.

The camp was beginning to stir. Men in old Lithuanian army uniforms, or in a mix of military and civilian clothes, were moving about, some stamping their boots to start circulation in their feet, others checking their weapons, some smoking and talking or heating water with which to shave.

The guide came to them, roused Vincentas, and took them to meet the leader of their band, a bearded forty-year-old called Flint. He was the oldest man in the group, one of a few with military training, and he kept a pipe between his teeth much of the time. He looked them up and down like the captain of a ship eyeing new sailors.

"Is Kaunas so crammed full of people that there's no room for you there?" he asked.

"That's right," said Lukas.

"Are you sure? It would be better for you if you went back, and better for us to have a couple of young undercover men we could count on in town. This is no kind of life you're choosing, and once you're in, there's no getting out."

"The Reds were starting to close in. They were going to come for us sooner or later."

Vincentas was letting Lukas take the lead, eyeing the camp and the other men.

"Did either of you have military training?"

"No."

"Know Morse code or how to use a radio?"

"Just to listen to the news," said Vincentas suddenly.

A partisan within earshot laughed at this answer.

"I'm glad you can turn a dial," said Flint. "But now you tell me what good you two would be to me. What do you have to offer?"

"I didn't realize we had to offer anything," said Vincentas. "I thought it was enough that we didn't want to live like slaves."

"What do you think this is, some kind of study group? The Cheka is looking for us now, as we speak. Or looking for me, anyway. There's a price on my head. Freedom doesn't come cheap. So what do you have to offer, if not military expertise or radio communications, or a machine gun? Do you have some inside information on a food warehouse? Or I'd love to get my hands on a small tank. Can you help me there?"

Vincentas shook his head. "I've had three years' training in the seminary. I could be your chaplain."

To Lukas's surprise, Flint nodded at this. It made some sense. They lived in a religious country where prayers were as common as sparrows, and everyone needed to tell his troubles to someone.

"What about you?"

"Our parents were farmers. I was studying to be a teacher."

"Can you write well?"

"Of course."

"I mean longer pieces, articles. News. Essays."

"That's the sort of thing I did at school, yes."

"All right, this is better than I thought. I have a lot of men who can pull a trigger. These camps are full of farm boys, but there are damned few men who can handle a pen or a typewriter. Mind you, everyone needs to be able to fight. But I want you to be sure about what you're doing. You could hide out with your parents, you know."

"We have another brother hiding out. Three of us would be too many."

"I only want men who have no other choice, you understand? No patriots, no hotheads."

"I'd rather be reading Maironis's poetry in university if I could," said Lukas. He looked around the camp. "And I wouldn't sleep outside in the winter if I didn't have to."

"You'll be glad enough to sleep outside after you've spent some time in a bunker. Listen, we own the countryside around here. We killed 170 Reds in a pitched battle in the Varchiai forest. The Reds stick to the main roads unless they're travelling in force. But it's hard to feed so many men at once. It puts too much strain on local farmers. We'll have to break into smaller groups eventually, and when the weather warms we'll dig some more bunkers in the earth. Are you claustrophobic?"

"No."

"Sure? You'll be buried alive for weeks at a time."

"But you're free here," said Lukas.

"Yes, that's right. We're free here."

"We want to be free too."

"There's a price for it."

"My brother and I are willing to pay."

This seemed to satisfy Flint. He nodded and relit his pipe. "Either of you speak English? No? Then learn it. We need someone to listen to the BBC and type up the news. You'll both work in writing newspapers along with other duties. Get something to eat, and then we'll do your oath."

Lukas and Vincentas walked over to one of the long log tables where the men were gathering to eat. They were served by a woman in a greatcoat. She ladled the barley soup into wooden bowls. She wore a Russian hat with flaps over her ears, but curly brown hair spilled out over her forehead and at the side of her face.

"Eat, men, eat. There's plenty where this came from. I'll be back to serve you seconds when you're done."

"What kind of meat is in this soup?" a partisan asked.

"Beef, of course."

"Again?"

"I'm sorry. I'll just run back to the kitchen and bring you pancakes and sour cream."

"I miss pork."

"Well, the Reds aren't driving the pigs out of Germany, my friend, they're driving cows. Think of yourself as an American cowboy."

"I'll eat the beef if you promise it's been cooked with love."

"You'll eat the beef or go hungry. And if you make any more smart remarks I'll knock your nose with my ladle."

Vincentas and Lukas sat themselves at the table and the woman served them as well. She smiled at them, but they were too shy to speak. For all her rough banter, Lukas saw that her hands were soft and the fingernails slightly long. This was no country cook.

Other men settled around them.

"Hello," said the man who sat beside Lukas. He was compact, with a strand of hair that stuck out from under his stocking cap, and cheeks bright red from the combination of cold and steam from the soup. From a pocket inside his greatcoat he took out a hand-carved wooden spoon as big as a ladle.

"That's quite the spoon," said Lukas.

"Beauty, isn't it? I carved it myself. And practical! It's saved me from starvation more than once."

"How did it do that?"

"Whenever we're short of rations, I ask for just one spoonful of soup or porridge, and then bring this thing out. It's the size of a bowl, see? My friend here, Ungurys, and I have both eaten from it more than once, tipping it from side to side. Of course, he has no trouble getting served now because his sister is visiting and she always gives him the best pieces of gristle."

The man he pointed to was thin and dark, with bushy eyebrows and a moustache and a quiet manner. He barely looked up when his friend said his name.

"Don't mind Ungurys. He has a good heart, but he doesn't know how to show it. He's the kind of man you can rely on in a pinch."

"He has an odd name," said Lukas. *Ungurys* meant Eel in Lithuanian.

"It's a code name. We all have them and try to use them so we won't know what our friends' real names are, in case we're ever taken alive. It doesn't really work over any length of time, but we do it anyway. You'll have to choose code names too. Mine is Lakstingala." It meant Nightingale in Lithuanian.

"That's an unusual name," said Lukas. "Why did you choose that?"

"The other partisans call themselves Falcon, or Vampire, or Tiger, trying to sound frightening or manly. It's embarrassing. Even Flint is only one of a dozen names of stones the others chose. Me, I just want to survive, so I've chosen a feminine name that will make the Cheka think I'm a woman, and a bird's name to help me fly away if I need to."

"It's an unlucky name," said Ungurys. "I warned you." He put his face back down into his soup.

"He thinks all bird names are bad because birds sing."

"Meaning what?" asked Lukas.

"That I'll confess if I'm ever taken alive. He thinks if he calls himself Eel he'll always be able to slip away. You'll each need to choose names before the oath. Have you thought about them?"

"I'll take *Salna*," said Vincentas. It meant Frost in Lithuanian.

"And I'll take *Dumas*." The word meant Smoke, but Lukas pronounced it without the final *s*.

"Both unlucky," snapped Ungurys. "Both impermanent."

"Not mine," said Lukas. "Mine is a joke. It refers to the French writer Alexandre Dumas, who wrote *The Three Musketeers*."

Vincentas laughed, but Lakstingala looked at them oddly and then turned to Ungurys for an explanation.

"I don't know what they're talking about either," said Ungurys. "They're intellectuals. They can't help it. I just hope they don't blow our heads off when they're learning to shoot."

"I actually shoot pretty well," said Lukas.

"Maybe," said Ungurys, "when you're aiming at a bird or rabbit. But those two don't shoot back. We'll see what kind of shot you are under pressure."

Lukas jutted his chin toward the woman who had been serving soup. "Are there many women among you?"

"Some," said Lakstingala. "They're mostly cooks and nurses, but others carry machine guns and fight if they're fierce enough.

Flint doesn't like to have them around much except as couriers. They're more useful to us in the city. The cook is Ungurys's sister. She comes down from Marijampole from time to time to visit her brother."

"Isn't that dangerous?" asked Lukas.

"I'm all she has left, except for our other sister," said Ungurys.

"What happened to your parents?"

"They had a nice house we grew up in, but a Red Army shell killed my mother and destroyed the house. The Reds had already sent my father up to join the polar bears."

"So what's she doing here?"

"I had to go into the woods to avoid the draft."

"And he's her little brother," said Lakstingala. "She comes down to make sure he's had enough to eat and brings him a clean hand-kerchief to blow his nose."

"What about Lozorius? I was hoping to see him around."

"Lozorius," said Ungurys, permitting a shadow of a smile to flit across his sour face. "Good man."

Lakstingala nodded. "He's the only one without a code name. He's off somewhere, trying to unite all the partisan bands. It's a tough job, and dangerous. There are thousands of us across this country. He's bringing us under a combined leadership."

"Now, *he's* the kind of man you can trust," said Ungurys. "He's been to Poland and then came back. You tell me who else would return here if he had a chance to escape. He woke up in a bunker once to find a Chekist bent over him, and strangled the man with his bare hands. If we had another thousand like him, the Reds would flee this country with their arses stinging."

"This must be some other man. The Lozorius I knew was a student with me in Kaunas. He was depressed for a while."

"Wide-set eyes, ears sticking out a bit?" asked Lakstingala.

"That's him."

"You knew him in the city, where he was just another student. We know him in the forest, where he's a different man altogether.

Listen, he broke twenty men out of prison. One of them is here somewhere." Lakstingala looked about and then stood and walked over to another table, where he went to a man with his back to them and clapped him on the shoulder. They talked for a moment, and then the man took up his bowl and brought it over.

The man was bundled up like no one else, wrapped in two coats and with a scarf both over his head and around his neck, the part beneath his chin wet with bits of barley on it. He scooped a couple more spoons of soup into his mouth before looking up. He was familiar, but Lukas could not place him.

"Lukas, is that you?" he asked, and by his voice Lukas recognized him.

"Ignacas?"

"That's right."

The fat young man with whom Lukas had shared a room in Kaunas had melted away.

"I thought you'd be in Siberia by now," said Lukas.

"I would have been, except Lozorius came for me."

Between spoonfuls of soup from the bowl that he refilled twice, Ignacas told them about how he had been in a holding cell at the train station in Pravieniskes when Lozorius led a band of partisans who shot the guards dead and blew out a whole wall to lead twenty men into the night. Lozorius had come for Ignacas in particular, and brought him to this partisan band when there was nowhere else for him to go. His own parents were already in prison. But Ignacas's joy at freedom was short-lived.

"Look at me," said Ignacas. "I'm a shadow of my former self."

"You were an elephant when Lozorius brought you to us," said Lakstingala, "and now you're a deer. You're healthier like this."

"But I'm cold all the time. I can't get used to my new shape, the lack of insulation. No matter how much I wrap myself up, I'm still freezing. I wasn't made for life in the woods."

"It's warmer here than in Siberia," said Lakstingala.

"Oh, I'm grateful all right. Don't get me wrong. The Americans had better hurry up and save us, though. I don't know how I'll make it through the winter."

Lukas and Vincentas swore their oaths later that day, promising to obey all orders scrupulously, not to desert, and to fight until the Reds had been chased out of the country. The entire band was brought together for the ceremony. One hundred and fifty men and two women stood to attention, saluted them, and then sang the national anthem as if they were living in a free state.

That night, the various squads prepared for their missions. Two were going out to assassinate a Red activist in the village of Nedzinge, where the priest kept a hidey-hole under the altar, and six others to raid a government dairy for butter and cheese. Three squads of four went out to patrol as country rangers, looking for Red thieves who descended on the farms by night to steal food or other goods.

Some of the rest sat around the bonfire, which had been set in a deep pit in the earth so the flames would not be visible from a distance. Here twenty men sat in a circle, talking and telling stories. Some of the men wrote poetry or songs in their free time, and they performed these pieces and then listened to the criticism of the others, who suggested changes in the lyrics or the rhymes.

Vincentas fell asleep almost immediately with his arms crossed on his chest. Lukas sat and watched the others, humming along when he heard a tune he knew. He sensed that he was among people primarily of the country, like the people who lived around the farm where he grew up rather than those he had met in the city. Country people felt certain obligations that city people did not. They kept up good humour and joked with one another. They were generous, giving away the last of their cigarettes freely, but expecting the same in return. They drank a great deal and they could pray for hours at a time, feeling the hand of God close by. Flint forbade drinking altogether, to the disgruntlement of some, and his common prayers were very short, to the disgruntlement of others. The men were fatalistic, having placed their lives in the hands of God, and sometimes met bad ends because they refused to evade trouble but faced it straight on.

Lukas wondered how he would fit in with these men. Never having been shot at, he was afraid he might be a coward. He also worried on behalf of Vincentas, sleeping at his side.

The bonfire was made of pine logs, which burned intensely but for a very short time. Small explosions shot burning embers out among those at the fireside, occasionally landing on a shoe or a coat hem to leave singe marks before they were extinguished. But mostly the sparks flew up into the night sky in swirling eddies that quickly burned out and fell to earth as specks of soot.

On the other side of the fire, Lukas watched as Ungurys came along with his sister and the two sat down to look into the flames and sing along with the others. Sometimes they talked to one another. He could see that the sister was asking questions, but Ungurys's replies were short. After a while they stopped this talking and began to sing with the others. Lukas went over to them.

"Do you mind if I join you?"

Ungurys shrugged, but his sister patted the place beside her and Lukas sat down. It was very warm by the fire and she lifted off her Russian hat, shook out her curls and ran her fingers through her hair.

"Do you have a cigarette?" she asked.

"Tobacco and papers. You smoke?"

"I never used to, but lately I need a cigarette sometimes."

Lukas was unaccustomed to women who smoked. They tended to be of two types, either tough market women or upper-class ladies. She didn't seem to be either of these.

"I'm the best roller of cigarettes in the whole camp," said Ungurys. "Pass over the tobacco and papers and I'll have three masterpieces ready in a minute."

"I don't know your name," said Lukas.

"Elena."

"So you're in the partisans too?"

"I'm semi-legal."

"What does that mean?"

"I'm a courier for the partisans, but I have a job in the Ministry of Trade Associations in Marijampole. I'm not from there. If they knew my brother was in the partisans, they'd fire me at the very least, maybe even arrest me, so I have to be ready to go into the forest full-time if there's too much pressure."

"You should work somewhere else."

"I get bits of information where I work. I can be useful."

"Yes, but it's risky."

"Every place is risky. My sister lives in Marijampole, and the job is easy. I can get away like this for a few days to visit my brother. Sometimes I carry underground newspapers back to Marijampole."

"Behold," said Ungurys. He held out three cigarettes on his palm, each perfectly uniform, looking as if they had come from a factory.

"Where did you learn a skill like that?"

"All it takes is time. When you're in a tent or a bunker for days at a stretch, you can perfect silly little skills like this."

Each took a cigarette and Ungurys lit them, beginning with his sister's. The tobacco burned at the back of Lukas's throat. He did not really smoke much, and when the tobacco scratched his throat like this he wondered why he ever bothered.

"Why did you join the partisans?" Lukas asked Ungurys.

"They tried to put me in the army to fight the Germans, but as far as I'm concerned, the enemy of my enemy is my friend."

Lukas looked at Elena. "How do you find life in Marijampole?"

"It wears on me. I feel unanchored with our parents gone. I was going to be a teacher, like my father, but I can't get into teachers' college anymore because they'll be more careful about checking my background. All I have left is my little brother here and my sister. Sometimes I wish I could do something to strike back at them."

Her brother laughed.

"Don't think I couldn't do it. I'm fierce, you know."

"I know, I know," Ungurys said. "When I was little, she'd beat up all the bullies who tried to hit me or our sister. Half the boys in my class were terrified of her."

This description of Elena was hard to credit. Her curly hair made her face look soft. There was humour at the corners of her lips and a little of it in her eyes too. Whatever fierceness she had was well hidden. Lukas's skepticism must have shown.

"I'd do anything to defend my family, and anything to avenge it."

Lukas shrugged. They finished their cigarettes and threw the butts into the bonfire, whose centre had collapsed and was now burning less intensely. Elena asked Lukas many questions about his life on the farm, and he told her about it.

"Why are you so interested in all this?" asked Lukas.

"I'm sick of life in town. It's so dreary there, and we have all these party meetings and education sessions we have to go to. I'd prefer to be on a farm or in the forest."

"That's the romanticism of city folk speaking," said Lukas. "I knew people in the countryside who lived in houses without chimneys, just a hole in the roof, and they walked around barefoot most of the year. Life's not so wonderful in the country."

"Don't patronize me, Dumas. I'm capable of almost anything."

"It sounds funny to me to hear my code name. Call me Lukas."

"All right. Don't patronize me, Lukas."

She had used his name, and it sounded good on her lips.

They talked for a while longer, and then she stood up.

"Leaving so soon?" asked Lukas.

"I'm going back tonight. My brother is going to walk me partway."

"We've barely had a chance to meet."

"I come by every once in a while. Are you going to be stationed here, with this band?"

"I think so."

"Then take care of my brother, will you?"

"She says that to everyone," said Ungurys. "It's embarrassing."

The fireside felt empty after they left. The songs the men sang became melancholy as the evening wore on, and Lukas did not want to let himself fall into that mood. He roused his brother and they returned to their lean-to for the night, but Lukas could not fall asleep for a long time.

FEBRUARY 1945

*L*IKE BEARS in hibernation, many of the partisans hunkered down during the winter, moving as little as possible to keep their footprints off the snow. Vincentas and Lukas were moved to a bunker three kilometres away where the rotary press, type-writer and radio were kept. Here they studied English grammar and practised listening to the BBC, and finally typed up the underground broadsheets and printed them for distribution to the villages.

Learning English was very difficult because the voice that came over the radio made noises that were barely comprehensible to some-one who had only a grammar book to study from. Lukas and Vin-centas began to take language lessons with the American farmer. This helped a little, but the American's accent was vastly different from that of the BBC announcer. The American's wife served them chicory coffee, black bread and butter, but her hospitality was grudging. She loved her children more than she loved her country, and if the partisans left tracks in the snow, the Cheka would ask questions.

Even in winter, the partisans carried printed sheaves out to the villages and towns to pass on to the couriers. The men posted hand-bills in prominent places and ripped down Red proclamations.

The couriers' houses were also letterboxes through which personal messages could sometimes be sent. Lukas wrote to his parents to let them know he and his brother were alive and well.

Lukas was used to hard work from his farm childhood, but he had never had to live out of doors for a long time. Even though he and Vincentas were privileged to work and live in a bunker that was heated by night, his fingertips never really warmed up and he hit the keys of the typewriter awkwardly.

There was so much to write about the progress of the war farther west, to exhort the people not to collaborate with the Reds, to forbid the young men from joining the slayers.

Slayers. Lukas found the Reds went straight to the point with their vocabulary. The word came from the Russian *Istrebitel.* It described Lithuanians who joined the Cheka as auxiliaries to hunt down "bandits" such as Lukas and Vincentas. In return, the slayers did not have to go into the army. Lukas could understand that a desperate man might become a slayer, but this understanding came without any sympathy. In order to preserve himself, the slayer had to hunt down his own people. Some of the slayers tried to play both sides of the game by acting incompetently, but their Red masters soon caught on to this. An incompetent could always be sent to the front. Ever the humane soul, Vincentas tried to moderate Lukas's hatred of slayers, but without much success.

Vincentas held prayer meetings because he was not ordained and could not say Mass. He listened to the confidences of troubled men, but he could not listen to confession, nor offer absolution. Those who were troubled or religious found their way to him and he offered them some comfort, even if his own comfort was in short supply. Like their friend Ignacas, Vincentas could not easily bear the cold. He was thin and developed a cough.

"Put another couple of sticks in the stove," said Lukas when he heard his brother's chest heave yet again as they were working in the bunker one night.

Lukas was typing up the stencil by oil lamp, and Vincentas was waiting to crank out the next issue of their "newspaper." It was a flattering term for a mimeographed sheet.

"Lukas," said Vincentas, "are you busy?"

Lukas glanced over at his brother. They were only a metre apart and both sitting at the small table where Lukas squinted at the stencil and typed slowly in order not to make any mistakes.

"I'm typing."

"Have you ever thought about what it's like to act ethically in war?"

"Not really," said Lukas. He spoke slowly between hitting the keys.

"We discussed it in the seminary during the time the Germans occupied the country. We discussed how the normal rules of behaviour were lifted during war."

"Yes," said Lukas, slightly impatiently. "People kill people in war."

"But not without cause. Even during a war, there is a system of values." This was exactly the sort of talk that Vincentas was known for. He used to wonder about all sorts of abstract notions even as a boy on the farm. He had wanted to know if birds had afterlives, if it was immoral to eat meat, even on non-fast days, if women, since they were not permitted to be priests, had fully formed souls.

"I think there is a system of values, yes," said Lukas, listening with half an ear. "Even during a war."

"So are we at war?"

"We fire at one another."

"But no one declared war between the Lithuanians and the Reds, did they?"

"No, because it's to the Reds' advantage not to. They call us bandits."

"And how is a bandit to act ethically?"

"But we're not bandits. I've just said to you, we're at war."

"I'm not sure I could ever kill anyone."

"With any luck, you won't have to. But I hope that if somebody is threatening me or one of the others, you'll defend us."

"I'll try."

Lukas became slightly exasperated with his brother. "Think of the world we live in. Think of what we've seen already—our people killed by the retreating Reds in '41, the Jews cut down, soldiers shot to pieces, children blown up under artillery fire. You're talking as if you've never seen violence."

"I've never had to carry arms before. I'm really a pacifist, you know."

"The Reds will thank you for not defending yourself. Then they'll shoot you dead or haul you away to Siberia."

"But I don't think I could ever shoot anyone."

"So you won't be covering my back?"

Vincentas ignored the question.

Lukas stopped trying to type. He turned to his brother, intending to give Vincentas a good talking-to, the kind their father used to give the boy when he was philosophizing too much on the farm. But Lukas held back. His brother was hugging himself for warmth even though the wood stove made the underground room quite comfortable. Lukas would have to speak to Flint about getting Vincentas out of the partisans. Perhaps there was some distant village where he could live semi-legally as a clerk.

On a Sunday night in February, when the air was so cold the trees seemed to cry out in pain, Flint called the brothers up from their bunker. Outside, they found Ungurys and Lakstingala, both of them swaddled thickly against the cold and wearing knapsacks and carrying their weapons. Flint's pipe was unlit, but his breath streamed like smoke in the air.

"All right, you two," he said, "you've been sitting around too long. You're going to get fat this way. Besides, it's time for your baptism."

"Baptism?" Vincentas asked.

"By fire. Don't worry—nothing too exciting. Two of my best men will be with you."

"Let's get moving," said Ungurys through the scarf over his mouth. "If we stand still, we'll freeze to the spot."

Vincentas and Lukas went with the other two and made their way to the market village an hour and a half away.

Lukas was glad to be going out, to be doing something besides listening to the radio and typing up news, if only to stretch his muscles. The mission was like a night game of the kind he used to play with the other farm children, but instead of a staff he carried a rifle strapped to his back; instead of a pocketknife, a long blade in his boot; instead of a flashlight, a grenade at his side. Still, it felt a little like a game. The men carried proclamations as well as other materials in knapsacks on their backs. The four walked across frozen streams and woods until they came to a spot along the main road out of the town, about a kilometre from the centre.

While Ungurys and Lakstingala kept watch from a hill alongside the road, Vincentas and Lukas nailed proclamations to each of three telegraph poles. They were posters depicting Stalin as a ghoul, consuming the country. Above each proclamation they nailed a warning sign forbidding passersby to remove the posters. At the third pole, the one farthest away from the town, Ungurys and Lakstingala took over, first wiring the poster to a device behind the pole and then setting up a primitive picket fence topped with barbed wire.

"What's that all about?" Vincentas asked.

"You do your job, we do ours," said Ungurys.

Lakstingala tended to be talkative, but Ungurys had a slightly determined air, as if his missions were more important to him than they were to others. It was a form of seriousness that made him curt at times. Lukas liked him well enough, but not as much as his sister, who had been by once and come to look for Lukas to share a cup of tea with him. They didn't really know each other well, and she had sat in the bunker with Lukas while Vincentas asked her questions about her spiritual life.

Lukas and Elena had twice shared glances as Vincentas spoke, and in the first sliver of time a trace of understanding formed between them. She sensed that the older brother indulged the younger one in the same way that she took care of her own brother. They looked at one another again and this time they sensed something else, which made it impossible to look a third time.

Ungurys and Lakstingala took a long time, and it was shortly before dawn when they finished. Vincentas and Lukas were very cold, and they trotted up and down the road to warm themselves.

"Now we withdraw to a vantage point and watch," said Lakstingala.

"Flint didn't say anything about that," Lukas said.

"Not to you he didn't. He only tells you what you need to know."

Using pine boughs, they erased their footprints and moved more deeply into the forest, up a slight rise and behind a thicket of bushes, which camouflaged them but permitted them a view of the road below.

Lakstingala and Ungurys lit cigarettes and smoked them, then buried the butts in the snow. They each carried a light machine gun, which they unslung from their shoulders and rested on their laps. Lakstingala instructed Vincentas and Lukas to ready their rifles, and they waited.

It was very cold, and they had been up all night, which made the cold bite even more. Ungurys gave Vincentas a dirty look every time he coughed, and so he tried to do it into his gloves whenever the need arose, muffling the sound.

An hour after dawn they heard a Studebaker coming out of the village, its exhaust a funnel of steam in the morning sunlight. The car drove past the first proclamation and then stopped and backed up.

Three slayers, the driver and a Cheka officer got out. The slayers cut the proclamation off the post with a knife. They did the same at the second telegraph post. When they came to the third, the officer and his driver stayed in the car and only the three slayers got out. Two of them, looking not much older than boys, stepped forward to remove the barbed wire and the poster. The third, considerably older, stood back to watch them work.

The explosion was so great that it blew the one man apart, top-pled the pole onto the second and made the third throw his hands to his face, which had had bits of barbed wire driven into it. One of the side windows of the car was blown out as well and from inside it the partisans could hear the officer shouting at the driver. After a few moments the car circled and drove back into town.

The wounded man was disoriented, blinded, turning around and around as if expecting help to come from the car. He moaned and shouted incoherently. Ungurys snorted.

"The fool's expecting help. The other two will be shaking in fear and looking through the back window all the way home. They won't return until they have thirty men with them."

"All right," said Lakstingala. "Let's go home."

"What about the poor man on the road?" asked Vincentas. Lukas looked at the man too. He was howling, his hands over his eyes and blood running down his cheeks.

"What about him?" asked Lakstingala.

"Aren't you going to take him prisoner?"

"We don't take prisoners. We have no place to put them."

"You can't just leave him like that," said Vincentas.

"You're right," said Ungurys. "Put him out of his misery."

"What?"

"If you feel so bad, you should shoot him."

"Vincentas is new," said Lakstingala. "He still has scruples. You can shoot him yourself."

"The machine gun isn't accurate at this distance, and I'm not about to go down and up this hill in knee-deep snow just to save some slayer a little pain. You, Vincentas, shoot the man."

Vincentas blanched and shook his head.

"I told you to shoot him."

"There's no need."

Lakstingala now sided with Ungurys. "You brought up the sub-ject. Anyway, he's your enemy. He's probably condemned priests to death. You'd better shoot the slayer or Ungurys will have you up before Flint. He said you were supposed to be baptized, so get on with it."

"I won't do it," said Vincentas. Lukas noted a sudden change in his tone, a supercilious air that might provoke a man. Lakstingala noticed it too, the arrogance of the superior man, the intellectual who will not stoop so low as others.

"*Won't* do it?" asked Lakstingala. He was the more civilized of the two, the more genial, but a partisan was a soldier. Soldiers followed orders and expected others to do the same, especially unbaptized partisans.

Lukas looked at his younger brother in wonderment. Did Vincentas not see what he was doing by this outright refusal? And couldn't he hear himself talking down to these men?

"Stop this nonsense," said Lakstingala, his voice as cold as the winter day. "I order you to shoot the slayer."

In one smooth action, Lukas lifted his rifle, sighted and fired, the crack of the gunfire a blow to the ears, the smell of cordite immediate.

Lukas lowered his rifle. The slayer had been shot in the chest and went straight down. Vincentas looked at him in horror.

"Lukas, how could you do it?"

"I put him out of his misery."

Lukas said the familiar words to calm his brother, but they did not reflect his own feeling, the strangeness of having committed an irreversible act. Before that moment he had been a student hiding out in the woods. Now he was something else, but the sensation was so new that he didn't yet know the creature he'd become.

Neither Lakstingala nor Ungurys was entirely happy about the way the morning had played out, but as the slayer was dead, there was no point in making Vincentas shoot him again. But Ungurys was still irritated, and he made Vincentas come up last behind them and reprimanded him twice for being sloppy in masking their footprints with the pine branch he was forced to carry.

MARCH 1945

T HE TRAVELLING SHOEMAKER from Merkine warily approached the wooden footbridge on his way out of town. He watched for movement on the country road on the far side of the river, high now with chunks of ice and spring runoff. He had heard gunfire upstream and did not want to run into a firefight or a group of drunken soldiers trying out their new weapons.

Gunfire in the countryside was as common as the cries of ravens. Rifles, hand grenades, pistols and bombs littered the forests and fields; one could find them in blueberry bushes, under stones or at the bottoms of rivers among the crayfish. The previous year, children had gone looking for them after the wild strawberry and mushroom seasons, when the ferns began to curl in the frost and revealed the scattered arms below their withered fronds. The children amused themselves by firing these weapons, sometimes shooting one another or blowing themselves up when trying to fish with grenades.

The lost and discarded firearms had lain hidden by the snow over the winter but were reappearing with the irregular melts of early spring, only to be hidden again at the next snowfall. The harvest of firearms was so common that no one remarked on the occasional gunshot or explosion in the forest or fields.

A red rocket arcing across the sky, on the other hand, festive as Stalin's birthday fireworks, was a signal to Cheka troops that a major concentration of partisans had been found and help was needed. Sustained bursts punctuated by single shots from various types of arms, as well as explosions of grenades or tank rounds, meant that a fight was going on. The partisans fought pitched battles across the country that winter and spring, taking on troops by the hundreds. The Reds ruled the cities and towns, but much of the countryside and some of the villages went back and forth between the hands of the partisans and the Reds.

The gunfire the shoemaker had heard was prolonged. It was a battle, but not a large one. He listened carefully before risking the narrow bridge where he would be exposed as he crossed six or seven metres in full spring flood, but he heard nothing more and stepped onto the boards. He stopped midway to look at the swollen stream, filled with clumps of ice and clods of earth. Something white was floating on the water, bumping against the far bank. The shoemaker hurried to the far side, found a stick and pulled the item to shore.

It was a prayer book, opened in the middle. He read the pages there, in particular the prayer for the dead: *Raise your eyes to the heavens and pray for me, for though my body has been consigned to the underground, we will rise again together in a better life.*

The book had not been in the water very long; the middle pages were not yet thoroughly soaked. Flint would want to see this. The shoemaker made his way onto the forest road and began to take various paths. He stopped from time to time to listen for the snapping of branches that would signal he was being followed, but heard none.

His home base was Merkine, but he did not spend much time there. The ancient town had once been a city, swept over by so many armies that military buttons from various centuries lay in strata in the fields nearby. The hill town at the confluence of the Merkys and

Nemunas Rivers had an ancient church with a steeple, a wooden Russian Orthodox church from the time of the czar and even a stately red-brick high school, two storeys high. It had once been a Jewish school, but since their murder no more Jews were left to fill it. The town was now a patchwork of a few old brick or stucco houses and many wooden ones.

The itinerant shoemaker had worked out of Merkine for over thirty years, walking to the farms within a radius of fifteen kilometres of his home, leaving the town trade to his lifelong competitor, a richer but older and stouter man who did not like to walk. With any luck the older town cobbler would die soon and the shoemaker could take over his trade. The travelling shoemaker was getting too old for so much walking, and it had become dangerous since the war started.

Someone had denounced him as a spy, and Flint had ambushed him on the road and taken him deep into the forest for interrogation. The partisans were ferocious with spies, who sometimes lay in ditches to watch the comings and goings of partisans and then sold the information to the Cheka. The shoemaker protested his innocence and even offered to fix the partisans' shoes to prove his good intentions. Luckily for the shoemaker, he had a straightforward manner, and some of the partisans had been in the forest for a year with the same boots.

The shoemaker had intended to stay in Flint's camp for a week at most, but he had so much work that he remained into December. He would have been working even longer if it hadn't been for the coming snows, which made the partisans stay close to their winter bunkers. The Cheka loved the snow, and awaited it with all the joy of a hunter anticipating the opening of his season.

It would have been better if the partisans had had wings to take them through the trackless sky. In that case they might have flown up to see that they were deep, deep in the Red-controlled zone, and there seemed to be no massing of American and West European troops coming to free them.

This lack of troops would have been perplexing. The French and English had gone to war over Poland, so why did the Westerners let their young men die if not to save that country? Surely the next to be liberated after Poland should be Estonia, Latvia and Lithuania, which thought of themselves as part of the European family.

No one else did. The English had decided to give the three Baltic countries to the Soviets if they ever asked, but the Reds never bothered. They believed they didn't need to. Had the partisans been birds, one of them might have perched on a branch in Yalta, where Roosevelt told Stalin he could keep the Baltics as long as he was discreet. As for Ukraine, where the partisan movement was much bigger and fiercer, Roosevelt did not even think it was worth mentioning.

And if the partisans could have looked into the future as well as into the distance, they would have seen a fog descending over Eastern Europe, a haze of ignorance in which much of what the Reds said was believed in the West. Anyone who had run away from the place, the Reds claimed, must have been a Nazi, and anyone who stayed behind to fight must have been one too. As the old archives were locked up, no respectable historian would write about the place because no respectable historian would work from secondary sources. As for what the partisans and émigrés wrote or said, their words could not be taken seriously. They were at best just pawns in a game they could not see properly, and at worst an entire race of criminals who hid out in the forests because they had nowhere to flee with their crimes.

But the partisans, of whom Lukas was now a member, were confined to the time they lived in, to the earth they walked upon, often living beneath it in bunkers, where the papered walls grew mould in the corners, the ceilings leaked drops in every thaw, and the air was thin during the day because it was dangerous to put in too many air vents, which gave off steam in the cold. The bunker was a home and a trap, safe if secret, but deadly if found out.

Now that the spring thaws had begun, the partisans could come out of their burrows from time to time, and the shoemaker could visit them. The shoemaker did not mind staying with the partisans as long as there was enough to eat and the men appreciated him, admiring his work and thanking him extravagantly, far more than customers who paid for their repairs with money. It was almost like being with a hunting party. The shoemaker spent his time more happily among these men than he had anywhere in years, even though his wife would scold him for being away so long and coming home with no money.

At his house in Merkine, his wife kept the vegetable garden, a cow and a goat, and he returned every week or two, depending on the season and his business. She was the only person who made him hesitate about retiring in town once the other cobbler died. Sometimes there were moments of tenderness when he returned from a long walk among the farms and hamlets, especially if he brought home a little money. What would happen to those moments of tenderness if they lived together all the time?

After finding the prayer book in the river, the shoemaker took half a day of circuitous forest travel to reach Flint's camp. He told Flint his story and gave him the prayer book, and then set himself up by the fire, opening the wooden box he carried on a leather strap over his shoulder. Soon he was working on a pair of boots that needed new heels, and three men waited their turn, having no other shoes but the ones they wore on their feet.

Flint sent a pair of scouts to find out how a prayer book had ended up in the river, and they came back with news soon enough. Three partisan couriers had stumbled upon a Cheka ambush and there was a firefight. The partisans withdrew as far as the river, and when their ammunition ran out, they opened their packages and flung their documents, letters and belongings into the river to keep them out of enemy hands, and continued to fire until they ran out of ammunition altogether. Then they blew themselves up.

Flint reflected on the news as the men stood about, downcast. "Did they manage to destroy their faces?" Flint asked the scout.

The families of dead partisans were singled out for harassment, sometimes for prison or deportation. Those killing themselves tried to destroy their distinguishing marks, particularly their faces, but whether the faces were destroyed or not, the Chekists set the bodies up in the marketplace as a kind of display. The Chekists took away their shoes and socks so the bodies looked poor, and sometimes they ordered people to beat the dead bodies with sticks.

The Lithuanians were somewhat used to these types of displays. As far back as 1863, when Murayev "The Hangman" had been sent by the czar to suppress rebellion and the dead were permitted to rot on their nooses, displaying corpses was a means of inflicting terror. The Chekists watched to see who reacted.

The job of identifying the dead was often left to old women, *bobos*, kerchiefed grandmothers, widows or beggars. Not even the Cheka bothered to imprison or deport them. Grandmothers knew the bodies of the young men well; they had taken care of them since childhood. A mole on the palm of the hand, a signature scar, a deformed thumbnail—any of these signs was enough. But how was an old woman to keep from crying out in grief if she saw such a sign?

Flint did not know these particular partisan couriers; his men were all accounted for. They must have belonged to a neighbouring band.

He couldn't let the spring begin like this, with a defeat within his territory. It would not do for morale. And the thought of the bodies lying in the town square was unpleasant.

"This is so very sad," Flint said to the men gathered around for a meeting at the camp where Lukas and Vincentas had first met him. "But being sad all the time won't do us any good. I think we should teach the Cheka some respect."

Lukas agreed along with the others that it would be good to act. He had not been away from the camp since the incident on the road. His study of English was not going well. Sometimes Flint would come to the communications bunker and listen to the French news, which he understood, and then translate it back to Lukas. But Flint wanted the BBC news. He believed that hope lay with the Anglo-Saxons, who were closer to the Americans.

And it would be good to get out for the sake of Vincentas, who was spending more and more of his evenings praying. Maybe this was natural for a man who intended to be a priest, but Lukas wondered what he could say to God over two hours that couldn't be said in half that time. Or less.

Lukas missed his home, but he missed his university residence and his student friends even more. He had been on the brink of a new and better life, but that life had receded from him now. The only hope of ever bringing it back was to fight.

It took a day to make contact with the neighbouring partisan bands and draw up plans to seize Merkine. It would show the Chekists they could not act with impunity. Six bands would attack different objectives simultaneously, and an assassin would shoot the two most ardent Reds in town. Others would bring back the bodies in the marketplace.

Flint sent the shoemaker home to Merkine and told him to take his wife to another town and visit relatives for a few days. The shoemaker tried to do as he was told, but when he got home his wife was not tender at all, and she was in no mood for travelling on the muddy roads of spring. She called her husband a fool to his face for trying to get her to travel. She repeated her complaints about her husband to the women she saw every day after morning Mass, and word of his pressing need to leave town began to filter through to his neighbours.

Vincentas and Lukas were in a small band of six men led by Lakstingala. Their job was to destroy the stone and stucco house that served as the main office of the slayers, and to make sure they could complete the task, they had been issued a *panzerfaust*, a rocket launcher to be fired by Ungurys. Lakstingala saw the prayer-obsessed Vincentas as the weak link in the group, and assigned him the job of runner, whose responsibility it was to get news to Flint's group, which was going to take the police station across town and destroy the records there.

The six men in Lakstingala's group stood behind a grove of pines on the edge of town, the first houses visible fifty metres away. It had been snowing, and there were already ten centimetres on the ground, which would make running hard, but if the snow kept up, at least it would mask their footprints when they retreated.

Lakstingala and Ungurys each wore white camouflage, but there had not been enough to go around for the others. The men had been standing in their positions since before dawn, waiting for the firing on the other side of town that would be their signal to attack. Lukas's feet and fingers were cold. He kept his hands tucked under his armpits, but he could do nothing about his feet.

A few shots came from the other side of town. These were followed by sporadic automatic fire. Finally the rate of fire picked up and a couple of grenades went off in the distance. Three hundred metres to the right, Flint and a dozen men began to run across the open ground toward the edge of town, hunched over and with their rifles and light machine guns in their hands.

"This is it. Forward!" said Lakstingala.

They were barely out of cover when the flash of gunfire from the window of a wooden house started up, and snow flew as the bullets struck about their feet. They were expected.

"Down," shouted Lakstingala.

The men were each a few metres apart and fell into the snow, and then began to crawl forward, returning fire.

In his grey woollen coat, Lukas felt all too visible against the snow. Some of it had flown up his nose, and the snow beneath him was so wet that he would be soaked if he lay there long. At this rate it would take many minutes before the others were close enough to throw a hand grenade into the open window, and even lying flat they would be all too easy for the sniper to pick off.

Lakstingala read the situation the same way, and called out Lukas's name while telling the others to hold their fire and so provoke the sniper to fire more often.

Lukas raised his rifle and aimed at the window. At the next muzzle flash, even before he heard the report, he fired, and then heard the incoming shot and a grunt from inside the house. Hearing the grunt, Lakstingala rose, struggled through the snow up to the house and threw a hand grenade inside.

Lakstingala waved them all over. None of the men had been shot, but Vincentas looked frightened. "They knew we were coming," said Lakstingala breathlessly, wiping the sweat and melted snow from his face. "Watch all the windows as you go into town. The doorways too. And don't bunch up. Now come on, Flint is far ahead of us and I don't want to fall behind."

By the time they made it onto the street, the inhabitants, both guilty and innocent, had taken shelter and hunkered down. Most of the shutters were closed; there was no movement except for a man in what looked like a uniform running toward the slayer headquarters. Without thinking, Lukas raised his rifle to his shoulder, aimed and shot the man in the back.

Vincentas looked at him and shook his head. Amid the tension and confusion, Lukas permitted himself a moment of exasperation for his brother and swore he would do nothing more to protect him. There was no time for other thoughts.

Lakstingala's group ran up to the dead man and identified him as indeed a dead slayer, his dropped rifle at his side.

"Take the rifle," Lakstingala said to Vincentas, "and check for grenades. Take those too. You," he said to Lukas, "hang back last and keep your rifle up. Cover us as we move forward."

Lukas did as he was told. The men went up to a crossroads with wooden houses on all four corners. The baroque church with its stone wall, iron gate and steeple stood nearby.

Lakstingala looked both ways and made it across, but the second man was hit by a burst of automatic fire. There was a machine gun up in the church steeple. The church was manned as a defensive position.

Lukas could not get a good shot at the steeple without exposing himself, and so stood little chance of hitting the man in there, but he harassed the sniper with short, three-round bursts of fire as often as he dared until the others made it across the open space. There was no one to cover him. He waited a few moments and then ran across, a burst of machine gun fire clipping at his heels until he made it to safety.

Lukas stood leaning against the wooden wall of a house, breathing hard, when the shutter creaked, opened, and a rifle barrel came out. Lakstingala fired two shots from across the road and the rifle clattered onto the cobblestones outside. Without pausing to consider if the man who had stuck out the rifle barrel had hidden himself among women or children, Lukas tossed a hand grenade into the room and waited for the explosion before looking to Lakstingala for further orders.

"Take the fallen rifle too," said Lakstingala to Vincentas.

"I can't carry all this."

"Just sling it over your shoulder."

There was no time to go back for the fallen partisan at the crossroads. He was not moving anyway, and he lay in the line of fire of the sniper in the church steeple. Intensely aware of not making themselves visible from the steeple, Lakstingala's men threaded their way to the one-storey stucco headquarters of the slayers in a small square not far from the centre of town. Along the way they came upon an overturned Studebaker, empty, with a leaking gas tank that had spilled fuel across the entire road.

"Be careful not to set the gasoline on fire," said Lakstingala, and the men walked through it gingerly, though Ungurys slipped and went down on his side before rising again.

By now sounds of rifle shots and machine gun fire came from many different places. The resistance of the Reds was sporadic, most of the local Communists having fled to cellars and pantries. The church steeple needed to be avoided. Whenever Lukas could see it from some new vantage point, he fired upon it in order to make the sniper more frightened, less vigilant in taking opportunistic shots at the partisans.

The slayer headquarters had a heavy wooden door. The building was full of men, with at least two rifles at every window. Lakstingala's band could not draw closer than the trees at the perimeter of the yard. One of the partisans had a heavier machine gun with a tripod, but even those bullets could not pierce the thick walls, and there was no way to get a good position to fire upon the wooden doors.

Lakstingala studied the building. "Concentrate your fire on the two windows on the east side," he said. "Don't waste all your ammunition, but try to shoot out all the glass and take out the crossbar of the window frame. I don't want any obstructions."

The five men fired upon the windows furiously, and soon they were only empty openings. They received no return fire while they were shooting, the men inside likely lying on the floor to protect themselves.

The partisans had to keep up sporadic fire to permit Ungurys the time to come to a kneeling position with the panzerfaust on his shoulder. It was a single-shot weapon, and they did not have another. It was essential that he shoot into the window to achieve maximum damage, and to do it quickly before the men inside had time to position a machine gun at that window.

"Remember that the men inside killed our partisans a couple of days ago," said Lakstingala. "Show them no mercy. Kill anyone who escapes."

Ungurys braced himself with this left shoulder against a tree and stayed within close coverage of the wall of the house behind him to protect himself from the sniper in the church steeple. Lakstingala had the others spread out to kill any survivors who might escape from the door or windows after the rocket was fired.

The missile entered the window perfectly, struck some obstruction inside, and exploded so strongly that all the remains of the other windows and the door blew out.

There were no survivors.

The partisans would have cheered, but they turned at the screams of Ungurys. None of them had fired a panzerfaust before, and none had been aware that the back flash was murderous if there was any obstruction behind the shooter. By staying close to a wall to keep out of sniper range, Ungurys had permitted the back flash to ignite him, and the gasoline he had trod through now burned as well. Lakstingala moved forward to knock him into the snow, but the church steeple sniper saw Ungurys and shot him.

Lakstingala and the three other men fell back into the cover of a house when Ungurys went down. His clothes continued to burn, but he did not move.

The smouldering hair and flesh smelled bad.

Lukas and the others watched helplessly for a few minutes until the snowfall began to thicken. It mixed with smoke that was rising from fires around the town. Then Lakstingala, masked from the steeple by the falling snow, stepped forward and patted down the flames that still burned on Ungurys's body. Lukas joined him and together they dragged the body within the protection of the wall.

Though he was tired and frightened, Lukas felt a pang for Elena, who had loved Ungurys so well.

Lukas had been sweating, and now he could feel the sweat cooling on him, making him shake a little. His brother's face was covered with dirt and soot and he looked stunned. Lukas would have liked to rest a little, but Lakstingala gave them no more than a few minutes.

The snow began to fall more thickly. With nothing in particular to shoot at, the sniper in the church steeple fired in short, random bursts, putting the men on edge. Although the sniper could not see them, they could no longer see him either and could never be precisely sure when they might fall in the line of fire.

They went back to the crossroads where the first partisan had fallen, and then they dragged the bodies of their two dead comrades to the town square. The three men killed days earlier were lying there too, their bodies sheathed in snow. Lakstingala tried to wipe down their faces to look at them, but the faces were just masses of ruined, unrecognizable flesh. One had a rosary draped around his neck, a form of mockery.

Intense gunfire came from two other quarters of the town.

"What do we do next?" asked Lukas.

"Flint was supposed to rendezvous with us here," Lakstingala said. "We were going to retreat with the bodies on a cart, but now I don't know if he'll make it. Lukas, go and see if you can find a sled or Flint. Come back with whichever one you find first. Vincentas, leave the extra rifles and go in the direction of the gunfire and see what you can scout. If you don't see anything, come back in ten minutes and we'll retreat with the bodies."

Each man did as he was told.

Vincentas did not know the town at all, and the smoke and snow made it very hard to see anything. He tried to keep closest to the walls of houses that came between him and the church steeple, but the town was not densely built and there were yards and other gaps that he had to run across.

He checked his ammunition and saw that he had not fired a single shot. And yet he remembered pressing the trigger. He examined his rifle and saw that he had never even taken off the safety. Some soldier he was turning out to be.

Vincentas wanted to pray as he walked into the obscurity, but it seemed obscene to pray with a rifle in his hands. And the intermittent sound of the sniper in the steeple enervated him, even though the gunfire was muffled by the falling snow.

He shivered. His boots, for all their good repair, were soaked right through and his fingertips were so cold he was not sure he would be able to pull the trigger even if he had to.

A burst of machine gun bullets hit the house behind him, and unsure of their origin he turned around the corner of the house, ran into a yard and then ducked around a couple more buildings. He listened for firing from the church steeple, but it had fallen silent.

Now he could not orient himself. The gunfire at the opposite end of town was diminishing and moving. He was lost, unsure how long he had been gone, unsure of which way to go back. He stumbled against a low fence and just managed to keep himself from falling into the unshuttered window of a house. Before he pushed himself away, he saw inside. Their shoemaker was there, sitting in the corner by a candle with his wife. They both looked up at him through the glass, fear on their faces.

They should have left town, as Flint had told them to do. Flint would have been suspicious of their presence, and all the more so because the partisan attack had seemed anticipated. The old couple were lucky Vincentas was the one who stumbled upon them. He waved through the glass, but they did not recognize him.

Vincentas walked on, found a road and followed it, but the snow was thicker, the visibility diminishing. He was afraid he might come across the Reds, but he came instead to the high school, a two-storey red-brick building. He was very tired and cold. He would step inside for just a moment. Two of the three classrooms on the ground floor were empty, but not the third. He found a senior class of high school students and their teacher, all lying on the floor. One of the young men jumped to his feet when he saw him.

"You're a partisan!" he said. "Have you come to liberate us?"

"Get back on the floor," said the teacher.

But the young man was not to be stopped. He wore thick glasses and a homespun suit, and was therefore from a poor farm. Vincentas smiled a little to see a younger version of himself.

"The boys in this room are ready to join you," he said. "We'll kill the Komsomol girl here and help save the country."

Poor boy. He would come to regret his words after the partisans withdrew and the Komsomol girl carried home news of what he had said. A harder man, someone like Lakstingala, might shoot the girl to save the boy's life. Vincentas could not do that, but he tried to do something.

"The partisans don't need your help now," said Vincentas. "You can serve your country by finishing your studies and learning how to be good men and women. And the first thing you have to learn is not to betray one another. You, young woman, is it true you're in the Komsomol?"

She could not reply. She was weeping.

"Well, it doesn't matter. As long as you never intended to hurt anyone. And even if you have joined the Komsomol, you must love your classmates. How can you love your country unless you love the people in it? Study hard, and be good students."

Vincentas suddenly became aware of himself, a dirty, wet man with a rifle in his hand giving a small sermon to the boys and girls. How long had he been gone from Lakstingala's band? He wasn't sure. He had to get out of there. He told the high school students to stay on the floor and listen to their teacher and not move until all the firing in the town had stopped.

Back out on the street, he heard very little gunfire. It occurred to him that the partisans might have retreated without him. Flint had drawn a rough map of the town and made them memorize it, and now that he knew he was at the school he might be able to orient himself and find his way back to the square.

But the snow and the smoke were bewildering, and soon he lost his orientation again. Two figures in white appeared in front of him, both of them dressed in battle gear, as Lakstingala and some of the others had been. He raised his hand to wave to them, and realized too late they were Reds. He raised his rifle at them and pressed the trigger but had forgotten to take off the safety. Rather than reach for it, he muttered the opening words of the last act of contrition.

AUGUST 7, 1945

*T*HE WAR had ended for the Westerners in Europe on May
8, 1945, after which Germans and Americans, English and
French and others all laid down their arms and began the
hard road to peace, the rebuilding of ruined cities, the denazifica-
tion that would clear away the old enemies, and the counting of the
dead that would lead to an understanding of the horror that innocent people had suffered through.

But in the East, no such end came. Instead, in Estonia, Latvia
and Lithuania, in Ukraine and Byelorussia and parts of Poland, the
war went underground. For a while the partisans fought pitched
battles from fixed positions, but now that Germany was defeated,
the Reds could turn and devote their strength to making the new
lands conform to their plan.

In the West, the demobilized soldiers went home to build homes
and garages and to fill them with refrigerators, washing machines,
televisions and cars. In the East, the project begun in the Soviet
Union twenty years earlier was continued, and the farmers were
stripped of their land. The mass deportations began in earnest again,
the cattle cars rolling northeastward with hundreds of thousands of
men, women and children, many to be starved, frozen or worked to

death. Whole categories of people were doomed: school principals, former government bureaucrats, former army officers all the way down to sergeants, policemen, train conductors, nuns, monks and many priests, shop owners, and any farmers rich enough to have had hired hands.

The Reds could sweep the countryside and hold it as long as they were present, but as soon as they left, the partisans came out of their bunkers again to assassinate the local Reds whose job it was to collect requisitions, police the streets and, in particular, check the myriad documents that the regime began to issue. These documents multiplied till they became like the strips used to wrap mummies, and with the same effect: the immobilization and entombment of the bodies of the inhabitants.

By now, Lukas was accustomed to sleeping outside day or night, in the rain or snow, to eating whatever he had foraged, from a fish found frozen in the ice to spring sorrel. He could sleep in the branches of a tree if he had to. He could shoot a slayer dead at a hundred metres, if he had the right weapon, or blend so thoroughly into the landscape that a Red could pass right by him and not notice he was there.

Since the death of his brother, Lukas had learned to bury all feelings as deeply as possible, although they sometimes rose up and clutched at his throat. Tears ambushed him when he was alone on sentry duty or scouting the fields for roving bands of slayers. These eruptions did not relieve his sense of loss, or help him in any way to come to terms with his new life. They only made him feel worse, and he did all he could to keep his untamed emotions buried.

He struggled with this project of turning himself into an automaton. On the one hand, he did not want to think about his lost brother, whose body was never found, and he did not want to humanize his enemies, because those kinds of feelings would make him weak in the work he must do. On the other hand, if he had no emotions at all, he would not love his parents or his country or anyone else. He began to understand poor Ungurys a little better now. He had been taciturn in the extreme, but his sister, Elena, was warm. Ungurys must have shared some of this warmth until his life in the partisans hardened him. And yet it was strange that love of country should make one a killer, that love should lead to its opposite.

The longer the partisans lived in the countryside, the more feral they became; a bookbinder, a teacher or a carpenter ceased to be any of those people in the forest and became another creature instead.

The genus *Partisan* adapted and differentiated according to the places where the fighters found themselves. Flint's band belonged in the species of *Field Partisans*. It consisted of foxes that ran along the roadsides, among the brambles and through woodlots to dart into the fields and granaries when opportunities presented themselves. Visiting farmhouses at night, they knocked on the shutters to ask for food and news of slayer squads and Cheka interior army forces. If their luck was bad, the field partisans found their enemies on the other side of the shutters.

When the Cheka interior army hunted them with hounds, the field partisans dabbed their shoes with lamp oil to throw off the dogs, and slunk into thickets or underground bunkers, some cavernous and others no bigger than burrows. They built hideaways whose entrances were halfway down wells, under woodpiles or haystacks, or right out in the open fields. They fought viciously when cornered.

Field partisans ate better than the other species because they ventured out among people so often, but sometimes they did not return from their sorties. Their bodies joined masses of carcasses thrown into the marketplaces, shoeless and bloody, heaped up like Red trophies of the hunt.

Flint's band was attending a parliament held in the forest, an attempt to forge an alliance among the last free beings in the land. It was safer for partisan bands to be free-standing units because they were less likely to be traced, but they also needed to know what the other bands were doing. Somewhere far away, Lozorius was reputed to be working to keep open the lines of communication among them, but no one was sure what he was doing or even if he was alive. He was like a miracle, more an article of faith than a fact.

The summit was hosted by the *Pine forest Partisans*, who carried themselves far less watchfully than their field cousins. The deep pine forests covered the poorest, sandy land in Lithuania, where farmsteads were few and the Cheka rarely dared to sweep. Whole forest counties remained untamed by the Reds, whose quislings slept together in fortified houses in towns by night, and went out by day only in armed bands.

Tanks could not pierce forests, and rocket flares did nothing to illuminate the deep shadows of the woods. As a result, these forest partisans held themselves more upright in stature. They were lively and good-natured by the massive bonfires they built at night, secure in their forest cover.

But for all their humour and easy-going nature, they were a hungry lot because there was so little food to feed them, and they had to rely more heavily on the few farmers nearby, who were not well fed themselves. Pine forest partisans foraged for wild strawberries and mushrooms, grazing on wild greens when they could find them.

The forest partisans were wood bison, a little slow and heedless, but well defended by their horns whenever they came under attack. Always slightly hungry, they forayed out in groups to strike at remote food warehouses or railway lines.

The *Bog Partisans* were yet another species, men who lived on secret islands in the swamps. The bogs were vast and deadly to those ignorant of the underwater bridges that the partisans had built. The bog partisans were beavers, industrious in their engineering. They hid in the reeds, kept boats among the bushes, and saved ammunition by leading their enemies into sinkholes of mud, where a fully armed Cheka soldier might descend into the bog to join bodies that had been resting there since the Iron Age.

But the bog partisans paid the same price for their security as the pine forest partisans, namely hunger. They fished when they could, cut down trees in which ravens had built nests, and snared whatever rabbits lived nearby. Their damp surroundings and lack of food made them pale and watchful. Persecuted by mosquitoes, they either grew indifferent to their bites or went mad.

The bog and forest partisans preyed on caravans heading east. Now that Germany was defeated, the Reds were stripping it to feed their own people. Disassembled German factories rolled by on trains, as did houses, including doors and windows and even nails, straightened by prisoners of war before being set in boxes. Food went the same way. No one thought too much about what the remaining Prussians would eat. They were going to be driven out of the country anyway, and if some died, there would be fewer to move.

At present the local partisans had robbed a food train of sugar, and sprinkled it on everything the other partisans had brought, from barley soup to cucumbers. A year later, when the sugar had all been eaten, they would regret the lack of partisan dentists, and cure themselves with pliers.

Lastly there were *Town Partisans*, but these were few. They lived legally, or semi-legally with false documents, and helped to bring word of army movements and deportations, as well as lists of traitors who had signed up to become slayers or Red functionaries. The city partisans were mice, secretive and silent, but susceptible to capture in the traps set for them.

Elena was a town partisan, an underground courier who had come into the realm of the forest partisans first in order to visit her brother and then to collect copies of the underground newspaper to circulate back in her hometown. Now that Ungurys was dead, her visits to the free realm of the countryside were coloured by melancholy.

She slowly became aware that her workplace lay in the heart of an experimental agronomical project, an attempt to uproot the native growth and to sow the land with seeds that made a new sort of person. But the uprooting was an ongoing problem. The native growth was stubborn. And she came to realize she was an ally in this project of uprooting, or, if not an ally, then at least a functionary in the apparatus of destruction.

She would have to get out. She hated them all, from the affable but slovenly Gedrius, who was to be avoided in the cloakroom, to her roommate, the born-again Komsomol girl. It amused her sometimes that so many important officials of the new regime did not know they had an enemy in their midst, the quiet woman working the abacus and adding columns of numbers.

At first she had enjoyed the thought that her brother fought against these people in the forest. After his death, her loathing of the functionaries grew so much that she knew she wouldn't be able to disguise it much longer.

Elena had very large brown eyes and was aware that men found her eyes attractive, but she usually masked them with unnecessary glasses when she was at work. In any case, she did not normally look up very much, because her workplace was full of wolves that could tear her apart. Even Antanas Snieckus, the chairman of the Lithuanian Communist Party and a hard-core Stalinist if ever there was one, the man who had deported his own brother to Siberia in 1940, the man whose own mother fled Lithuania in 1944 before he returned with the Reds—even he had paused to look at Elena's eyes during an official visit.

Now she was sorry she had not taken the opportunity to kill him.

Elena's gentleness and simplicity were fading, and she was transforming into something different, hardening around the lips. She kept her shoulders square and wore a working woman's business suit and carried a leather satchel, altogether like a secretary on her way to work.

The partisan newspaper that Elena was supposed to pick up was three days late due to a lack of ink for the rotary printer, and the parliament of partisans was four days late because the bog partisans had had to make it through two separate swarmings of Chekists.

The parliament gathered in a forest meadow with a few trees inside the clearing, and in the shade of one of these Lukas was running off the last of the newspapers and laying them out in the sun to dry. He worked with the radio on a stump beside him, listening to the BBC, much of which he could now understand after a winter and spring of study with the American farmer. Nearby on the grass sat Ignacas in a jacket with a ripped collar and only one button. He had a switch in his hand and was idly whipping it back and forth in the air to keep off the flies. The BBC announcer said something in a voice slightly more inflected than the usual monotone.

"What did he say now?" asked Ignacas.

"Nothing much."

"But what nothing in particular?"

"They were announcing the scores of the British football games."

Ignacas sighed, partially in resignation and partially in envy. There were no football games in this part of Europe, not even high school against high school. The football coach might have been deported to Siberia, a child's parents might have fled to the West, and countless others had simply disappeared. Ignacas wished he could disappear as well.

He was hopelessly inept and never sent out on missions. He was not a good writer, dithering over his sentences too much to be of any use on the partisan newspaper. Worst of all, he was perpetually hungry and had been reprimanded once for stealing food from the stores. One more such incident and he might get court-martialled, which could lead to only two possible results: a further reprimand or execution by firing squad. And yet he considered himself a patriot.

Lukas pitied Ignacas and helped him when he could, but the man had become mournful unless he was eating, and Lukas could listen to only so much misery without having it weigh him down.

Ignacas looked about them to make sure no one was within earshot. "There are a few more days to go until the amnesty runs out," he said.

The Reds had declared an amnesty after the war ended in Germany, and many partisans had taken up the offer. Some of the bands forbade it, but Flint let his men make their own decisions. The only rules were that they leave behind any good weapons they might have and take poor ones, and that they not betray their old comrades. The first part was easy, but not the second. How was one to placate a new master without betraying a former one? Lukas asked him this very question.

"Here's my plan," said Ignacas. "I'll wait until this parliament is over and then I'll slip away. When I turn myself in, I'll do it in some village, where it will take a while for them to work their way up to the proper authorities. Then I'll bring them here as a sign of my sincerity. But all of you will be gone, you see? I'll have betrayed nothing."

"The Reds aren't stupid. Do you think they'll believe that?"

"I'm a good liar."

"Even under torture?"

"They wouldn't torture me, would they?"

"They do sometimes."

"But not ones who give themselves up. I don't think they do. But even if they did rough me up a little, by the time I told them anything, all of you would have moved on."

"Except yourself."

"What's that supposed to mean?"

"You know they never keep their promises. You know your father owned too much land. You're an enemy to them by category—anything you say won't change that."

"I can't think like that. I need to believe in something, and I need to believe they're at least partially sincere. They're building a new world, but they're still fighting a war with people like us. They'll become gentler over time."

"You're sounding more and more Red with every sentence. Maybe you do belong with them."

"Oh, come on, don't turn on me like that. You knew me back in school. You knew what I was like then. But let's face it—I'm useless as a partisan. I wasn't meant for this kind of life. It'll kill me in the long run."

"If they don't kill you first."

"I never realized you were such a hard-liner."

"I'm not. I'm just cornered. I know I have to fight because I have no other choice."

"You do have a choice, and so do I. Why should our generation be sentenced to death? What did we do? We need to find some way to live, some way to go on."

"Taking amnesty won't do it."

"Maybe not for you, but what about me? Would you hold it against me?"

"Each of us has to do what he must."

"But will you tell Flint about my plans?"

"What you just told me isn't a plan, it's an idea. And I don't want to hear any more about it."

Ignacas nodded, seemed about to speak again, but decided against it and turned to waddle away. He was no longer a fat man, but he still carried himself as if he were. No matter how much he gave in to them, the Reds would find he stank of "bourgeois."

Elena made her way past a small group of older partisans by a smokeless fire where Flint was speaking with the leaders of the other bands. They fell silent as she passed. Farther on, a trio of young men sprawled on the grass, two cleaning their rifles and a third writing a letter. They tried to engage her in banter, but she did not have time to talk. She was looking for the latest newspaper and sought out Lukas among his newspapers laid out on the grass.

Absorbed with his work, Lukas did not look up from the press he had been cleaning. He had his sleeves rolled up and wore an apron to protect his clothes from the ink. Sensing someone nearby, he began to speak without glancing up. "I didn't have enough alcohol to thin the ink properly. It's still sticky, and I'm hoping the sun will dry it out. It would be a waste to let the newspapers smudge after all this work."

Lukas's hair was long, curling over his ears. Like the other partisans, he was a little feral, but he wasn't coarse. He looked swift and comfortable, though there was trouble on his face. When he finally did look up at her, the trouble evaporated and his beautiful mouth broke into a smile.

"It's you," he said.

They had not seen each other since early spring, just before the seizure of the town of Merkine.

"I was afraid you might not come anymore," said Lukas, "after you lost your brother. I'm very sorry about that, but I'm glad to see you here. I lost my brother that day too."

"You did?"

"Yes."

She had hardened her heart to help get over the loss. She had thought she could get on with things now, but when she heard of Lukas's loss it reminded her of her own and she could barely speak. Lukas sensed her feelings and came forward and took her hands in his. She looked down, surprised yet gratified, and saw that the ink of his hands had smudged onto hers.

"My brother's real name was Tomas," she said finally, squeezing his hands before letting them go. "I didn't like his code name—it made him sound slippery and cold. He wasn't like that at all, at least when we were younger. After he went into the forest, he changed and started to become taciturn. I think he was killing his old self in a way because he was afraid of being soft. I never had a chance to see him much in the winter because it was so hard to get around. And then the next thing I knew, I received word that he was dead. Now I wish I'd tried harder to see him."

"How could you have known? None of us knows when our time is coming."

"No. You say you were with him on the final mission?"

"Yes."

"Can you tell me what happened?"

It was not that Lukas didn't want to be with her, but he wished they could talk of something else.

"Lakstingala was there and they'd been friends for a long time. Why don't you ask him?"

"I already have. He told me in his rough, country way, his soldier's way."

"What do you expect me to add?"

"I don't know. Why don't you just tell me what it was like?"

"All right."

Lukas took off his apron and they sat down on the grass. The radio was playing on the stump nearby, and the conversation of men murmured indistinctly at the other end of the clearing like the sound of a brook.

"Do you have a cigarette?" she asked.

"I gave them up. The smell of tobacco smoke carries quite a distance, and I didn't like the cravings for it when we were on a mission and I couldn't smoke."

"Then tell me what happened."

Lukas stretched out, leaning on one elbow, and related the day's events in Merkine. He trod carefully through the story, leaving out the part about Ungurys catching fire. He told Elena he was shot cleanly by the sniper and died before knowing what hit him.

"And you retrieved his body?"

"Yes. We buried him a few kilometres away, in a forest."

"How did you dig the earth in the winter?"

"We used an old bunker."

"I would like to visit that place someday."

"I could show you, if you like."

He looked at her then and thought he would like very much to travel with her to that place, sad though it might be. A pair of bees flew slowly about the field flower she held absently in her hands, and she observed them for a moment, and when she looked up, she caught him staring at her face. He was embarrassed, and she blushed in turn.

"Did you bury your brother near mine?" she asked.

"No, we couldn't get the body. I didn't even know he was dead for a couple of days. I kept waiting for him to find his way back to me."

"Are you sure he wasn't captured?"

"It doesn't seem likely."

"Miracles happen sometimes. I've heard of people surviving and showing up much later. I almost wish I knew less about the death of my brother, just so I could have a little hope. Lakstingala tells me I should be very proud of him. Everyone knows about the day the partisans took Merkine. There are stories about it all across the country. He's some kind of hero, I guess."

"Of course he is, but that doesn't make it any easier to live without him. Life is hard." He hadn't meant a great deal by the statement, but it seemed to strike her in some way. She let the flower drop and reached forward and took his hand and squeezed it. For a moment he was afraid he might burst into tears. He crushed the emotion.

"Yes, it's very hard," she said. "Sometimes I think it's unbearable and there's no escape from it. I feel like I'm in a vise that's being tightened by a quarter turn each day." She let go of his hand and looked away to the newspapers lying in the sun. "If the ink won't dry, why don't you blot the sheets?"

"Paper is scarce and I can't be wasting every second sheet."

"I had farm cousins," said Elena after a while. "Their mother laid out linen on the grass to bleach it in the sun."

"My mother used to do that too. Maybe she still does," he added.

"You haven't seen her for a while?"

"About a year now. Not the rest of the family either."

"At least you still have them. I just have my sister."

This was the sort of conversation she could never have in the city anymore. There it was unsafe to say too much, but here she could say whatever she pleased.

"What happened to your family?" asked Lukas.

"Our house took a direct hit when the Reds were coming in the second time. My mother died right away and the house was destroyed."

"And your father?"

"The Reds took him the first time they came."

"So they deported him to the North?"

"I think so. He was in prison in Kaunas for almost a year. I know they knocked out his teeth. His body wasn't there with the others the Reds shot when they pulled back before the Germans, so they probably took him to Siberia."

Or they might have shot him on the way, but Lukas did not say this. "He must have been important."

"He was a high school principal, but his brother owned a car dealership in America. It was enough. They took him in the first days. Then, when the deportations started, my mother and I went to Kaunas and walked out among the boxcars to look for him. There were a lot of people like us, carrying packages with clothes or food for the families stuffed inside the cars. We called up to the air holes, where there was always someone listening. But we never found him. It was a hot day and the guards were getting irritated. They threatened to put us on the trains if we stayed around any longer."

Elena was going to say more, but Lukas heard something and rose to go to the radio and bent over to listen.

"What is it?" asked Elena.

"Be quiet a moment."

She watched him listen, two furrows of concentration forming between his eyes. "Get me a pencil," he said, and she went to the partisan who had been writing the letter when she first arrived. When she returned, Lukas took the pencil and began to make notes.

"Well?" she asked, but he shushed her and continued to make notes until the radio broadcast ended.

"Good news," he said. "I'll tell you later."

"Tell me now."

"I have to speak to Flint first."

He walked to where the partisan leader was talking with the others, and the two of them conferred. A little breeze came up and stirred the newspapers laid out on the grass. Elena tested the ink to see if it had dried. It had, and she stacked some of the sheets carefully, leaving others to dry more.

Flint called the men together and all came around except for the sentries. Flint gave the floor to Lukas, who stepped forward and spoke from his notes.

"The Americans have dropped a bomb on a city in Japan," he said. He repeated what he had heard in the broadcast. "It's a very big bomb. It destroyed everything."

"How big?" one of the men asked.

"Half a city was wiped away."

"What do you mean, 'a city'?"

"I don't know, but the radio said over a hundred thousand dead."

"That's impossible. A bomb that big could never be loaded into an airplane."

The men broke in with many technical questions, most of which Lukas could not answer. He knew only what he had heard on the radio.

Elena was unsure of what to make of the news, but the same was not true of the other partisans. Once they had understood properly what Lukas had said, they took the explosion of the atomic bomb as very good news, the best news they had heard in a long time. They began to cheer and applaud.

Elena elbowed her way through them to Lukas. She took him by the sleeve and pulled him aside.

"What are they so happy about? Think of all those dead civilians."

Lukas was flushed and happy. "We hoped the Americans would go to war with the Reds once the Germans were beaten, but they didn't. Probably this means they weren't strong enough to finish off the Japanese while taking on a new enemy. But now they are. Now that the Americans have this bomb, they can destroy the Reds. They can beat them back. We might be on the verge of freedom."

"In that case, God bless the Americans."

He looked at her and found her beautiful. How had he missed this before? All it took was a moment of hope and he could see clearly again.

"Do you think you could help me?" Lukas asked.

"To do what?"

"You work in an office. Your typing is probably better than mine. If I wrote out the news story, could you type it up on the stencil for me?"

"Yes, I can do that."

Elena waited as Lukas wrote out his summary of what he had heard on the news. The entire camp was buzzing with conversations about the announcement and how soon their lives would be changing. She listened for a while to the news from Warsaw, but there was no mention of the bomb on that station. Moscow said nothing about the bomb, but it did repeat word of its declaration of war against Japan.

Elena typed out the stencil with a typewriter set on the stump, with Lukas hovering over her. He was so anxious about getting the words right that he kept suggesting changes to his own handwritten article. She drove him away until she was done. When he returned, he read over her work carefully.

"I'll start printing these up now," said Lukas, and then he paused, slightly unsure of himself. "Will you wait? If you do, I can walk you to the train station."

By the time Lukas finished the printing and set the newspapers out to dry, evening was drifting into night. The men who had been scanning the radio stations for fresh news had heard nothing and tuned back to Warsaw, which was playing popular music, a foxtrot with a fast beat.

Lukas felt regret that he could not quite understand when another man asked Elena to dance. There were no other women in the camp, but three other couples formed, the men dancing the women's roles, hamming up their femininity, others waiting their turn as the only woman was passed from one partner to another through foxtrots, polkas and waltzes until she broke the heel of her shoe and had to sit down to rest. Lukas would have liked to dance with her too, but there were too many men who wanted her attention.

Soon it would be dark and the dew would settle on the newspapers Lukas had printed. He walked over to where they lay in the fading light, like rectangles of snow on the grass. The ink was not as dry as he would have wished, but the papers had been printed on one side only, so he stacked them back to front, trying hard not to shuffle them so they wouldn't smudge. He put the typewriter back in its case and cleaned the press.

Euphoric, the partisans celebrated by building a bonfire. They sang and danced like a forest hunting party, wishing they could drink as well. Lukas was just finishing when Elena came to him, limping slightly on one foot.

"Are the papers ready?"

"Do you still want them?" he asked, unable to keep out of his voice his envy of the men who had danced with her.

"Of course I still want them. Do you still want to walk with me to the train station?"

"You're limping."

"I broke my shoe, but I can go barefoot if you come along with me."

His envy evaporated in a moment. "You city people aren't used to walking barefoot, especially at night. I have a pair of bast slippers I could give you."

"But how would I return them?"

"They're made out of bark. You could throw them away, or you could return them to me when you come back."

"Do you want me to return?"

"I do."

"Then I will."

Lukas brought the bast slippers for her, but she was unaccustomed to bark shoes and, sitting on the stump in the darkness, could not see how they were fastened.

"Let me help you," said Lukas. He knelt at her feet. The slippers were too large, but he could fold them in a way that would do to get her back to town. The straps were of bast as well and needed to be wound in a particular way to hold the slippers tight.

Lukas felt a slight tingle as he handled her feet. She was shy of her feet, but Lukas delighted in their touch. "How do the slippers feel?" he asked when he was done and she stood up in them.

"Very well. Thank you."

Lukas told Flint his intentions and received reluctant approval to walk Elena back to the train station as long as he stayed off the main road and did not approach the station itself. Like a shepherd, Flint liked to keep his flock close; Reds and slayers prowled day and night.

It was not good to speak while travelling at night because one needed to listen for the snap of branches under other feet, and to keep one's own feet as quiet as possible. But they talked a little in murmurs when they passed running water, which helped to cover the sound of their voices and the noise of the forest floor underfoot.

It was hard to see because there were only stars in the sky and no moon. Elena put her free hand under Lukas's arm and he pressed it to his side. He had not been touched in a very long time and he enjoyed the pressure of her hand on his arm.

"I'm very happy about the news of this gigantic bomb," whispered Elena, "but I hope they use it soon. I can't go on like this much longer." She stepped on a branch that broke with a loud crack, and the noise set off the baying of a farm dog somewhere not far away.

Lukas touched her shoulder to make her stand still as he listened for other sounds. She stirred and he touched her again to keep her still. He removed his rifle from his shoulder and waited, listening intensely, but after the dog stopped howling all he could hear was the sound of her breath in the night, and he stood still a little longer in order to drink in the sound. He bent toward her to tell her quietly that they could go on now, but as he moved forward she turned her face up to him, and with her lips so close to his he kissed her.

He set the rifle against a tree and she put down her sack and leaned back against another tree. The touch of her felt very fine, the smell of her hair something vaguely sweet and feminine mixed with woodsmoke from the fire and the outdoor smells of leaves and grass. They kissed for a long time, and he let his lips go across her cheek and up her neck to her ear.

"Let's sit down," he said.

It was dry on the earth and for a moment he wondered if she would permit him to continue to kiss her. She did, and more than that, she put her arms around him and they lay side by side, sometimes kissing and sometimes just holding each other. After a while he shifted a little, but she pulled him in tight.

"Don't let me go," she said.

"I won't."

He squeezed her very hard and she did the same, and something about the tightness squeezed out some of the pain of the death of his brother.

"Let's sit up now," she said after a while.

"Be very quiet. We're not far from the road." And then, after they had sat up, "Can you stay here a little longer?" he asked.

"Not much. There's only one more train to Marijampole tonight."

"Go tomorrow."

"No, I can't stay. I wish I could, but I have to be at work in the morning and I need to leave these papers at home."

"When will you come back?"

"As soon as I can."

Time was running out. They stood and she brushed herself off. He took her in his arms one more time, kissed her, and let her go.

SEVEN

VILNIUS

NOVEMBER 1945

*T*HE CITY OF VILNIUS, the new capital of the Soviet Socialist Republic of Lithuania, was a city of ghosts and a city of strangers. The ghosts originated with the Jews and the old Polish ruling class, dead or deported but haunting the city, alarmed by its drastic changes, not so much in architecture, although whole neighbourhoods had been bombed, as in the wholesale disappearance of survivors.

The Polish Home Army had helped seize the city from the Wehrmacht in 1944, only to be disarmed by the invading Reds and deported north to die for their trouble. The Reds gave the city back to the Lithuanians and deported whatever Poles remained to within the new borders of the new Polish state. The Jews, of course, were mostly dead already.

Vilnius had been a provincial city for three hundred years, but now it became a capital again. The Lithuanians who streamed into the city to work as teachers and bureaucrats functioned under the tight leash and watchful eye of their Red masters. The bureaucrats had jobs to do: counting the square footage of destroyed apartments, forming work brigades to clear the rubble where the city had been shelled, and removing religious paintings from the churches so the buildings could be changed into warehouses and museums. Much as the Vilnius residents despised their new overlords, they were under too much scrutiny to organize resistance. Opposition lay with the partisans in the countryside.

As for the ghosts, their sadness went unnoticed by the new inhabitants. If anyone knew about the sorrow of these ghosts, it was those who had managed to escape and live elsewhere, in New York, or Tel Aviv, or Warsaw. With no one to haunt properly, Vilnius's ghosts were malnourished and sickly, doomed to fade more quickly than phantoms at other sites.

As a result of the war and the emptying of the old inhabitants, Vilnius was both a free city and a dangerous city, empty in so many quarters that a vagabond could live unnoticed for weeks in the rubble yet be subject to unpredictable sweeps by militia, Chekists and Red Army soldiers, who pointed their rifles first and asked for documents second. The detritus of the war, the widows and widowers, the orphans and the estranged, the hurt and the unhealthy, the angry and the mad—all of these pools of people appeared in the city as if from nowhere, speaking languages unrecognized locally and thus as lost as the ghosts.

For all the policing, the place was also full of thieves: desperate men, women and children who could not leave, because either they had no documents, or their offences were too well known, or they had a natural taste for crime and longed to be among others of their kind.

Lukas walked into the city just after dawn with a rough cigarette on his lips, a cap over his eyes and a basket that contained eight cooked beets in their shrivelled skins. He arrived unremarked, among country people who straggled into town to sell whatever they could spare in the marketplace or, better yet, to barter for things they needed.

He made his way across town, through the ruins of the larger Jewish ghetto and over toward the Dawn Gate, one of the medieval city gates where a miraculous painting of the Virgin hung in a shrine untouched by the Reds, the better to attract suspicious elements. Lukas ducked into a side street before he reached that choke point where there was bound to be a documents check. He had false documents, but he did not want to test them.

He walked through the first courtyard and looked for the chalked circle on the archway, found it as expected and then walked into a ruined building, following broken stone steps down to a closed cellar door.

When Elena opened the door, she didn't recognize him at first, and spoke sharply in Russian and then Polish.

"It's me," said Lukas.

She pushed the cap up off his face to reveal his hair falling on his forehead. "Shame on you for frightening me like that."

Elena pulled the hand-rolled cigarette out of his mouth and threw it on the landing outside before taking him by the sleeve and pulling him into the room. Then she took his face in her hands and pulled him forward to kiss him on the lips.

Each meeting was a gift now that they had found each other. But every joy was sharpened by the knowledge that it might be the last one. The sheer luck of their survival, to say nothing of the ability to meet, was like a small miracle. Lukas pulled away, put down the basket and held her in his arms for a while before kissing her again.

The cellar was dark and cool and smelled of mould. An artillery shell had come through the roof and both floors to embed itself unexploded in the cellar. It would lie there quietly until 1971, when an ambitious and ahistorical home renovator would tap its side with a hammer and blow up himself and the old woman living in the flat above. But for now it lay quiet, waiting.

The only light in the cellar came from the hole the shell had left in the floor above, a miniature skylight.

"No one else came with you?" asked Elena.

"No."

"So what happened to that atomic bomb of yours? I haven't heard anything about Moscow in flames, have you?"

"Not yet. That's what this meeting is going to be about."

"Do you think there's still hope for a war?"

"Oh yes, eventually. We just have to keep our spirits up."

"Easier said than done."

It was hard to see Elena clearly in the dimness, especially with the light from the air shaft to her back, but he didn't really need to see her face in detail. He felt her presence, her warmth, an emission of tenderness that needed no light to be seen.

"My spirits are good," said Lukas. "If you feel bad all the time, the Reds have won. I want them to feel the sting of my whip on their asses. That uplifts me. When I looked around the city on my way into town, I saw nothing but downcast people on their way to work. We're becoming a nation of serfs. I, for one, refuse to be downcast."

Lukas looked at Elena, slightly embarrassed by this speech. She stood up on her tiptoes and kissed him. "You lift my spirits too, when we're together. Sometimes I think we should make ourselves some very fine false documents and then find a forgotten corner of this country and settle down to live." She said it quickly, knowing he wouldn't like the idea.

"That would make me a deserter. If Flint or any of the others caught us, we'd be shot."

"I know it's impossible. But on the other hand, the partisans of one district never really know what's going on in the next one. If we moved over two provinces, we might be able to do it."

"To hide from the partisans and to hide from the Reds—we'd be double fugitives. What kind of life would that be?"

"At least we wouldn't be doomed."

"Doomed?"

"You can sting the Reds all you want, but they won't go back home because of you."

"Maybe not, but at least I'll have the satisfaction of knowing they didn't go unpunished."

"That's what I want too. When I think of my brother, and yours as well, I rage and rage, but feel impotent. Why are the Americans so selfish with their bomb? Why can't they help us with it?"

"I don't know."

A table and four chairs stood in the corner of the ruined cellar, trash left behind by other scavengers. The chairs looked wobbly and mean. Lukas set his basket upon the table.

"What do you have there?" Elena asked.

"Just some beets, but they're cooked. Are you hungry?"

"I'm always hungry. I have half a loaf of bread and some cold tea in a bottle."

"Then let's sit down for a moment. How much time do we have before the others arrive?"

"Maybe an hour, if everything goes well. Do you know what this is all about?"

"I do, but let's wait a bit first."

By the light from the air shaft, Lukas laid out his eight wrinkled beets on the table and watched as Elena removed a small loaf of dark rye from her briefcase as well as a stoppered half-litre bottle filled with sweet tea.

"Please, have a seat," said Lukas, as if he were a waiter in a fine restaurant.

"Let me do this," said Elena. "Do you have a knife?"

Lukas passed her a small pocketknife with which she peeled four of the beets and cut them into quarters, the way a mother might quarter a small orange for her child. She cut two slices of bread for each of them. Even in the bad light, her fingers were bright red. She stuck one of the beet quarters and offered it to Lukas off the end of his knife. He took it and put it in his mouth. When he reached down for the second piece she offered him, his fingers were bright red too.

"More than anything else, this is what I'm fighting them for," said Lukas.

"Beets?"

He laughed. "No. Some kind of normal life. We shouldn't be down in a basement like this, hiding away, just because we want to eat together."

Elena didn't reply. She unstoppered the bottle of tea. "We don't have any glasses," she said.

"That doesn't matter."

She lifted the bottle and drank from it and then passed it to Lukas, who drank from it too.

"Flint asked me to come here first," said Lukas, "because he wanted us to have a chance to talk to one another for a while in private."

"He knows about us?"

They had met only three times since the night they had first kissed, but each time they had managed to find a little time together.

"Flint knows everything. We live very close to one another in the bunkers and not much stays secret for long."

"Have you talked to the others about me?"

"How could I not?"

"And what do men like Lakstingala advise in matters . . . like this?" She had almost said "matters of love" but was too shy to use those words.

"Lakstingala is not exactly a romantic, but he has a good heart."

"So what is this thing that Flint wants us to talk about?"

"You work in an office in Marijampole, a place where the Reds congregate."

"Yes, I know that. What about it?"

"There are some terrible Russian Reds there and some converts from the Lithuanian side. These are very bad men, as you've told me. They've sent hundreds to the camps in the North. They've sent others to Cheka prisons and permitted the men and women to be tortured. They have tortured people themselves."

"Yes, yes. What about them?"

"We intend to execute them."

"All right. Of course. I have no problem with that. But why are you telling me this? Do you need my permission? I can find out exactly where they live, if you like. I could look at their registration cards at work and tell you anything you want."

"We'd never get them all. They go about with guards during the day and they sleep in safe places at night. We need to lure them out."

"All right, so we'll lure them out. How?"

"You could invite them to a party."

"I could invite them? To what kind of party?"

"I don't know. A name day, maybe."

"My name day is the second of March, but the Reds don't like name days much because they come off the Catholic calendar."

"We'll think of something else. The details don't matter yet. It's just the principle. Could you do it?"

"Be clearer on what you want."

"You would invite your colleagues and as many important Reds as would come to a party in your flat. Once they were there, we'd liquidate them."

She listened to him and did not reply, falling silent as the meaning of the words sank in. He'd used a euphemism unusual for him. How did one "liquidate" a human being? When she did not speak, Lukas carried on.

"You wouldn't have to do anything yourself, but I have to say it wouldn't be pretty."

"And after it was over?"

"You'd have to flee into the woods with us. Your legal life would be over. One unknown is whether they would come to the party if you invited them."

"If I can find some liquor, food and women, they will come. They are very simple men. Roll me a cigarette, please, as I try to understand this."

Lukas did as he was told, taking out his supplies. The tobacco was homegrown and rough, and glued papers were hard to find, so he twisted the ends of the paper to make a tight cigarette that would be hard to draw on. He gave it to Elena, who examined it. They both remembered the fine cylinders her brother had made for them the first time they met.

"I thought you might have come early to this meeting because you missed me a little," she said.

"I miss you a great deal. I wish I could be with you always."

"But there is business that has to be done first."

"The two are intertwined. I didn't choose the life I'm living now. You said to me that you wanted to leave your old life. You said they were getting suspicious of you at work. This would be your chance to strike back at them, to avenge your brother. And I'd be avenging mine."

"And afterward?"

"We'd be together then. It wouldn't be an easy life, but we'd have each other."

"There aren't many women right in the underground."

"But there are some. Listen to me. I love you. I want to be with you every moment of the day and night."

She paused to let the words sink in. "I love you too, but is this the only way we have to be together?"

"What else could we possibly do?"

"I don't know. And if I don't agree?"

"Then it's just one plan among many, a plan we never carried out. That's all," said Lukas.

"And the two of us?"

"We see each other whenever we can."

"What about my plan?" asked Elena.

"Your plan involved treason."

"And yours involves murder. But if we do nothing, we continue to see each other like we have until now, every few weeks, as the situation presents itself."

"Yes. I can't promise you anything better than that. I'm a soldier. We're at war."

"How would you kill them?"

"Flint and I thought about using poison, but it turns out poison is harder to get than we imagined."

"So?"

"Flint says I'm the best shot he has. We would bring them into one place, feed them and get them drunk, and then I would shoot them while their guard was down. I understand you have a roommate. We could find a way to keep her away."

"She's as bad as the others at work. She's discovered the Komsomol."

"Then you could invite her, and as many women like her as you can think of."

Elena smoked the last of the cigarette and threw it down onto the earthen floor. Lukas stamped it out.

"Your face is an open book," said Elena. "Do you think you could mask it?"

"I don't know."

"You'd have to be all cheerfulness on the surface and a fox beneath that."

"You're speaking as if you've made your decision," said Lukas.

"I have, almost. But I need you to tell me what's in your heart. You Lithuanian men are all silence when it comes to your feelings. I have heard that men in other countries are not so circumspect with their thoughts."

"Do you want me to say again that I love you?"

"Yes, of course I want you to say that. The words are very sweet to my ears and I never tire of hearing them. We're living in an ocean of lies and melancholy, and sometimes I think I can't bear it anymore. I have to have hope of some kind. I'll do this thing if you want me to, and I'll do it for you because you love me, and only for that reason."

"I do love you."

She took his hands in hers and examined his fingers, now just as red as hers. She shook her head and laughed a little, and then pulled him forward, kissing across the table.

LATE SUMMER, 1946

P ETRAS was an alcoholic forger who had stumbled into Flint's realm and now chafed under the restrictions of the teetotalling partisan leader.

"No liquor, no work," said Petras, crossing his arms and looking to his wife, who sat pale and trembling at the kitchen table of the American farmer. To the unease of the American, the partisans used his house more and more often for rendezvous. He wished he could send his children somewhere, but there was nowhere to send them. Thus he became the ambivalent host to partisan meetings and a post office for underground messages.

The forger's greasy black hair had several cowlicks at the ears and the crown, and his suit, tie and collar were both dirty and badly mended. Lukas wondered how such a man, such a couple, ever came to exist. The war gave birth to unlikely pairings: Petras was a country teacher on his way down whereas his wife had been a village slattern who was improving herself with him until the liquor took the upper hand.

Flint stood over the couple at the long wooden table, with Lukas and the American by the door and Lakstingala outside, watching out for Reds.

Petras and his wife were now itinerant forgers, who travelled from village to village creating false documents for payment of samagonas, the home-distilled liquor that every farmer made from whatever was at hand. Petras could re-create official-looking imprints of government stamps out of wood blocks, and his wife had a large collection of blank government forms and suitable paper, as well as the punch used to attach and seal photos to passports, travel documents and military exemptions.

As far as Lukas could see, the man and his wife never ate, but never looked drunk either. Their skill was marvellous, but when they made their way into Flint's realm, he forbade their travelling any farther and kept them under his control. A forger was useful, but a drunken one was dangerous. Sooner or later he would be caught by the Cheka and tell everything he had done for a glass of vodka. Flint kept him at various safe farmhouses and tried to wean him off alcohol. None of the partisans was permitted to drink, and Flint hated to make an exception for the forger.

"The alcohol will kill you both," said Flint. "I'm doing you a favour."

"And how do you expect us to work?" asked Petras. "Look at my wife. She's trembling so much it would be a waste of paper to have her touch anything. And I'm not much better."

"These are petty, personal problems," said Flint. "We're at war."

"If you have a sliver under your fingernail, it hurts whether you're at war or not. If you're starving, you can't fight."

"Alcohol is not food."

"It is to us. You're starving us to death. Every animal has its own needs. The fox wants flesh and the crow wants grain. Only the pig will eat anything, and we're not pigs."

Flint hated to forgo his principles. His principles had brought him into the forest. His principles had kept him there for two years while dozens of his best men died in battle, or were taken prisoner, or blew themselves up to avoid capture.

"One small glass each," said Flint, tapping his pipe on the table to underline his concession.

"One large glass before and one large glass after," said Petras, and so their haggling began, resulting, after much bickering, in medium glasses before and after the job.

Flint put his pipe in his mouth and lit it. He looked at Lukas through the pipe smoke with a hint of accusation. So much trouble just to get the forger to make a top-quality pass for Lukas's personal trip. Although Flint had promised the trip to Lukas, he was not happy about it.

Flint was grudging about giving leaves to his men. Partisans went off on private business and never came back. They stopped for a drink at a former neighbour's house and drank themselves into a stupor, and then wandered the streets until a group of slayers took them down. They went to attend family weddings and exposed themselves to the whole neighbourhood, and were followed back to their bunkers by spies. Time wore the men down, and some betrayed their former comrades for the promise of a soft bed.

But Lukas was something of a special case, and for him Flint was prepared to make an exception. Like Lozorius in the past, Lukas had developed a reputation. He shot dead a roomful of Reds in Marijampole with the help of his fiancée. He was good for the morale of the people, whose only real news came through whispers and the underground newspapers, and whose news was almost invariably bad. A man with a reputation could be given a little leeway.

And finally there was the matter of Lukas's growing signs of distraction. He had fallen irredeemably in love with Elena, from whom he had been separated to keep each of them safe. Flint had managed to keep them apart for four months, hoping Lukas's feelings would cool, but his ardour hadn't cooled at all.

On the night of the engagement party the previous April, Flint was waiting for them with the sleigh as planned.

"How many dead?" he asked as soon as they stepped into the sleigh and the driver cracked the whip at the pair of horses.

"Five dead and one wounded."

"You let him get away?"

"The accordionist."

"You should have killed him too. Now the Chekists will be on our tails very fast."

Elena and Lukas had melted into one another under the woollen blankets, but they came alive again when the sleigh met another one a few kilometres away at a crossroads.

"Lukas, into the other sleigh," Flint had ordered.

Elena shot up. "Where are you taking him?"

"I'm separating you for your own good. The pair of you will be a prize the Reds hunt hard."

"I want to go with him," said Elena.

"You'll do as I say."

"No. You made a promise. I did this to help you and to be with Lukas. You're breaking your side of the bargain. Do that and I quit you right now."

"You cannot quit the partisans. There is no quitting once you're in."

"Then shoot me dead right here. I refuse to be separated."

"Lukas," said Flint, "tell her I'm right."

"I won't do any such thing. You promised."

"Yes, I did. But not to let you stay together right away. We need to disperse for a little while."

"How long?" asked Elena.

"A few weeks at most. Now, come on."

"Wait," said Elena. She took Lukas by the hands. "Do you promise to come back for me?"

"I will. As soon as I can."

"Don't die. Be very careful not to get yourself killed or captured, if only for my sake. You owe me that."

He kissed her, and then stepped into the other sleigh and sped down a branching road.

It had taken longer than a few weeks, but now he was going for her.

After drinking their glasses of samagonas, Petras and his wife regained their colour and set to business, laying out their stamps, inks, pens and papers. Lukas went out to join Lakstingala on sentry duty, finding him seated near the barn with his back against a haystack. Like a sailor, Lakstingala wore his stocking cap in all weather, even the summer heat. He was a comforting man to sit beside because, although he was compact, he seemed to contain great strength, a reserve of potential energy that he could harness if he needed to.

"The smell of hay always reminds me of harvests and afternoon naps. It makes me sleepy," said Lukas, settling in beside Lakstingala. "Aren't you afraid you'll drop off?"

"I never fall asleep on sentry duty," said Lakstingala. "If I did, I would have been dead long before this."

They each knew many dead, in addition to Vincentas and Ungurys. Almost a dozen men had fallen that day in Merkine, and twice as many in the year afterward. New men came to join them, but Flint, Lakstingala and Lukas were among the veterans, men you could be sure of, not only because of their experience but also because of their luck. Caution and skill were important for survival, but so was luck. Why did some fall in a firefight and not others? At any moment the three dice of skill, caution and fate were tumbling; a partisan could control two of the variables, but not the third.

In the last year Flint's band had broken into smaller units of five, very few with the knowledge of where the others had their bunkers. The era of bonfires and dancing in the forest was past, and as well the time of massive attacks upon towns and garrisons. The last really bold act had been the engagement party massacre in Marijampole. That act had been both gratifying and stupid. It lifted the spirits of the Lithuanians as word got out about it, but it excited a whole hornet's nest of Reds, Chekists and slayers, who combed the woods looking for partisans.

The latest partisan battle was against the settlers, Red soldiers who were encouraged to demobilize in Lithuania and take up the farms abandoned by those who had been deported or fled to the West. Lukas wrote public proclamations in Lithuanian and Russian, warning them not to take up the farms, and then letters to the new settlers, giving them a month to vacate their land. Lakstingala led the enforcement brigades that frightened off the settlers, or executed them if they did not heed the warnings.

This type of fighting was more damaging to the soul than battles with Chekists or slayers. Sometimes the settlers resisted, barricading themselves into their houses and shooting it out. It was important to remember that these were the enemy, that they had been warned, that they could have surrendered with a white flag and been escorted with their wives and children out along the road. Still, it was hard to drop a grenade into a house with women and children inside.

Lakstingala and Lukas did not have that much in common, but they had been together in Flint's band for almost two years, and so they had become comrades. It was easier to talk to someone like Lakstingala than it was to some to the newer recruits.

"What if the Reds come up on us from the other side of the haystack?" asked Lukas. "You won't see them coming."

"The rest of the American's family is working in the fields that way. They'll come running if anything's up." Lakstingala took out a pouch of tobacco and some papers. He rolled a cigarette but did not light it because of the haystack. The smell of the hay at his back reminded Lukas of home.

"Going to do a little travelling?" Lakstingala asked.

They compartmentalized each other's lives, knowing some parts and staying intentionally ignorant of others. The question itself was a sign of their intimacy and comradeship.

"Personal business."

"You're a fool," said Lakstingala without a moment's hesitation and without a great deal of inflection.

"What do you mean?"

"Anything personal will put you at risk. You'll be caught in a moment."

"I'll be careful."

"There's no being careful in a trap. Once you're inside, they'll spring it on you and that will be that. And you take this risk to see Elena?"

"That's right."

"You'd give her a better chance of survival by staying away from her. Don't you think the Reds would love to catch the two of you together? You'd be a real prize. If they caught you alive, they'd put your photos on the cover of the local *Pravda*. If they killed you, they'd set your bodies up side by side in the market square and put a wedding veil on her body to satisfy their sense of humour."

"You're sounding a little too angry, my friend. I can't help it that I'm in love."

"What kind of love could that be? You hardly know one another. A few meetings and one mission and your head's been turned."

"People fall in love at a dance in one night. It happens."

"No, you're confusing comradeship with love."

"You're my comrade, but I don't love you."

"Don't make fun of me. I'm serious."

Lukas took off his hat and ran his fingers through his hair. "Look who's talking about love! A bachelor soldier like you!"

"I'm no bachelor. I'm married."

"What? You never told me that."

Lakstingala shrugged. "You never asked me."

Lukas looked at him with new interest. "I had no idea. And you've never seen your wife all these years?"

"Not much."

"But a little, right?"

"A little," Lakstingala conceded.

"So why do you begrudge me?"

"Because I'm worried that you're turning soft just as things get harder, just when you should be getting tougher. We're not the first ones to go into the woods, but we've lasted longer than anyone else. How are we going to survive unless we turn our hearts to stone?"

"I don't understand you."

"It's not the Reds that worry me. It's your feelings. Those are what are going to get you killed."

"How is it possible to live without feelings?"

"It's not, but you have to bury them in order to fight. If you become soft, you'll see the eyes of his mother in every Red you kill and you'll hesitate, and one day you'll die yourself. The only feelings you should have are a thirst for revenge and righteous anger."

Lakstingala looked at Lukas's face, deeply tanned now in the summer, the eyes uncannily bright against the darkness of his skin. He could see a hint of a smile in Lukas's eyes, and the condescension annoyed him.

"You take over sentry duty," said Lakstingala. "I'm going for a smoke."

Lukas couldn't understand why Lakstingala was so angry. He was going to get his fiancée, and if possible show her to his parents before bringing her back to Flint's band.

At the train station in Lentvaris, a town on the outskirts of Vilnius where he slipped back into the aboveground world, Lukas beheld the daylight movement of normal townspeople for the first time in a long while. The forger had assured him that the false documents could pass any inspection, but Lukas carried himself cautiously, even in this unaccustomed mass of people so large that it seemed they would breathe up all the oxygen in the air and leave none for him.

He had been a free animal, and now he stepped back into the zoo and found it stifling. Unaccustomed to wearing a shirt and tie, he felt as if he were being strangled, but did not dare loosen the knot or open the buttons of his jacket for fear of giving away the package that hung on his chest from a string around his neck.

He carried a worn leather satchel with a change of socks and underclothes, a physics textbook, notes, half a loaf of heavy black bread and two thick pieces of country bacon he might eat or use for bribes. He also had binoculars, which were slightly suspicious, but if he was searched he could say he was trying to sell them. He had no weapon except for a paring knife that he kept in his jacket pocket.

The world had changed since he last travelled through it openly, and the Lentvaris station was not as empty as he had hoped. There were dozens of new draftees, those born in 1927, as well as Red Army sergeants and officers who kept an eye on them to make sure they did not desert before reaching their training base. The draftees clutched packages of food from home and wore sturdy civilian clothes, as they'd be neither dressed nor fed during basic training. Nor issued live ammunition, because the AWOL rate was so high.

The tiny station, platform and entranceway were packed with other travellers, from Communist Party workers to demobilized Red Army soldiers, prisoners travelling with guards, beggars, and black market speculators from Byelorussia. Some had been waiting for days for a train, and they slept with their heads on their brown paper packages, pillowcases stuffed with used clothing, and suitcases full of hand soap or woollen socks or other items in short supply in one place but abundant in others. Lukas had to pick his way over them to make it to the ticket window, where dozens of travellers jostled for the right to bend down in front of the low grille and entreat the stony-faced seller to let them buy a ticket. Only the more persistent Cheka operatives with extravagantly foul vocabularies managed to squeeze tickets out of him.

Lukas searched carefully among the shouting, disgruntled travellers, the despairing old women hoping to visit their sons, the soldiers, the bewildered farmers going to appeal to government officials, and he finally identified the weary stationmaster, who walked out occasionally among the masses waiting for tickets or trains. He was slovenly and unkempt, frustrated and irritated by the impossible task of keeping order.

"Excuse me," said Lukas, and the man looked at him, slightly pushing up his cap by the bill and then placing his hands on his hips like someone preparing for another fight. Lukas explained that he was faculty from the technical university in Kaunas and needed to make it to that city by early the next morning to give a lecture. The stationmaster shrugged and waited, and finally he did extend his hand to shake Lukas's when it was offered. Then he turned away to study the size of the bill Lukas had placed in his palm—a hundred rubles. The stationmaster turned back to him.

"Wait over there," he said, motioning to a corner with his head. "I'll see what I can do."

He returned in ten minutes with a ticket, for which Lukas had to pay, and asked for another fifty rubles to pay off the guard, as each car had one, whose job it was to throw off the pressing masses. Lukas suffered a twinge of guilt for the country folk, whom he knew would not get tickets. These meek people would never get what they wanted until they learned to pay bribes. They were a very long way from inheriting the earth.

The train arrived an hour later, guards standing on the steps of each car and holding on to the handrails on each side to block the way of anyone trying to get on board without their permission.

The train was full. Even those with tickets and those who had paid bribes were not permitted aboard, and immediately there were shouting matches as high officials showed their tickets and swore at the guards. Some of the bigger men, or those in twos and threes, pushed their way past the guards only to find that all of the compartments inside the cars were full, and so they settled themselves in the corridors. Others leapt onto ladders only to be beaten back by guards. But there were more wanting to travel than there were guards to beat them off, and no sooner was a ladder cleared of two or three men clinging to it than it filled again as the guard moved on to beat those who had slipped up to the open platforms between cars.

Lukas waited until one such guard had cleared a platform and moved off and then hoisted himself onto it just as the train wheels began to turn. Another man was already standing there, a clerk or government official of some kind who could not bear the crush in the corridors and had stepped outside. Lukas offered him a pre-rolled cigarette.

The man nodded, took it and lit up. "Safer out here anyway," said the man between puffs of smoke.

"Why's that?"

"Two men were murdered in this wagon last night, and their bodies thrown out the window. Killed by demobilized soldiers having a little fun, I think. They let a couple of civilians into their compartment and then robbed them during the night and ditched their bodies."

The distance to Kaunas was only a hundred kilometres, but the train moved very slowly and stopped at every station along the way, and at each station the scene at Lentvaris was repeated. By the time the train was halfway through its journey, it was already the middle of the night and the outdoor platform where Lukas, the clerk and half a dozen others stood was very full.

Lukas was leaning with his back by a broken window when a hand came up from inside and seized him by the neck. An opportunistic thief must have seen him as easy to kill, but many Reds had tried to kill Lukas over the last year and none had succeeded yet. Lukas crouched down as far as he could, putting pressure against the assailant's forearm, pulled the paring knife from his jacket pocket and cut across the top of the hand at his throat. He heard a yelp of pain and the hand withdrew back inside the door.

Rubbing his neck, Lukas pushed himself slightly away from the window and looked at the faces of his fellow travellers, who had

watched the scene without expression or making a move to help
him. Even the clerk who had told him about the murders stared at
him indifferently.

Lukas stepped off the train at the country station of Mauruciai,
walked out of the village and hid himself just inside a wood and
slept for a while. He stayed there until nightfall, cut off a piece of the
smoked bacon and ate a chunk of bread, drinking at a stream to
take off his thirst.

When Lukas made it to the farmhouse deep in the Kazlu Ruda
forest where he was supposed to meet Elena, the fields and yard
were dark and he banged on the door a long time before the farmer
appeared with an oil lamp in his hand.

"What do you want?" he asked. He had a white beard and moustache and would have looked like Father Christmas in his night-
gown if not for the sour expression on his face.

"Any Reds around?"

"How should I know?"

"I was supposed to meet someone here."

"That's your business, not mine. There's no one here but my
family, and you're disturbing their sleep as it is. Good night."

"Just a moment," said Lukas, slipping his foot into the door
before the farmer could close it. "I've been travelling and I'm hungry. Do you think you could give me something to eat?"

"My children went to bed hungry. I have nothing for you."

"Then maybe a bed."

"Every single pillow is spoken for."

Something was wrong. He had arranged to meet Elena here,
but the farmer was being too aggressive. He acted as if Lukas were
a bandit. The most intelligent thing would be to slip away, find a
place in the hay in the barn and burrow in deep until the morning.
But the attitude of this farmer did not please him. Lukas had been
travelling two nights and was tired.

"I'm a partisan," said Lukas.

"Good for you. You go about your business and I'll go about mine."

Lukas lifted his briefcase. "I'm armed. Make me a bed here on the floor by the front door, and be quick about it. Keep the other doors closed until I tell you to come in."

For a while he wondered if the farmer would make him show the non-existent weapon, but he sullenly did as Lukas commanded.

Lukas spent a restless night and rose just before dawn when he heard the farmer begin to move around. Lukas sat at the long table and drank milk and ate bread with the grim farmer and his wife. Two girls and a boy were interested in him, but the parents would not let them speak at the breakfast table.

A face appeared through the imperfect glass in the window. Lukas recognized Elena and his heart leapt up. She waved and then walked around the house and he went to the door, which he threw open to find her in an army uniform jacket and skirt with a hand-made Lithuanian tricolour patch on the shoulder.

Lukas looked at her face, half afraid that he might find coolness there, or caution, or, worst of all, determined friendliness. But instead he saw a mixture of hope and fear that mirrored his own feelings. He took her in his arms, awkwardly, for she had a rifle on a strap over her shoulder, and he held her and kissed her face.

He heard the farmer behind him and pulled away, embarrassed now in the moment after their embrace. She stepped inside and shut the door behind her.

"If I'd known you were here I would have come earlier," she said, taking off her hat and shaking out her hair, "but I expected you two days ago and thought something had happened." Every plan that the partisans made was contingent—on the ability to travel, on the local risk, on messages being delivered accurately.

The farmer was grasping his hand and apologizing. He had been warned not to give anything to suspicious men who appeared in the night. There were *agents provocateurs* among the Reds and the slayers, and he had assumed Lukas was one of them. His wife tried to make amends as well, heating the previous evening's soup for them, cutting squares of bread and spreading them thickly with butter, making tea.

They talked of things in general over the table, of the harvest and weather, of politics and the trainloads of goods that chugged through the forest on the railway from Germany, where the Reds continued to strip the towns and cities to rebuild their own. The farmer listened attentively, trying to glean whatever information he could. There was no real news to be had in the ordinary way, so he tried to piece together details to create some picture of what the future might hold for him.

As for Lukas, he spoke in the optimistic, encouraging way of the partisans, who saw it as their duty not only to fight the Reds but also to preserve the morale of the people. Elena did not speak much. He sensed that the farmer knew her. He looked at Elena as much as he could but tried not to stare.

After they had eaten, Lukas and Elena went out to the garden and sat on a secluded patch of grass behind the currant bushes so they could speak freely. It was the season of grasshoppers, which leapt from the newly dried grass in the morning sun. Bees hummed around the flowers in the garden by the house, and a single cricket sounded from near the foundation.

Lukas looked closely at Elena. She did not have the worn, pale look of those who spent most of their time in bunkers. It was summer, and she must have been coming out to bask in the sun, which was good for her skin but bad for her life expectancy. He intended to admonish her, to beg her to take better care of herself for his sake, but when she looked up at him he lost all need to speak and laid one hand on her shoulder to hold her as he kissed her. He held her tightly against himself for a while, stroking her hair. She smelled good to him, and he lifted her hair to nuzzle up against the side of her neck. He had been away from her for so long.

"Is there a place where we can be alone?"

She took him by the hand and led him out through the gate in the yard. She led him down the lane toward the forest, and then across a piece of scrubland along the banks of a brook to a place where the bushes grew in a dense mass and the brook flowed into a small river. At a bend of the river they came upon a high bank with a beard of roots and grasses hanging down. Elena reached down and pulled aside a mat of branches that had been woven together to camouflage the hatch of a bunker, and then pulled open this door and motioned for him to go ahead of her.

The bunker was dark except for the light cast by the open hatch. It was tiny, a temporary hiding place for two with nothing more than a narrow wooden bed frame and a little space beside the bed for a table built into the corner and a stool beside it. The walls were rough boards papered over with newspapers to keep the grit from coming through inside.

"I didn't realize bunkers could be private like this," said Lukas. The life of partisans, for all its fugitive nature, was the life of people in groups. One was never alone.

"I've been expecting you. I made arrangements. Sit on the stool and take off your shoes."

He set down his briefcase and did as he was told while Elena pulled the hatch shut most of the way, leaving it open a thumb's width so a narrow crescent of light could seep in. He reached for her, but she squeezed his hand and pushed it aside. She pulled an open box with two down comforters from beneath the bed. One she placed on the bed frame as a mattress, the other she pushed to the far side of the bed so they could pull it over themselves later.

Lukas had taken off his shoes and now he reached up for her again, and she bent to kiss him. She undressed quickly, lay down on the bed and held up the comforter like a tent. The crescent of light fell across her face, barely illuminating her body. As Lukas climbed in beside her, she drew the comforter around themselves.

"Are you all right?" he asked.

"I'm nervous."

"Are you afraid?"

"I've wished for this for a long time, but I might not be good at it."

"Then we'll practise together."

Afterward, they lay quietly for a while.

"How was your life after you went underground?" asked Lukas.

"I missed you while we were apart," said Elena. "At some of the harder moments I wondered if we would ever have a time like this."

"Now we do."

"At last. Before you came it was nothing like the day we met last summer, when the camp was big and the men sang and danced. The group of partisans who took me here were so worried about my safety that they kept me in a bunker for the first three weeks. They never let me go farther than a hundred metres away unless a pair of men escorted me. They were so careful with me that I felt like I was being smothered."

"The Reds must have been combing the forests for you."

"Oh, they looked long and hard for you and me, but the trail is cold and they have other things to worry about now. So do we, I might add. My band attacked a train. Eventually the slayers and the Reds will come through here, looking for revenge."

"When?"

"No one knows for certain, but soon."

"We'll get going back to Flint's when it's dark. But along the way I need to look in on my parents by Rumsiskes. I want them to meet you."

"Your parents?"

"Yes."

"Does that mean you want to marry me?"

"Yes."

She laughed a little sadly.

"What's wrong? I thought you'd be happy."

"Oh, I am. I need a new family. I've been thinking of you for months, ever since the night we shot all those people in my room in Marijampole. I shudder to think of that now."

"Do you regret it?" Lukas asked.

"Yes."

He misunderstood and was stung. "What part?" he asked.

"I shot two men that night. Two on my first night. Imagine! I've killed more since then, but that was at a distance, in firefights. I'm not the same anymore. That night changed me forever."

"None of us chose this. It was thrust upon us. What else do you regret?"

"What we did to my sister. I thought the authorities would grasp that she wasn't involved with the executions. If she had known, we wouldn't have left her behind. But now she's been deported to the Komi Republic."

It was a bad place—very cold, worse than Siberia.

"And is there anything else you regret?"

"I don't regret anything else, no."

Lukas kissed her again.

"Do you really want to marry me?" Elena asked.

"What a strange question."

"I mean, where will you find a priest to do it?"

"I know one in a small parish in Nedzinge."

"I have another idea as well."

"What is it?"

"There's a new amnesty coming out. Stop! I know what you're going to say, that the Reds can't be trusted. But listen to me. If we married first and took the amnesty, and if they did betray us and deported us, at least we'd be together."

"The men and the women who were deported in 1941 were separated," said Lukas. "It takes cattle cars a month to reach Siberia. Some of them would have been dead before they got there."

"But we don't know what happened to them. Maybe they were reunited in the North. Maybe the labour camps are not as bad as we've heard. And who knows, the amnesty might even be real."

"But we'd have to betray all the men we've been fighting with."

"They could take amnesty too."

"Elena, listen to me. You and I shot a roomful of Red commissars. They will never forgive us for that, you understand? They won't just deport us."

"Lukas, I love you, but the future doesn't look very bright for you and me. We could throw in our lot together. I'd be *like* your wife and you could be *like* my husband. We could sleep together. We could even tell the others we were married secretly. Wouldn't that be good enough?"

"Why are you saying this? Why don't you want to marry me?"

"I do, I do. But we live with violence, you and I. Our relationship started with violence and it will end that way too. Maybe it's better if we're not married."

"How is it better?"

"We wouldn't bring bad luck upon ourselves."

"I don't believe in luck. Besides, what we did wasn't a crime. We were striking back at enemies."

"I know, I know. But it was horrible. I keep picturing Vinskis. Earlier that night he'd said someone's head was going to roll for mistakes at work, and then I can see his head dropping after you shot him through the neck."

"Why are you reminding yourself of these terrible things? Put them out of your mind."

"I wish I could put them out of my mind. I wish I could wash my mind of that whole night, but it keeps coming back to me, especially the picture of poor Stase in the moments before you shot her."

"If I hadn't done that, they would have executed her."

"I don't sleep well anymore. I thought I would go out into the countryside and live free, but it feels as if the Reds have captured my soul."

"All the more reason to marry me, then. I'll take care of you."

"Listen, Lukas, you've made me a good offer. But I've made you a good offer too. We could live together as man and wife, no strings attached. We'd be free as long as we could. But if I married you, you would be responsible for me and I would be responsible for you. If you were captured alive and imprisoned, I would die trying to free you, and you would have to do the same for me."

"I would anyway."

"Maybe you would and maybe you wouldn't. But if you were married to me, you'd need to act against all reason."

"You make marriage sound so difficult. I think it's more difficult to live without you."

"We'd be living on the run."

"That's the way we live anyway."

"We'd have hardly any time alone. We'll be in bunkers with other men."

"But at least we'll be together. I've been thinking of you since we first met, and then again from the moment I put the bast slippers on your feet. Even in the presence of other men I can at least touch your hand."

"And what about the battles we might fight? Don't you think Flint will be unwilling to have a couple fighting with him? We'll be a weak link."

"Flint would let us fight together again. We've proved ourselves once. Now stop raising all these objections. What about me? Do you love me?"

"I do."

"Then that should be enough."

There was no way they could travel by train together, so they made their way overland toward the Jewish Pine Forest, skirting the villages and towns and staying as close to the woodlands as possible. Elena had given a rifle to Lukas, and they each carried a pair of grenades.

It felt good to have Elena at his side. She had been in the forest long enough to know how to carry herself. And whenever they settled down in a quiet spot at dawn, in a thicket of bushes or tall grasses, they made love again and again, delighting in the discovery of one another's bodies. Then he would watch over her as she slept first, studying her in the quietness of the morning, secure in the knowledge that she would do the same when he slept later.

They searched for a long time before they found a rowboat to carry them across the Nemunas River. Once safely across on the fourth morning of travel, they made their way into the Jewish Pine Forest.

Lukas scanned the town of Rumsiskes with his binoculars, making sure that no sunlight reflected off the lenses to give him away. The town looked peaceful enough at this distance, though there was a red flag on one of the buildings by the market square. The square was too quiet for this time of day. Something was up.

When he was a child, Lukas had gone to the square with his father on market days, to be treated to bagels or "sailor" candies with a picture of a sailor on the wrapper so attractive that he pinned it up on the wall in his room. When they'd return from the market he'd tell his mother about all the things he'd seen: the farmers selling eggs or piglets off their wagons, the horse market, and the fights between the men who spent their profits in the tavern.

Lukas scanned the square again with his binoculars.

"What do you see?" asked Elena.

"I can't make out much—just two men in the marketplace, leaning up against a wall. Drunks, I think."

As they made their way through the sand dunes of the Jewish Pine Forest, Lukas recounted his childhood memories to Elena, about a fort in one tree, a goat caught with horns tangled in a thicket in another spot. It felt good to talk to her about his life before the time with the partisans. He wanted to remember himself in his childhood, a time not that long ago yet utterly remote, a time before the war, which had been going on for his entire adult life.

They made their way down to the perimeter of the forest. All was quiet on his father's farm and near the house. A single cow was chained in a field, slowly grazing in the range of its reach.

"This is the place you grew up?"

"Yes."

Elena squeezed his hand. She felt very close to him now, filled with nostalgia for this place even though she had never seen it before.

For all they knew, a spy or a soldier might be watching the farm from some other vantage point. The strangeness of his situation came upon Lukas. He had never been away from home for so long, and for the first time he could see the world of his previous life laid out before him, etched all the more sharply because Elena was seeing it too. The house and fields were both familiar and unfamiliar, like a dreamscape. He half believed he could simply walk up the farm lane and re-enter his old life.

They had been underground long enough to know to practise caution, so they established themselves in a thick clump of bushes near the edge of the property and watched, first to make sure there were no Chekists or slayers around and finally in the hope that one of his family might come outside. To Lukas it seemed a little too peaceful; there should have been more movement around the house at this time of day. If the Reds had discovered his true identity, as they might have, they could be waiting for him. Lukas and Elena needed to watch the house until they could determine if the place was safe.

They waited a long time, watching the seas of grass shimmer in the wind, pitched one way and then another. The grass showed the wind currents, not only the general direction but the tiny swirls of microclimate as well, the sudden flattening in some places, the parting as if of a sea. Soon the grass would be cut down, but until then it was the measure of the day, an ongoing performance that left no lasting impression.

The shadows grew short as the morning advanced toward noon, and then lengthened again in a different direction in the afternoon.

"Who's that?" Elena asked when someone finally came outside.

"My sister, Angele."

She had come out to the well. As far as Lukas could see, no one else was around.

"I want to get a little closer," he said.

"I'll come with you."

"No. I'll come back for you if it looks all right."

He made his way toward Angele, his back bent low in the hay-field to keep his profile down, like a thief in his own home. When he was close enough to call Angele's name, he startled her. She dropped the bucket down the well and put her hand to her mouth.

"Come over here, by the hedge," he hissed.

"Lukas? Is that you?"

"Are there any soldiers around?"

"Not anymore. They're gone now."

He was going to go back for Elena, but something in Angele's voice made him wait. She came to him then, and stood with him on a patch of earth between the currant bushes and the apple trees where they were masked from any spying eyes. She threw her arms around his neck and covered his face repeatedly with kisses. Much as he enjoyed the moment, he finally pulled her away and held her at arm's length, laughing at her enthusiasm, and she burst into tears.

"Let's go inside," he said.

"No, wait. You need to know something first."

She had a hard time speaking through her tears, and Lukas was forced to wait, his unease growing with every moment.

"What are you crying about?" he asked.

"The slayers found Algis yesterday, right here. He'd been hiding all this time, not even with the partisans, just hiding in various places throughout the county. He'd beg for food or people would give it to him."

"What happened?"

"He came to see us. He did that sometimes, appearing out of nowhere, like you just now. You frightened me, you know—I thought you might be him. Sometimes I'd look for him in the bunker under the hayfield, and he might be there or he might be gone. He'd come home to get food. He was hungry, thin and dirty. He'd just had a glass of milk by the kitchen table when the slayers appeared in the yard in a car and an open truck. There was no time to hide. Algis jumped through a window and ran. One of the slayers outside had a machine gun mounted on the truck and shot him."

"Wounded? Killed?"

"Cut in two. It was terrible. Father came out and began to cry when he saw the body, and he didn't stop sobbing until early this morning. We can't talk to him. He doesn't see us. He just mutters and stares at nothing."

"What happened to the body?"

"The slayers took it away. They put it in the marketplace with another one. It's terrible. They took off their shoes and socks and put bibles in their mouths and rosaries in their hands. Mother sopped up some of his blood with her shawl from the place where he fell. She says she's going to bury the shawl so at least he has a decent burial."

"Who did this?"

"I told you, four slayers."

"Did you know any of them?"

"Two are Rumsiskes men. The others were from somewhere else."

"Tell me their names and where they live."

"They were a father and son, but forget that now. You have to go in to see Mother and Father quickly. Maybe your face will help Father. Then you have to get away from here as fast as you can. It's not safe."

"It's not safe anywhere. Calm down. Stop crying. Tell me how it's been since we left."

"Terrible. They want more in grain than this farm produces. They're trying to kill us. Some of the farmers have been deported. Some are in prison. There's talk of collectivization. Father said he'd rather sweep the streets in Kaunas than be a serf, but you can't just leave your own farm. You need permission, and no one gives it, and there's nowhere to run away to." She wiped her nose on her apron. "Do you have news of Vincentas?"

He shook his head. There was no use in telling her any more bad news. She looked at him searchingly.

"Don't tell Mother and Father that. Make something up. Anything." Angele was holding his hands and staring into his eyes. Her face was etched with despair.

Lukas let go of her hands and cautiously entered the house. He was immediately overcome with the familiar smells of home—recently baked rye bread, boiled potatoes, smoked meat.

His father sat in a dark corner in the shadows, near the broken window through which Algis had leapt. The window was now patched with cardboard. His father's back was upright and his hands were crossed in his lap, making him look like a man waiting patiently for a train. He looked very old, with his thinning grey hair cropped close to his head. His mother was washing dishes, wearing an apron and a scarf over her hair. She was frightened when she first saw Lukas, and crossed herself to make sure he was not a vision.

"Mama," he said, and her tears began to fall.

Markulis and his son worked their spades well, given that it was dark and they were wondering if the graves they were digging were for themselves. The boy, barely twenty, was silent and afraid. The father was nervously talkative, though no less frightened.

"It's pretty here, by the forest's edge. You couldn't have picked a better place."

Lukas had asked them to dig three graves. The bodies of Algis and the other partisan were in a cart behind them. Two bodies. Three graves.

Elena stood beside Lukas. He had not brought her into his house after all.

"I hope your sister told you that it wasn't either one of us who fired the machine gun at your brother."

Lukas knew that, but he didn't know the other two slayers, and the convenience of a father-and-son team had given him an advantage. Lukas had held a knife to the boy's throat as he explained to the father that he was to go to the market square that night, tell the guard he had been given instructions, and load the bodies up and bring them along.

Markulis had been a small landholder, ten acres and two children, both of whom worked as hired labour as soon as they were old enough to shepherd geese, and then pigs, and finally cows. Markulis hired himself out too. He had been an angry man, prone to getting into fights, perpetually frustrated by his poverty. Joining the slayers had given him a regular income and kept his son out of the draft. It was a dirty business, but he had helped slaughter pigs and spread manure, so he was used to dirty work.

And now this.

"I've known you since you were a boy," said Markulis. "I remember you as a child on market days, chewing on bagels."

"Did you remember Algis too?"

"He should have given himself up long ago. He let two amnesties pass. Armed resistance just brings down the wrath of the Reds. You have to play along with them in order to survive."

"What about your country?"

"That's over now, and if you think it isn't, passive resistance is the thing."

"That's not resistance at all."

"You mean you're loyal to that bourgeois dictator who ruled before the Reds came?"

"There's more to a nation than the man who rules it."

Markulis rested his spade for a moment. Lukas kept his distance. The safety on his rifle was off.

"There's no one but the Reds now. The czar ruled here for a hundred years. The Reds are going to rule here forever, and we'd better get used to it."

"The Germans said they'd rule forever too, and look how long they lasted. You haven't even matched their record yet. What do you think is going to happen to you when the Reds fall?"

"They'll never fall. If I believed they would, I wouldn't be here."

"Get back to work," said Lukas. "I want to be done before dawn."

Lukas had brought linen sheets from his mother's house. He had the Markulis father and son wrap each body, place it in a grave and cover it over. His brother's body caused some problems because it was in two pieces, but he tried not to dwell on that.

When they were done, he told them to stand beside the empty grave. The boy was crying now. His father put his arm over his shoulder.

"This is your grave," said Lukas, "waiting for you if anything happens to my family or anyone else in this town. Now fill it in." He took a deep breath. "And remember, it will be easier to dig out a second time."

Markulis looked up with relief that changed to confusion as he first felt the bullet rip into his stomach and then heard the report of Elena's rifle. He looked to his son and saw the red stain spreading across his chest. The two slumped awkwardly at the side of the grave, not falling in. Neither was dead yet, each moaning in the tangle of arms and legs. Elena walked around closer to them and fired a bullet into the head of each.

"I was going to let them off with a warning," said Lukas.

"If there's to be no amnesty for us, let there be no amnesty for them."

"We kill only when we have to."

"Think of your brother, cut in two. Think of my brother, and of your father's grief. I will forgive no one who strikes at my family."

"I never knew you could be so cruel."

"I *am* cruel. And you helped to make me this way."

"But someone may have heard the shots."

"Leave the bodies here, where they are. Let them take care of their own dead."

NINE

NOVEMBER 1946

*T*HE MOON shone so intensely through the clear church
windows that the priest could read the marriage ceremony
from the book in his hand. The wedding party huddled by
the south wall, avoiding the skewed columns of light that lay across
the nave. These guests were always wary of exposure, careful of the
cool radiance inside this small church in the remote village parish
of Nedzinge, in a forgotten country.

To the priest, this midnight marriage was just the latest sign of
the world turned upside down. In his darker moments he wondered if this inversion of custom could be a sign of the Second
Coming. The priest had heard that some of the evangelical Protes-
tants believed the good would be taken away to heaven in rapture
before the physical end of the world while the others were left behind. Was this withdrawal of good people into the darkness a sign?
Stalin was said to have a diabolical sense of humour. Certainly the
people running the country were imps, small demons, servants of
Stalin, the village bullies and drunkards now ruled the streets. One
sort of village tough had served the Nazis and now another sort
rose up to strip the farmers of their land, the shopkeepers of their
shops, the religious of their God and the patriots of their country.

What kind of people would be left once this work was done?

The priest looked at the couple before him. A young man filled with the ecstasy of love, a little nervous, trembling even, at the gravity of the marriage act. The woman was beautiful in the way of young women, glowing as if she were going to move to a new life in a safe home.

The priest's thoughts made him stumble through a few of the Latin phrases he should have known so well. He was more than a little anxious himself. If the Reds discovered this marriage, he would be shipped out in a cattle car. A third of the parish priests were already dead or in the North, and the priest himself was a little ashamed not to be one of them, but also terribly grateful. He tried to shift his thoughts away from himself and onto the couple before him. Poor young man and woman, he thought, in love while the world lay in ruins.

He glanced up at the guests. Pale, pale, the faces of the wedding guests—Lakstingala, who had left his automatic outside in deference to the church but was nervous without it; tearful in the darkness, the drunken forger and his wife, extra burdens to the partisans because drunkards did not travel well; fearful the American, as farmers did not go out at night. And Flint, who crossed his arms and then uncrossed them, ill at ease in the knowledge that they would have to make their way back to their bunkers in this full moonlight, which he had always avoided and had warned his men to avoid as well.

"Are you sure you want to do this?" Flint had asked Lukas. "It will only make life harder. It will only make the pain worse if something happens to one of you."

They were sure. Against all the odds, both Elena and Lukas had survived this long, through firefights, betrayals by partisans who were giving up the fight, and winters without enough food.

Flint had so many things on his mind. The partisans would need help soon. None of the foreign radio programs mentioned Lithuania or the other two sister Baltic States. They had disappeared so thoroughly from the Western public eye that soon no one would know they ever existed, and whatever happened in a land that did not exist did not matter. Unless the situation turned around, all of the men and women in that church would soon be as inconsequential as the ghosts of Vilnius.

As for the couple up at the altar, they were not thinking of strategies or politics at all. They were only thinking of one another and of some of those who could not be with them. How much Lukas would have liked his brothers and sister and parents and all the tribe of uncles and cousins to be there, but half of them were certainly dead and the others so far away, maybe dead as well. He would have liked to swell the numbers in the country church, to fill the nave with dead souls. As for Elena, her dead had died earlier, and so she did not think of them as much as she did of the man beside her, the one who was so in love with her. She loved him too and needed him and could no longer distinguish between the two.

The nighttime ghost of a ceremony was comforting to Elena. It was the remains of something normal, a shadow ceremony but at least a shadow—something, instead of the blasted nothingness of the new world outside. The future did not bear consideration. She had only this moment on the altar with him. No rings, just a moment's security as they held each other's hands.

The reception took place in a big bunker, one with two rooms, three hatches, stools and benches, and dug so deeply that a short man could stand upright inside. The air was good because the bunker had been built with clay-pipe ventilation holes, unlike some of the other places where a candle would go out from the lack of oxygen. It was too dangerous to have a bonfire aboveground as they used to in the old days, but they could have a few candles and a little low singing. Flint cut slices from a side of smoked bacon; Lakstingala had brought a loaf of heavy black bread. In addition to the litre of samagonas that the forger had for himself and his wife, he had managed to bring a bucket of milk. They all drank, and then laughed at one another's white moustaches as if they were children. They sang a few songs together and ate the rest of their food, and then there came an awkward moment when there was not much more to do.

"Come on," said Lakstingala, "your wedding gift is a night in a special bunker."

The others hooted, making jokes about checking up on them, and encouraging them to go straight to sleep and get a good night's rest.

The gift of privacy was the best wedding present they could receive. The moon was far below its zenith, below the treeline, and so the light was not quite as terrible as it had been earlier. Lakstingala led them through some reeds and into a spot with a high riverbank. Then they walked for a long time until they came to the edge of a wood where it met some farm fields. Beside a large stump stood a small pine. Flint lifted this sapling, moved some mosses and opened a hatch.

"Get inside," he said. "I'll replace the moss and tree once you're in there. You can't budge during the day without messing up the entrance, but the advantage is that they'd need to look very hard to find you here."

Lakstingala shook Lukas's hand and kissed Elena on the cheek. She held him for a moment, hugging him.

"Thank you," she said.

They crawled inside a short passageway and could hear Lakstingala covering up the hatchway behind them.

They came into a room much smaller than the massive bunker they had left behind, actually not much bigger than a large closet turned on its side. It held two narrow bunk beds and two stools. The ceiling was so low that the person on the upper bunk would have difficulty turning himself on his side without scraping the top. Lukas lit a candle stub and found some gifts placed on a stool: a small square of chocolate, some kind of liqueur in a tiny bottle and some dried flowers in a glass.

The fall rains had already begun and the bunker smelled damp. Even so, they had not lived in this kind of luxurious privacy since they had met again in Kazlu Ruda.

Elena lifted the small bottle and turned it every which way, and then laughed. "It's an Eiffel Tower, filled with cognac."

It was many years since anyone could have gone to Paris to pick up such a souvenir. Either it had belonged to a German during their occupation or it had come to Lithuania a very long time before that. Someone had been saving it, and now that someone had given it to them as a wedding present.

"Let's taste it," said Lukas.

The cognac was not the best ever made, just brandy designed for tourists to take back home, but neither Elena nor Lukas had tasted liquor for a long time, and what they had tasted was all home brew or rough vodka. To them it made the dream of Paris into something real. If there was still cognac, there must still be France as well as Paris.

"Should we eat the chocolate?" Lukas asked.

"Let's save it for later."

They rearranged the bunker so the straw pallet from the upper bunk lay beside the lower one, enlarging their bed to make room enough for two. Elena undressed and Lukas did the same, and they kissed for a while before making love.

TEN

DECEMBER 1, 1947

T O THE PACING SLAYER, the forest floor seemed undis-
turbed, a thick bed of pine needles overlaid with curled
leaves of ash and poplar. He looked up. A lone rowan stood
at the edge of the forest, its red berries bright against the grey sky,
the leaves of the tree all fallen now. The December branches were
awaiting snow—bones awaiting cover.

Beyond the forest lay a pair of farm fields, one an abandoned
tangle of weeds, its owners either fled or shipped away, the other
planted with winter rye by an owner who might not live to enjoy the
fruits of the harvest.

The slayer was studying the forest floor for some sign. It was
hard to see how the ground cover could be so untouched. No ants
stirred on the knee-high anthill, all aslumber for the season in their
tiny burrows.

Winter was coming, and the slayer had not even been issued a
decent pair of boots. And his employers knew he suffered more than
others when it was cold. *Slayer,* he thought, such a dramatic title for
someone who wore such poor clothes. Looking down, he could see
the grey sock where it protruded at the split seam of one of his miserable shoes. The locals despised him for taking up arms for the

Reds. Not that the Reds treated him particularly well. They seemed to believe that his bourgeois background made him untrustworthy. His uniform was cobbled together from an assortment of clothes: an army tunic, his own linen shirt beneath it, and a baggy pair of trousers, the last remains of a good suit he had once owned.

His face was scratched along the right side, small scrapes from a drunken fall onto a stony road. He had never been much of a drinker before, but now drink was the only consolation when his clothes were too thin, his stomach half empty and his tobacco in short supply.

The slayer felt his grievances keenly. *They* did not even let him carry his rifle on this particular mission. A rifle in his hands would have been another consolation.

They were a Cheka lieutenant and twenty-three internal army soldiers in two rings around this patch of earth, the second ring all the way at the forest's edge, by the farm fields. No one was sure exactly where the bunker was, and his examination of the forest floor had not revealed anything. The Cheka lieutenant did not speak Lithuanian, and so the slayer had been sent out to reconnoitre. An excuse, he thought. He was being used as bait. If the partisans decided to fight, he would be the first one they killed.

Empty of birds, the forest was very quiet except for the squeak of leather on leather and the occasional rustle of forest debris as the soldiers shifted in their positions. The soldiers were as dangerous to the slayer as anyone underground. What if a trigger-happy soldier was hungover, or needed a cigarette, or was nervous and suspicious of him?

The crunch of the leaves beneath his feet was unnaturally loud. He could use a drink, but he had been given two mouthfuls before he stepped out onto the forest floor and there would be no more until his job was complete. He looked to the lieutenant and shook his head to show that he had found no telltale signs. The lieutenant signalled that he should talk.

The slayer sighed. The partisans would know what he was as soon as he opened his mouth, perhaps even who he was, and they hated his kind more than they hated the Reds. It was so unfair to be treated like this. He was as much a prisoner of circumstance as they were—he'd rather be doing anything but this. He would need to find some common ground with those hiding down below.

"Brothers," he said loudly, and waited a moment. At least no one was firing at him yet. "Here we are, you below and me above. Let me tell you, it's better up here than down there. I know. I've been there. I'm twenty-six years old. Don't do anything hasty. Listen to me."

He walked as he spoke. If someone were to fire from below, he did not want to be standing still in one place.

"There's no need to panic. A new amnesty has been declared. Come out unarmed and you'll be pardoned. You can't shoot your way out of this one. We have three machine guns and a hundred men."

There were no machine guns, and he exaggerated the number of men because he knew they would think he was lying and would cut his number in four. In his own manner he was telling them the truth. He did not mention that he had taken amnesty himself and this was where it got him.

"Think of your mothers and fathers. I did. I'm a patriot as much as you are, but my patriotism began with my parents. What will happen to yours if you try to shoot your way out? Your mothers raised you in hope. What will they do if you die?"

He had been told it was important to get them out alive. The web of the underground ran along threads that could be followed if one did so carefully. His own parents had been deported, and much as he loved them, he was in no hurry to follow them.

"Who will help your fathers with the planting in spring? They grow old. They need your help. And if any of them has been deported, come out and talk it over with us, and we'll bring them back. You could still have a life here."

It was important to give them a choice.

"Reconcile yourselves to the way of the world. Listen, I don't like the world I live in either. I could imagine a better place than this, but I'm a realist. The Americans are far away. The English and the French have their own problems. No one will help us, and in any case Moscow has a plan. We'll build a better future together. They've made mistakes, I know. We've all made mistakes. The important thing is to learn from them and move on. Maybe going underground was the right thing to do when you first started. But that time has passed. Give yourselves up now. Be reasonable."

The slayer walked and talked for so long that he began to feel like a fool. A light rain started to come down and then grew heavier, drops gathering and falling from the bare lower branches of the pine trees. A degree or two lower and the rain would turn to snow. He was cold, and the boredom of this task irritated him more as the vodka wore off. He was becoming hungry too. But the lieutenant signalled to him to keep it up. The lieutenant was a patient man.

The faint smell of smoke reached him. Not tobacco. The slayer looked around carefully, but he could not see where it was coming from; the wisps were too small to be visible in the rain. He looked up to the lieutenant and signalled to him. The Cheka soldier could smell the smoke as well.

There were men below the ground somewhere, burning documents.

The slayer followed the smell to where it was strongest. The damned rain was dripping off the end of his cap, distracting him, but he cleared away a few leaves, scraped aside a sheaf of pine needles and revealed a clay pipe set in the earth. The ventilation hole showed the smoke more clearly once the leaves were gone. The pipe was too narrow to drop a grenade down it, but a shot fired below might get lucky.

He gestured for the lieutenant to come over and see for himself, but the lieutenant refused. Instead, he had four men go back to the farm, and they returned with rakes. They set about clearing the leaves and pine needles from the ground, exposing two more air vents and, finally, the lid of the opening, which had been covered with a woven matt of moss and pine needles. Once it was exposed, the lieutenant assigned three men to cover the exit.

"Keep talking," said the lieutenant, and so the slayer walked from air vent to air vent, cajoling the partisans, urging them to give up. As the hours passed, the soldiers became ever more restless. The light was already noticeably poorer by early afternoon. Finally the lieutenant instructed the slayer to stuff a rag into each of the air vents to speed up the deliberations below.

"Did you recognize the voice?" Lukas asked.

Elena shook her head.

"It's Ignacas. I'm sure of it. I just wish I could get my fingers around his neck."

"Let's find a way out of this," said Elena, her lips pressed close to Lukas's ear. He looked into her eyes. There was only a single candle burning inside the bunker, its light unreflected by the bare wooden walls. He looked to see if any of the others had heard her. What she said was almost treasonous, a suggestion that they should take their chances with the amnesty.

She understood his disapproving look but refused to avert her eyes. They had talked often of this moment, trying to anticipate how the end would come—to lessen their fear by rehearsing it. But there was no way to accustom herself to her own death, especially not now.

Life had become harder and harder over the past year. So many of their kind had died. Some were taken prisoner and Flint's band had had to relocate more than once in case the captured partisans broke down under torture and betrayed the locations of the bunkers. But in a way it had been an exhilarating time too. She and Lukas fought together and slept together, and she had never imagined she could live so wholly in a relationship. Flint sent them out on missions together, because the anxiety of one was always high if the other was gone. They were both husband and wife and comrades, and she was not afraid as long as he was with her. Until now.

She had hoped that death, if it came, would catch them un-aware—a swarm of bullets in an ambush. These last few hours and this slow reflection on their impending death had been unbear-able. The danger nauseated her. Before she married she might have accepted it, but now she wanted to hold on to life more than ever before.

Elena was the only woman among ten people who sat tensely in the bunker. The most important documents were burned and the air was getting scarce since the slayer had plugged the air vents, but they did not spread out, although someone should have been lis-tening by the other two trap doors to determine if they had been uncovered as well.

The bunker was a command post, with a small storage room and a latrine in addition to the room where they were huddling. It was a fine piece of work, for all the good it did them.

The fact that they were still alive was contrary to standard oper-ational procedure, which called for partisans to blow themselves up with grenades as soon as all documents were burnt. The grenades were to be held close to their faces.

The thought of destroying Elena's features was intolerable to Lukas, but what choice did he have? Elena's brown hair curled to her shoulders, though she gathered it with a band at the back. He knew her brown eyes and lashes, the fine nose and strong cheek-bones. He should not think of details like that. One should simply do what one must do. Lukas held her hand as they waited.

The feel of her hand in his was bittersweet.

Flint should have made sure they were dead by now. Lakstingala would have reminded him of his duty, but Lakstingala was not there, off on some mission. It would be within Flint's rights to drop a grenade to stun them and then finish them off. But he seemed unwill-ing to do that, delaying as long as he could, having them search the bunker's two rooms for the smallest piece of paper, empty their pockets of anything that might give them away.

There was precious little air in the bunker now. The partisan named Vilkas had wanted to fire a shot up through the air vent to dislodge the rag that blocked it, but that would have been a fool's game. He was restless and needed to do something.

"The longer we wait, the harder it's going to be," he said. He was the toughest of them all, a realist. "Let's get it over with."

"Just a moment," said Lukas. "They found the main hatch but not the back ones. We could take them by surprise and try to shoot our way out."

"Too risky," said Vilkas.

Flint should have been leading the discussion, but he hesitated. No one talked about accepting the amnesty, but it was hard not to consider it.

"What are we waiting for?" In one smooth movement Vilkas drew his Walther from his pocket, put the barrel in his mouth and pulled the trigger.

The smoke and the noise made them jump, but even in his shock Lukas noted that the shot blew out the back of Vilkas's head but not the front. To protect Vilkas's parents, Lukas reached for the butt of his light machine gun and smashed in the face of his dead comrade. The others looked away, but Flint did not stop him. Elena made a sound of disgust in her throat and moved to the far corner of the bunker.

The slayer formerly known as Ignacas walked up to the lieutenant.

"They're starting to kill themselves. I suggest we throw a couple of grenades through the hatch and then wait. Some of them will survive and we can take them for questioning."

"How many did the farmer say they were?"

"He didn't say. A lot, whatever that means."

"Once the hotheads have shot themselves, the others might give up. We wait."

"How long?"

"As long as it takes."

Just before nightfall, the hatch flipped open and a stick came up with a white handkerchief on the end. It seemed unnaturally bright in the last light of day.

"You've made the right decision," called the slayer. He stood behind the three men whose automatics were trained on the opening. They lay on the ground, but he knelt behind to see over them and to speak to the surrendering partisans as they stepped out of the bunker.

"Remember your discipline," the lieutenant shouted in Russian. He didn't want anyone getting nervous and firing.

"Show your hands first as you come out of the hole," said the slayer.

There was some kind of movement he could not make out in the poor light. The slayer heard a thump and looked to his feet, where something had landed. It was a German grenade, the kind with the long handle. In the moment before it blew, he considered that he had always been unlucky. Why should the end of his life be any different?

The explosions of the grenades set all the guns firing, and the greatest danger for the Red soldiers inside the first ring came from their compatriots behind them who might fire right into the backs of their heads.

There was no way to kill the person throwing up the grenades unless someone tossed a grenade into the opening, but before this could happen another lid opened some distance away, grenades came flying from it, and men scrambled out, firing in a circle. Yet another lid opened and the melee was unleashed. Bullets flew in every direction, and many of the Cheka soldiers huddled down to protect themselves from the undisciplined fire. Finally the lieutenant himself threw a grenade into the first opening, the one from

which the white flag had appeared, and with one less centre of fire
the Cheka soldiers were able to still the other two as well.

When the lieutenant called for a ceasefire, he saw the bodies of
half a dozen partisans on the forest floor. Some had probably gotten away, he thought, although it would be hard to tell for sure until
the smoke cleared and he questioned the other men.

Out in the weed-filled field, Flint and Lukas huddled down.

"Did you see what happened?" Lukas asked. He had lost Elena
in the firefight.

"I saw her fall and then reach for a grenade. I'm not sure where
it blew. I'm sorry."

Without a word, Flint pushed Lukas ahead of him and forced
him to escape through the overgrown farm field. Flint would have
to get him away from the scene before the terrible fact of his wife's
death sank in, and before the others began to look for them.

PART TWO

ELEVEN

LITHUANIA, PRUSSIA, POLAND
JANUARY 1948

SIX MEN MARCHED in single file through the snow of the winter night, all but the first stepping in the footprints of the man before him; the last one swept the snow behind them with a pine bough. They stayed close to cover whenever they could—copses of trees or bushes, where once a startled owl flew out before them and another time a hare raced out across the snow.

They came to a river at the former border, found a rowboat by a stretch of open water and rowed across. The men made their way onward into the abandoned fields of Prussia, now filled with frozen weeds as thick as fingers and as tall as men, prickly grasses that tore at their clothes and faces as they passed and threatened to pull the grenades from their belt loops. When they approached a particularly dense patch of grass, a troop of feral pigs rose squealing from a flattened place and fled.

Five partisans, Lakstingala among them, had volunteered to take Lukas into Poland through East Prussia, and from there he would get himself to the West. The border with Poland was easier to cross at East Prussia because all of the former inhabitants had been expelled by the Reds to pay for the crimes of the Nazis. Prussians had lived here for hundreds and thousands of years, but now they were gone. The new Red settlers had not arrived yet. There was still a place called Prussia, for the time being, but there were no more Prussians. All of them were dead or gone, and soon the name would be gone too.

The men marched steadily. They had a long way to go.

Although it was very cold, Lukas was sweating, weighed down by his automatic rifle, the grenades on his belt, and the backpack filled with photographs, declarations, summaries of the atrocities by region and a letter to the Pope. He was tired, but grateful both for his fatigue and for the mission.

They found no footprints on the road when they finally reached it. No light shone from the ruined farmhouses they passed, and all the Prussian milestone markers lay fallen at the crossroads. The roads did not follow the direction the men wanted, so they cut cross-country, tiring quickly by trudging through the snow, hoping to find a place to rest. In some places there were canals or broad ditches, which they crossed using logs or fallen trees. One man slipped off one of these and fell into the water up to his chin.

After he extricated himself, he and the others ran awkwardly through the snow in order to keep him warm until they finally found a cellar two kilometres farther on, where they hunkered down for a rest and built a fire to warm themselves, allowing the wet man to change and partially dry his clothes. They made raspberry cane tea, their mothers' recipe against catching cold, and then they rose again and marched until dawn, when they came upon a ruined manor where they decided to spend the day. The manor and its outbuildings were empty of living souls, some of the various roofs collapsed or burnt, the windows broken, the yard full of empty tins and papers half covered by blown snow. The doors and even their hinges were all gone, packed up and sent to Russia as war reparations.

On the second floor of the main house they found a room with a view on three sides and a fireplace on the fourth. They jammed boards into the window frames to keep down the draft, found a battered tin oven and brought it inside, running a pipe into the fireplace chimney. A nearby tree masked the smoke. They had intended to eat first, but they were too tired to wait for the water to boil and fell asleep in the sudden heat emanating from the thin walls of the tin stove.

Lukas took first watch. When the kettle boiled, he tossed in some raspberry canes and set the kettle on the floor. Then he took the lid and set it upside down on the stove and cut in some pieces of bacon and laid a few small sausages on top. As he had expected, the men woke from the sleep they had so recently fallen into, ate and drank, and were asleep again as soon as their empty cups hit the floor. Lukas sopped up the grease from the lid with a piece of bread, ate it and then set himself up by a window in order to keep watch. It was a little colder at the window, all the better to keep him awake.

A dog barked in the distance and he could see a thin column of smoke to the east, but not the house it came from. A Red Army truck drove by but did not turn into the lane. Shortly after that a man walked by carrying a hunting rifle over his shoulder.

Elena came to him then, leaning into his side so he could almost feel the weight of her. He did not want to look that way, preferring to think she might really be there, just outside his peripheral vision, and hoping against all reason that she might move into some place where, out of the corner of his eye, he could at least catch a glimpse of her.

Two weeks later, Lukas stood out on the sidewalk at the corner of the street in the city of Gdynia, waiting until a lingering woman left the bakery. She was an old woman, probably chatting up the cashier.

From where he stood on the cobblestones he could smell the sea, but he could not see it, the port one block over but obscured by the backs of the warehouses at the waterfront, some still shattered. A crane swung into view between two buildings, but he could see neither the ship nor the pier from where he stood, just the finger of steel and the cable hanging from it.

The smells of the city were coal smoke, dust, tobacco, diesel exhaust and, beneath them all, the salt tang of the sea. He could hear the call of seagulls as they fought over scraps, their harsh maritime tune the nautical equivalent of the screeches of crows in the countryside.

"I'm not going out to the West," Lukas had said to Flint when he first received his orders. "Elena died here and I'm going to die here too, but before I do I'll find her body and give it a proper burial."

"You'll never find her body if you haven't found it by now, and as for dying here, what good is that supposed to do?"

"At least I'll be in the same country."

"Others would leap at a chance like this."

"Not me."

"No. But you'll follow orders like anyone else."

"Why choose me?"

"Because you have some English and a little French. Because you're wallowing in depression. You're dangerous to me here."

"Then release me from my oath and let me go."

"And lose a good fighter? Absolutely not. Listen to me. We need to re-establish ties with the West. At this rate we'll be crushed slowly and no one will ever know the difference. Get to Sweden and find out if Lozorius is still alive. Contact the Americans and the English. Carry a letter to the Pope."

"I'm not a diplomat."

"No, but you speak well enough and you can write. Lakstingala will help you get out."

"Is he coming too?"

"Only as far as Warsaw. I need him here."

"And what happens once I get news out to the West? How am I supposed to get back here?"

"Any way you can."

The old woman finally left the bakery, and through the window Lukas saw the shopgirl at the counter begin to take the short, dark rye loaves from a basket and set them out on a shelf. She turned to face him as soon as he came in, a working woman, economical in movement, a little reserved to discourage male banter.

She was a few years older than him, her dark hair tied up under a baker's cap. Her name was Sofia, but he did not address her.

"Yes?" she asked.

"Andrew's cousin sent me along," said Lukas.

"What for? I don't know anybody by that name."

"Julius said I should come too."

Lukas heard the knob of the bakery door turning behind him. The cashier leaned toward him to speak quietly before another customer entered.

"We close for lunch in an hour. Come to the back door then." She set half a loaf of bread on the counter. Lukas took it and left the bakery.

He walked down to the quay to look at the ships being loaded out on the piers. The port had been heavily bombed during the war, but most of the damage had been cleaned up, if not repaired. There were inner and outer harbours, a distant breakwater, and long piers with ships at their sides. It would not do to draw attention to himself by dawdling, so he walked as if he had some purpose, trying to memorize the layout of the port in case he ever needed it. After twenty minutes he turned back up toward the city and bought a glass of tea at a kiosk and ate some of the bread with it. Then he made his way back to the alley behind the bakery and knocked on the door.

Sofia unbolted the door and opened it, looked him over and beckoned him inside. They were in a warm antechamber with steps leading down to the bakery ovens below. She took him downstairs, where the baker was sitting at a small table with honey cake and three small glasses set out before him. The baker was a barrel-chested man named Dombrowski, a Pole, Sofia's husband. He beckoned Lukas over and Sofia joined them at the table. He poured three measures of Zubrowka into their glasses, they drank it, and then Sofia poured tea.

"I have some bad news first," said Dombrowski. "We might as well get that out of the way. One of your companions was killed on their way back in to Lithuania."

"Which one?"

"I don't know."

Lakstingala or someone else? One more to join the ranks of the dead. Lukas felt as if a kite string had been snipped and he was now in danger of zigzagging down to earth. He held the edge of the table to maintain his balance.

"How did it happen?"

"An ambush of some kind. Maybe the border patrol expected them."

"So some of them got away?"

"We're not sure. Someone might have been taken prisoner. But the point is this: if one was taken prisoner and he talks, there will be a description of you sent around to the police stations. There's some chance we're going to be watched, if we aren't being watched already. Whatever the case, you can't come back here."

"I won't put you in any danger," Lukas said, and stood up and reached for his bag.

"Don't be so dramatic. Sit down. Where would you go, anyway?"

"I have to get out to Sweden. I have a contact there."

"Yes, I know. His name is Lozorius, and you're in luck. He's not far away, though not in Gdynia. He got tired waiting to see if you made it here without getting killed."

"Lozorius is alive?"

"He's had a few close calls, but he's lucky. Sometimes the dead rise again."

"But usually they don't," said Sofia.

Her face clouded. There was something bothering her. Dombrowski put his hand on her shoulder and Lukas wondered about the two of them. They were speaking Polish because Dombrowski had no Lithuanian; his wife was the Lithuanian one. How had he come to act as a letter box for the Lithuanian partisans? As a favour to his wife, but for what?

"How do I find Lozorius?"

"I'll tell you, but keep this in mind: you must not come back here, no matter what trouble you might find yourself in. For all we know, the Polish secret police are sniffing around already."

The modest city of Puck was a fishing port up the coast. Lukas was to ask for Lozorius at the kitchen door of a convent that housed a tuberculosis hospital just outside town. A sour old doorman in a torn cap barred the door, but the man was swept away by another, younger man who threw his arms around Lukas and embraced him as if they were brothers.

"Thank God you made it!" Lozorius said, and kissed him, an old-fashioned gesture more common among their parents than their own generation.

Lukas had had no such welcome for some time, one reserved for close friends or family, and he was overwhelmed by it and gratified. Lozorius was a demigod, the man who had moved a printing press across Kaunas while the rest of them were quivering in fear of deportation.

Lukas looked at the doorman, who watched them warily. Lozorius followed his gaze.

"Forget about the old man. He can't do you any harm. Nobody knows who you are in this town, and nobody cares. You're free here. Get used to it. Besides, none of them understands Lithuanian."

Lozorius was not a big man, but he had the energy of a host at a country wedding, all good humour, and this exuberance made him seem larger than he was. His ears still stuck out from his head and the hair was receding at the part, making his skull seem very large. Lukas thought of a gambler on a winning streak; cockiness and well-being came off him like a glow, brightening Lukas in its light.

Lozorius had not aged much since Lukas had last seen him on the streets of Kaunas in 1944, but he looked fuller, more substantial, and certainly well fed. His skin had a healthy sheen to it even by comparison with the Poles, who looked better than the Lithuanians.

"I'm glad to find you alive. You've become some kind of legend," said Lukas.

"Legend? For what?"

"You're famous, our man in the West, but everybody thought you were dead because no news of you has come in for some time."

Lozorius laughed. "They can't kill me. I sent letters in, but the lines must have broken down somewhere. Did you bring things out for me too?"

"Yes, I have them in my bag, checked at the train station."

"We'll get them later. Let's find you a room and something to eat and then we'll have time to talk."

In a whirl of activity, often assisted by distracted nuns who seemed to want to indulge him, Lozorius found Lukas a room in the hospital on the third floor, where Lukas could see the people coming in and out of the front door. It was a simple nun's room, with a narrow cot and a table with two chairs, but it was warm and dry, the best room Lukas had stayed in for weeks.

After he had eaten and rested, Lukas walked up to the station with Lozorius, who seemed to have a torrent of words locked up in him that he could let flow at an astonishing rate. Lozorius described the history of the town, once Poland's only window on the Baltic, the number of patients in the hospital and the incidence of tuberculosis, life in Poland and in Sweden, and half a dozen other subjects. Lukas was bemused by the man's words, but relieved as well because he didn't want to talk until they were in some private place.

When they were finally back in Lukas's room, Lozorius put a half bottle of vodka on the table as well as some sausage and bread.

"Now I need you to tell me a few things about the West," said Lukas. "That's what I was sent out here for. First, when can we hope for the war to start?"

"What war?"

"The war between the Americans and the Soviets."

Lozorius cut off two pieces of sausage, offered one to Lukas on the point of a knife and took the second piece himself. "There isn't going to be any war, or if there is, it won't be any time soon. Everybody out here has their own problems."

"How is this possible?"

"The West is sleeping. It's like some kind of madhouse, where everyone is going about his own business on the second floor while a fire is burning on the first floor. But you can't reason with them. They think *we're* the crazy ones. They think that nothing is going to happen. If you push them, they concede that it might, and if the Reds attacked, they would take all of Europe to the Pyrenees. But they won't prepare for it, as if ignoring the problem will keep it from getting worse."

Lozorius cut another piece of sausage, but Lukas turned it down. "The West has the atomic bomb."

"And what do you think they'll do with it? Blow up Moscow?"

"Why not?"

Lozorius laughed in the most frightening way possible. It made Lukas realize he was being ridiculous, yet his line of reasoning was shared by almost everyone he had left behind. It was depressing to know he and the others were so out of touch.

Lozorius poured each of them a shot of vodka. "The world looks different from this place. You'll see. The first thing you have to learn is that everything important to you is unimportant here. Nobody knows who you are. Nobody cares. The ones who do know about you sold you to Stalin. Don't feel bad. You might be able to get something out of them if you prod their consciences, but for the most part they don't want to see you and they don't want to hear you. Believe me, I have seen the future. In a decade there will be children who have never heard of the Baltic States, or if they have heard of them, they will mix them up with the Balkans. Already most people think the Ukrainians are the same as Russians, and as for Byelorussians, you might as well forget about them.

"And all of us out here in the West, all of us who came from those places, if we're noticed at all, are supposed to be fascists and war criminals. Stalin told Truman that there were no Russian prisoners of war, only deserters. So our first problem is that we don't exist and the second is that if we do, we're murderers and traitors."

"Traitors to what?"

"Traitors to the Soviet Union, your homeland and the ally of the Americans, though that last part is getting a little tired now."

"How can we be traitors to an occupying army?"

"Everything you say is bourgeois rationalization, the intellectual machinations of fascists. The West made a deal with Stalin to defeat the Nazis, and the deal was the Reds can do anything they want. We annoy the West, Lukas. We irritate them and we look funny to them. Especially the intellectuals, who love the Reds better than they love the Americans. It will become clearer to you over time." Lozorius poured them each a shot of vodka and toasted Lukas wordlessly. Lukas found he needed the alcohol. When he looked up at Lozorius, he saw that the man's prominent ears turned red when he drank, a trait Lukas remembered from their student days.

"I don't see how we can ever expect to free ourselves if there isn't going to be a war between the Reds and the West," said Lukas. "What about help with arms for the partisans so we can keep harassing the Reds? Will they at least supply us in our own fight?"

"You're going to have to pique the interest of the spy agencies if you want to get anything at all."

The words made Lukas uneasy.

"We'll speak about that later. Tell me what it's like in the country now," said Lozorius.

Lukas began to talk about the new partisan tactic of limited engagements, and of the old dream of centralizing the partisan command structure. Even as he spoke, he could hear himself dramatizing the situation, making the organization seem stronger than it was. He felt as if he were describing his family to an outsider and wanted to cast it in the best light possible. He did say they would not last very long unless the West came through with some kind of support.

"I tell you, you won't get any support unless you offer them something."

"Like what?"

"Information. Red Army troop disposition, airfield locations, fuel dumps, the number of ships in port and where they're from, train schedules, economic news, lists of names and command structures . . ."

"We don't have any of that."

"What did you bring?"

"A letter to the Pope from the partisan command. Photographs of dead bodies laid out in marketplaces. Rough numbers of deportees. There have been thousands sent away, tens of thousands. We have identity card samples and various other blanks—passports, police identification, as well as samples of stamps of all sorts."

"That's not bad. That's a good start. I like the letter to the Pope, a nice touch. But then, the Pope doesn't have any divisions, does he?"

An appeal to the Pope as the highest moral authority had seemed to make perfect sense in Lithuania, but now Lozorius made it sound naive. Lozorius saw Lukas's discomfort and made him swallow another glass of vodka.

"So what exactly do you intend to do out here?" asked Lozorius.

"To represent the partisans to the Lithuanian government-in-exile, to get help, to raise funds."

"I'm already doing all that. Too bad communications are so poor—they could have saved the lives of some good men if they hadn't tried to get you out without checking with me. I could use your help here, of course."

He let the moment hang in the air. Lukas sensed there was a control issue here. He didn't care.

"That's what I'm here for," said Lukas. "To help."

Lozorius nodded, accepting the concession.

It was late at night by the time Lozorius finally stood up to go. He left two fingers of vodka in the bottle.

Lukas was tired and this was the first good bed he had been offered in some time, but after Lozorius left he hesitated to lie down until he was sure he would fall asleep quickly. Otherwise, Elena would visit him in his mind. She wasn't the only ghost—an entire trail of dead had somehow brought him to this comfortable cot in a Polish coastal town. He could not quite understand why they had died and he had lived.

He drank the last of the vodka, took off his shoes and lay down on the bed. But when he closed his eyes, sleep did not come for a long time. Elena was there, always there. First in his waking mind and then in his dreams, until he mercifully fell into unconsciousness.

In the four days that followed, Lukas was visited often by Lozorius as well as by a mute nun who brought him trays of food. Once he had eaten he felt restless, and so Lozorius took him for long walks by the winter sea.

They talked about how long the partisans could hold out. Of the importance of contacting the Ukrainians and other Baltics, the Estonians and Latvians. Of the Polish resistance. Of the terrible killers of Jews, collaborators who had tarred the reputations of their own countries in the West. All of this until the wind off the seas became too much and they returned to drink tea in Lukas's room.

At the end of the fourth day, Lozorius told him to be ready to leave the next morning. "Write a letter to go back into Lithuania. We'll drop it with the Dombrowskis."

"The Dombrowskis asked me not to go there. They said they were being watched."

"Bakers are nervous types. I'll do the drop-off on the way to the harbour."

The following morning, they boarded the train and rode back to Gdynia. Lukas was to wait on a street corner as Lozorius took his letter to the Dombrowskis, but from the distant corner Lukas could see that the door of the shop was locked.

"What does it mean?" Lukas asked when Lozorius returned.

"Who knows? It's odd to close a shop on a Tuesday, though. I'm going to drop this off at the post office." He left Lukas at a tea shop and then returned half an hour later and they headed out into the port.

"How is this 'leaving the country' done?" Lukas asked.

Lozorius laughed. "Simple. Just watch me."

It was a windy day, and although the harbour had not frozen in, there were lumps of ice in the eddies around the piers and slick spots on the quays where an unwary walker could slide under the chain at the edge and into the sea. The pier Lozorius took him out upon was empty of people, but there were two ships tied up a hundred yards apart. Lozorius led Lukas up to the second one.

"This is it," he said.

"You know someone on board?"

"No, but it's a Swedish ship and it will be going back there eventually. We'll just set up under a tarp and wait until we get there."

"Just like that?"

"Just like that."

The drop down to the ship was over three metres, and Lozorius went first so Lukas could drop his backpack down to him. After they had scouted around to make sure no one was looking, they made their way under a tarpaulin on the deck that covered odd pieces of heavy machinery.

"Now we wait," said Lozorius. "I hope you remembered to put on your long underwear."

TWELVE

SWEDEN

FEBRUARY 1948

*T*HE LARGE twin-funnelled ferry upon which they had stowed away sailed from Gdynia in Poland to Trelleborg in Sweden, hauling rail cars and trucks. The winter wind seemed to find every gap between the tarp and the deck, and the rocking of the ship made Lukas sick. Lozorius did not seem to be affected, or he didn't show it. The journey lasted only twelve hours but it felt much longer, and Lukas could barely straighten out his legs for their numbness when it came time to disembark.

The guard at the gangway in Sweden seemed unsurprised when two half-frozen men with large knapsacks appeared at the bottom of the gangplank. Lozorius addressed him in Swedish and the guard escorted them to a small, self-contained room at the customs shed onshore and locked the door behind them.

The whole process had seemed very relaxed, but Lukas did not like being locked up.

"Don't worry," said Lozorius. "These are all formalities."

"In the old days you didn't like being locked up either."

"You're in a new place and you have to adapt to it. The dangers out here are not the same as they were back home." Lozorius smoked cigarettes and looked out of the window as they waited.

Lukas studied the man across the room from him, draped comfortably across a bench as if between trains in a railway station. Lukas had not known him well when they were students, and it seemed odd that this slight and unpretentious man should have developed such a reputation among the partisans. Maybe it was his very ease in unfamiliar circumstances that gave him his standing. Lozorius knew he was being looked at, but it didn't seem to bother him. He even seemed to enjoy it.

A policeman came and Lozorius surrendered a revolver he had in an inside pocket of his coat. The policeman set the revolver on a desk and wrote out a receipt for it. A woman appeared with two tin cups of sweet tea and a ten-pack of cigarettes, and then locked them in again.

"What a country," said Lukas, looking at the burning end of the cigarette. Even the paper seemed fine, almost too fine to burn up. Everything back home was coarse in comparison.

Another policeman came and took Lozorius away for a while.

Lukas had felt comfortable enough in Poland—it was a neighbouring and familiar country—but Sweden was completely unnerving. He was in a foreign country where the rules were utterly unknown to him. The calm proceedings to deal with stowaways seemed odd and a little intimidating, as if he had stumbled into a country of lords and ladies where his peasant background would make him seem uncouth. He was accustomed to watchfulness and danger, yet even when there was no danger the habit of vigilance would not leave him. He felt restless and uneasy. Some part of him wished he could withdraw to the underground again.

Lukas looked out upon the port from the very small window. There was not much to see; a series of carts on steel wheels blocked his view. Sweden was a good country, he hoped, but he really didn't know.

Two hours later, the door was unlocked and the tea lady took him through the blustering winter wind to a long black car with a driver, where Lozorius was waiting in the back seat. When Lukas got in, he found a boxed lunch with sandwiches and a Thermos of tea as well as a small bottle of aquavit on the seat between them. It was a right-hand-drive car, the first that Lukas had ever seen.

"How did you manage this?" Lukas asked as the driver put the car in gear and drove away.

"They know me here. We're in for a long drive to Stockholm. Have something to eat and then try to get some sleep. We'll be driving through the night."

Not for the first time that day, Lukas wondered how he ever would have managed without Lozorius.

Lukas intended to stay awake, but once he had eaten, it became dark, the fantastically early night of the northern latitude. Then he drank some aquavit and fell asleep with the taste of caraway on his lips. It was a flavour very common in this part of Europe, one that reminded him of home.

Lukas spent the next eight days in an empty warehouse on the waterfront of Stockholm, writing reports about the political, economic and social conditions in Lithuania. Lozorius would take the papers he had written and disappear for hours, sometimes overnight, and then return with questions or requests for rewrites.

"Why is this taking so long?" Lukas asked.

"You arrived from *terra incognita*. They need to figure out the place you come from and what kind of animal you are and if they can trust you."

"Couldn't you just vouch for me?"

"It's not so simple. They never trust anyone completely. And people change. The man you knew a year ago might be a different man today."

"I haven't changed. I'm still the son of a farmer."

"Don't pretend to be simpler than you are. You're the one who took part in the seizure of Merkine. The one who shot down a whole tableful of dinner guests. The one who evaded capture for two years while others were dying or being taken prisoner, and then crossed the border successfully. You're almost too good to be true."

"What does that mean?"

"Just that you're quite a prize. You even make me look good. I was getting a little stale for them."

"Stale?"

"I've been here for a long time now. I haven't had much new news since Lithuania's been closed up tight. Just the odd letter was coming out before you appeared, and I couldn't find a way back in. You've given me a new lease on life."

The warehouse where Lukas lived was at least a hundred years old, all weathered red brick. He had a bed and a table in a corner of the vastness of the space. When he turned the light off, the interior was as dark as any bunker. He felt the vertiginous emptiness of the warehouse, whereas in the bunkers he had felt the oppressive closeness of the earth.

A small door led out to the street, with a canal on the other side of the road. Lukas could walk around all he wanted, but the city was a confusing arrangement of bridges and islands, a metropolis that stymied him. Twice he had become lost for well over an hour, wandering deep into the suburbs. He could not make himself understood to the locals when he asked for directions. He asked Lozorius to write down the warehouse address, and he tried showing this paper to pedestrians whenever he was lost, but he could never understand their explanations. Finally he lost the scrap of paper and reconciled himself to going astray each time he went out.

The city was old and unbombed, a novelty of preservation. Compared to Gdynia it was a museum, with charming old parks and cafés, picturesque in a storybook way. But it was also impenetrable. The people who walked the streets did not seem to have any problems, or at least no problems that showed on their faces. Lukas stared at them intently, as intently as he dared, but he could not see through their strangeness. On the fifth day he was caught staring at a young mother and she looked back at him angrily in a manner that made him understand *he* was the strange one, not they.

He had no money. There was no lack of food or drink back at the warehouse, and he found a new suit of clothes and a fresh pair of shoes laid out for him one day on his bed when he returned from a walk. Yet it felt odd to be unable to buy the simplest things, a coffee or a newspaper. Was he being sent a message? The shoes and suit fit perfectly, which was both comforting and a little disturbing.

On the eighth day he returned to find a man with steel-rimmed glasses and swept-back hair sitting at his table and smoking a cigarette. He seemed to be in his mid-thirties but could have been older. The man rose as soon as Lukas came in and extended his hand and addressed him in Lithuanian.

"Hello. My name is Zoly. Just my nickname, really, short for Pranas Zolynas. I hope I can call you by your first name?"

"Who are you?"

"A friend of Lozorius. Yours too, I hope, in the long run. We're on the same side. I worked with the Lithuanian embassy here before the war, and the Swedes took me in after it was all over."

"That was kind of them."

"In a way, yes, but the Swedes don't waste their kindness. Let's not forget, the Swedes immediately recognized the incorporation of Lithuania into the Soviet Union and gave our embassy to the Reds. That wasn't so kind. They put me out of a job in the first place. Since that time I've tried to be useful to the Swedes in small ways, and they are useful to me in return."

"Where's Lozorius?"

"Not in Sweden at the moment, I'm afraid."

"What? He didn't tell me he was going anywhere." Lukas felt abandoned.

"He does that all the time. One is always happy to see Lozorius, but one should never expect him to be around for long. Like the Holy Spirit, he moves in mysterious ways."

Zoly smiled and Lukas realized he had made a joke. Lukas was unaccustomed to this kind of playful talk except in the presence of women.

"But Lozorius gave me the reports you wrote, and I have to say I'm very impressed. The Swedes are interested. The West needs shaking up and the news of all those partisans still fighting almost three years after the war is just the thing."

"Four years."

"For you, yes, but here they don't count the war as ending until May of 1945. If the Red Army killed you before that time, you were a German collaborator. What did you say you had—forty thousand partisans?"

"I said thirty thousand, and it was an estimate, and I don't possess them personally."

"Even if you're only half right, that's inspiring."

"What's going on? Why am I being held here?"

"Nobody expected you, and the Swedes are trying to figure out just what kind of fish Lozorius reeled in. Your reports are being translated into Swedish. Don't worry, you're on the verge of being figured out. In the meantime, I'm here to help you."

"How?"

"In any way you like. Do you want to see a ballet? Go out for a few drinks and some female company?"

The offer sounded better than he cared to admit, but he didn't dare to admit it, especially to himself.

"I'm on a mission to the West, not a pleasure trip."

"Very serious, I see. Commendable. But you say 'the West' as if it were some kind of monolith. There is no such thing. There are the Swedes, the French, the English and the Americans, and they often don't agree on matters among themselves."

"So who should I be speaking to?"

"Well, the Swedes first, obviously, since that's where you are."

"And what's taking them so long?"

"Long? You call this long? You haven't been around government very much, my boy. They're moving with lightning speed. With any luck you'll be summoned sometime soon."

"What does that mean?"

"It means I don't know. Ask me something else."

Lukas had many questions. Were there any émigrés in Sweden that Lukas might know, people he could talk to? Some, it turned out, but Lukas should not mix with them yet. How big was Lozorius's information bureau and how tightly was it connected to the Swedes? By the look of Zoly, very tightly indeed. What steps should he take to make his case to the Swedes? Follow Zoly's instructions and wait.

But it was hard to wait. Where would he make the most impact? These were the sorts of questions one asked of people one trusted, and while Lukas did not distrust Lozorius or Zoly, he did not wholly have faith in them either. Lukas missed, for a moment, the clarity of life in the underground back home, where a friend was a friend and an enemy was an enemy.

Zoly offered him a cigarette, which he turned down, but he did ask for a map of Stockholm, which Zoly did not have. Instead, Zoly gave him a detailed verbal description of the city. It did not help. When Lukas went out for a walk that afternoon, he became lost again. As he wandered, he looked to see if the men who must be following him could be identified on the street, but they knew their craft too well. Lukas could not find a recognizable face, and wandered about for an hour and a half before he found his way back home to the warehouse.

After two more days, Zoly came in one morning and asked if Lukas would mind meeting someone from "very high up" for lunch.

"Very high up where?" Lukas asked.

"Among the Swedes, where else?"

"What part of the Swedish government?"

"He's the deputy director of intelligence, and he'd like to lunch with you."

"Here?"

"No, at his apartment. It's a great honour."

Oskar Ramel lived in a flat on the island suburb of Lidingo, a few minutes from Stockholm's city centre. The three-storey building was twenties modernist, all the space calculated squarely and rationally, without waste. Ramel's flat was in the southwest corner on the second floor with a view over the water. The sky was low and overcast, but there were large windows on both the south and west walls and the place was filled with cool winter light.

Ramel had been a commodore in the Swedish navy, an attaché in Buenos Aires before the war. He was tall and straight of back, middle-aged and elegant. He spoke several languages, and they chose English at first to test Lukas's command, and then German in deference to Zoly, who was clearly going to sit through the meeting with them. One end of the dining room table was set with openfaced meat and fish sandwiches, and Ramel mixed up aquavit cocktails for them while recounting his experiences in Argentina during the war.

Having eaten a couple of sandwiches, Ramel brushed the crumbs off his fingers with a napkin and got down to business. "I've read your reports and I'm intrigued. Are you really the one who shot all those Reds during the so-called engagement party?"

Lukas shifted uneasily. It seemed barbaric to hear the words out here, in Ramel's mouth. He felt like a murderer. "That was a long time ago."

"Still, very remarkable. What happened to the woman who worked with you in that operation?"

"She was killed."

"I'm sorry to hear that. Were you close to her?"

"She was my wife."

An awkward silence ensued. Ramel sighed, proposed a toast in her memory, and they finished their drinks. He rose, mixed fresh cocktails in the glass shaker and refilled their glasses.

Then he asked many questions, cross-checking what Lukas had written in his reports, sometimes asking for information that Lukas did not have. Lukas had no idea how many military bases the Red

Army had in Lithuania. He had no idea about any rocket installations. He did not know the state of East Prussia beyond what he had seen when he crossed it to get to Poland.

They had been talking for a few hours and the pale grey light in the apartment was growing weaker, although it was still only mid-afternoon. They were on their third cocktail by the time Ramel finished asking questions. He had been thorough and courteous without committing himself. Either he was masking his heart or he did not have one.

"There's no doubt that the Allies made mistakes during the war," he said. "We all did." As a former supplier to the Nazis of war materiel, there was no way to avoid accepting some of the blame for Sweden's actions. "But Roosevelt made too many concessions to the Soviets. As a result, the whole of Europe has been thrown off balance and the fate of small nations is at risk. A country like Sweden has no option but to manoeuvre between the great powers. It's true that we have recognized the incorporation of the Baltic States into the Soviet Union. That was regrettable, but necessary for us. However, we are still your friends."

"You let the Reds have us. How can I think of the Swedes as my friends?"

He had not intended to be so rude, but he was slightly drunk now and getting exasperated. He felt as if he had come to say his child had fallen into a well and his neighbour was giving him a dissertation about the high cost of rope.

"I need you to understand *realpolitik*," said Ramel, unperturbed. "There's no need for me to meet with you at all. We could stop talking this moment and I could find a spot for you at a displaced persons' camp."

"Maybe I'll take you up on that offer. But first let me hear what else you have to say."

"We're democrats in Sweden. We think you should have the same rights too. Emotionally we're on your side, but the Soviet Union is very close to us here, just across the sea.

"Furthermore, the political situation is unstable. We might stay as we are for some time or Europe might go back to the borders of 1939. On the other hand, the Soviets might sweep right across Europe and end up ruling us all. We don't look forward to this sort of tyrannical orientalism.

"However things turn out in the end, the Estonian, Latvian and Lithuanian states and their partisans are important players in the future of Europe. I'm honoured to pay my respects to the movement through you. Lozorius, the old rascal, has been filling my ears as well.

"Here is what I've been authorized to do. I can help you get in contact with the wider world. Sweden can take no direct action, but we might be able to put you in touch with people who can. I should remind you that we helped you during the Nazi era, even though we were supposed to be neutral then."

Ramel stopped at this point and it seemed polite to thank the Swedes through him, so Lukas did so, although it was hard to be diplomatic. His friends were dying and Ramel was talking about measured action.

It was almost dark outside now, but no lights had been turned on inside the apartment. Although all their glasses were empty, Ramel made no move to mix fresh cocktails. The business was nearing its end.

"You know, there is no way you could carry on any clandestine activity here without our knowledge. Do you have any ties with other agencies? Say, the French or the Americans?"

"You're only the third person I've met in this country," said Lukas. "The fourth if you count my driver from Trelleborg."

Ramel nodded vaguely. "Well, I feel better now. At least we understand each other."

Zoly was rising from his chair. Lukas did the same.

"It's been delightful speaking with you," said Ramel.

"Maybe we'll have a chance to speak some more another time."

"Perhaps."

A car was waiting for them when they reached the street.

Neither he nor Zoly spoke until the driver pulled up to the warehouse. Lukas got out of the car and Zoly stepped outside too.

"Well?" Zoly asked.

"He's a cold fish," said Lukas. "These Swedes are calculating. Look at this beautiful city, a living monument to their neutrality. If you're neutral, your heart never catches fire, you don't believe in anything. God, how do these people even procreate?"

"I'm sure he's passionate about other things besides the fate of the Lithuanians. Do you expect others to risk their security for you?"

"I think I do. Or let me put it another way. I don't care all that much about their security, which gives them the right to live in beautiful cities like this. Am I supposed to worry about their not wanting to provoke the Reds? What does that get me, except the right to be annihilated?"

"I think you have to find a place where your interests coincide."

"I don't see where that place is. He didn't offer anything."

"Not exactly, no, but he didn't close the door either. I think you were being assessed, and I think you passed your exam with flying colours, including being a little abrupt with him."

"That wasn't calculated."

"Then you should think of calculating a little more often."

"I just want someone on our side."

"Be patient," said Zoly.

Lukas looked at him in exasperation. He half liked Zoly, but he also had a deep desire to take him by the shoulders and shake him very hard until the diplomatic veneer shattered and revealed the real man beneath.

THIRTEEN

STOCKHOLM

FEBRUARY 1948

T WO DAYS LATER, Lukas heard Zoly's characteristic knock,
a discreet, slightly less than obsequious *tap tap tap* on the
warehouse door. The man might have been a concierge,
both invasive and ingratiating.

"Hello, hello!" Zoly let himself in and waved from the doorway
to Lukas at his desk beside the bed. The warehouse was in cavernous
darkness except for the two lights, the one over the door where Zoly
stood and the other on Lukas's desk.

"How would you like to come out for a walk?" Zoly asked.

"I'm in the middle of writing something now. Can it wait?"

"Maybe not."

Lukas put on his coat, not intending to take his scarf and gloves,
but Zoly insisted. They might be away for some time.

They stepped outside onto the street and began to walk along
the sidewalk under the grey February sky.

"Where are we going?" asked Lukas.

"It's all fairly complex, you see. Ramel had to look you over. After
all, you're in Sweden and he has responsibility for what goes on in
this country. And it's true the Swedes are on our side, in a way, but
their range of activity is limited because of their neutrality during

the war and their caution about the Reds. They can't actually do anything, so they're passing you over to someone who can."

"The Americans?"

"No. The Americans could do something, but they don't seem ready. We're going to meet the Brits. Their power isn't what it once was, but the Baltic used to be a British lake, so they're familiar with the territory. The British managerial class go back for generations here.

"Just a word to the wise. You have to be a little bit careful about the British because they make distinctions among themselves. The man we're going to see was born in Moscow, and his father was born in Archangel, but if you call him an Englishman he'll be insulted. You'd be better off calling him Estonian than English. He ran a timber business in Tallinn before the war. But he considers himself a Scot. They're a very proud people."

"Meanwhile, most Brits cannot distinguish a Latvian from a Lithuanian."

"Foreigners always seem so silly, don't they?"

"What happened to this Scotsman's business?"

"All swept away when the Reds came to Estonia the first time, back in '40. He fled to Finland with his Estonian wife, and then to Sweden. I think he must hate the Reds more than you do."

Zoly took Lukas to a remote part of the harbour and along a quay that had three boats tied up to it. Two were fishing boats, but the third was a sleeker craft, something like a large customs patrol boat with a bridge, two lifeboats and quarters down below. Asking no one's permission, Zoly took Lukas onto the deck and they climbed down a ladder to a narrow corridor with two doors. Zoly rapped on one of the doors and opened it.

"Close the door behind you," a voice said. "The cold air is blowing in here."

Zoly brought Lukas into a low cabin with a small table and four chairs. There was a bottle of whisky on the table and a Thermos of tea beside it. A large man in shirt sleeves was standing up, his broad, weathered face serious but the eyes genial. He had thick white hair, a little too long, and the girth of a man who enjoyed his food. He wore suspenders and his suit jacket hung on the chair behind him.

"Leonard Dunlop," he said, extending his hand. Lukas had worked on the farm since he was a child, and he had lived in the forest, so his hands were not exactly soft, but Dunlop's were very big and meaty and hard, as if he handled rough goods often.

"Zoly, I think the captain has some coffee on the bridge upstairs. He might enjoy your company."

Zoly nodded and went out, closing the door behind him. Lukas could hear the metal ladder creak as he made his way back up on deck.

"Drink?" Dunlop asked in Russian.

"Why not?"

"What language do you prefer to speak?"

"I have some English."

"Good for you. We'll start in that, but we can speak Russian or Polish if you want, or Finnish or Estonian, if you speak those."

Dunlop poured small glasses of whisky for each of them and glasses of tea as a chaser. They drank the whisky neat and sat down and Dunlop launched into a talk about Lukas's reports and then asked questions about the state of the partisans in Lithuania. They had another two glasses of whisky as they talked and Lukas felt the alcohol go to his head. Dunlop did not show himself to be any the worse for the drink.

Where Lukas came from, and throughout the whole of Eastern Europe, alcohol was as common as tea, and had been more common during the war. It had caused the undoing of the best of plans, but was consolation for the failure of those plans and the murderous nature of history. Drinking was a way of life for Eastern Europeans. Although he had not been drinking much over the previous years with Flint, Lukas could hold his own as long as the drinking didn't go on too long, in which case Dunlop's superior body weight and years of practice would give him the advantage.

"What do you think of this boat?" Dunlop asked suddenly.

"I don't know much about boats."

"It's a refitted German E-boat. Now attached to the British fishery protection service, but it has the same German captain it's had since it was launched in 1943. They used it to patrol the Baltic and drop agents behind the lines, and to torpedo our ships. Let me tell you, the captain saw a few of our own boys drown. But that's all in the past now. We're fighting a common enemy. This boat has been stripped of its armaments—no more torpedo tubes. It was overhauled in Portsmouth—twin Mercedes-Benz 518 diesel engines. We can guarantee a speed of forty-five knots, the fastest on the Baltic, and the quietest. The exhausts have been installed underwater."

"Do you use this boat very often?" Lukas asked.

"From time to time. We hope to use it again."

"And what, exactly, are the English views on the Baltics in general, and Lithuania in particular?"

"First, I need to know if you're working with the Americans."

"No, not yet."

Dunlop smiled and poured them each a shot. "Good. The Americans don't understand the subtleties of the Baltic. It's too far away from them."

"I'm not sure I understand them either. I'm a simple man. We need allies, not diplomats."

"Unless you learn subtlety, you'll just stir up the Reds."

"My people are dying, Mr. Dunlop. We aren't concerned about stirring up the Reds. We'd like to annoy them so much that they pack up and go home."

"I know something about the Reds and the Baltic. I've lived here my whole life and I'd never be involved in anything that would harm you. My wife is Estonian. The real interest of Britain is to make the Baltic States independent again."

Dunlop was likely using some kind of mixture of truth and lies, but Lukas could not distinguish one from the other. His sixth sense, his nose for deception, which had served him so well back in Lithuania, did not function properly out here in Sweden. It was clear enough that Dunlop wanted Lukas and the partisans for some purpose. The question was, did Lukas and the partisans want the British, given that they would do nothing to free the country and were so much weaker than the Americans since the war?

"We appreciate you," said Lukas. "At least someone knows we're dying and knows what we're dying for. But what I need to know is what you can do for us. I'm beginning to understand that we shouldn't hope for a war?"

Dunlop's look answered that question.

"In that case I need to know what you can deliver. We need weapons, for example. With every passing year it gets harder to find new weapons, and ammunition for the ones we have. We need regular radio contact, crystals and at least two sets of radio transmitter/receivers, as well as men who can operate them and who have been trained in ciphers. We need money, preferably rubles, to buy food and other supplies, like printing presses. If there were some way of getting duplicating machines into the country, that would be very good for us too. We need medications: gramicidin for wounds, aspirin and morphine for pain, ether for operations, as well as cyanide capsules."

"That's quite an order. Why should we give any of this to you?"

"For compensation, for one thing, for letting us drop out of your conscience for so long. And you said you wanted to see the Baltics free."

"Spare me the discussion of my conscience. You're not going to free the Baltics, not alone. We need something too. We need train spotters who will let us know the schedules. We need to understand the movement of troops, especially any massing that could mean mobilization. We need the command structure of the Baltic Red

Army, including names of officers and descriptions of ones who can be turned if possible. We need general economic news—five-year plans and so on."

"You need spies."

"I need people who are clear they work for me first and for themselves second."

"I work for my country first."

"A very noble sentiment. We can discuss sentiments later."

Dunlop started to tell stories of the Russian Revolution, which had happened when he was a young man. He had intended to throw a bomb at Lenin himself, but his father, a Moscow merchant, had hustled him out of the country and soon enough there was no going back.

Lukas listened to Dunlop with half an ear, wondering what the right course of action was. On the one hand, he was making contact with a representative of the mythical West, as he had been instructed. It was not much of a reception, but it was something. But if the British were so eager to have him, maybe others would be too. And maybe they would provide him with a little more than what Dunlop was willing to give. The British were losing power, their empire deflating like a balloon with a slow leak, whereas the Americans were rising. Who knew, even the French might be interested. Back in the twenties they had provided training to the new diplomats of Estonia, Latvia and Lithuania. And this business of being a spy for the British stuck in his throat. He didn't want to be a mercenary in his own country.

There was a gentle rap on the door and Zoly came inside. "I was just wondering if you wanted anything to eat," he said. "It can't be good, drinking on an empty stomach like this."

Dunlop told him to sit down and join them. Ever the diplomat, Zoly took off his coat and accepted two fingers of whisky. The suggestion of food was ignored.

Dunlop did most of the talking and Zoly did most of the listening, prompting Dunlop and laughing appreciatively at his anecdotes.

Lukas looked at Zoly, and the more he looked, the less he liked what he saw.

"Are you out of your mind?"

Lozorius walked in, leaving the warehouse door open behind him. He had his coat, gloves and hat still on, and he had not even greeted Lukas.

"Close the door and we can talk about it."

Lozorius slammed the door behind him and threw off his overcoat. It was the middle of February, but the cold had not let up yet.

"I'm just keeping my options open," said Lukas. "Why should I go with Dunlop? There are sixty thousand Lithuanians in Europe in displaced persons' camps. The government-in-exile is in Germany and the remains of the diplomatic corps are in Rome. What business would I have committing myself to the British when I haven't looked around thoroughly yet?"

"But I have. What do you think I've been doing out here? The DP camps are full of people who want to emigrate to America. They don't care about your war anymore. And the ones who do are not the best ones. They want to go home and rule the country once the Americans free it for them. You have to be a realist. The Brits are the only ones who are committed."

"I didn't like the smell of him," said Lukas.

"I've been sniffing around longer than you have, and Dunlop stinks less than the others."

"Who pays your salary?" Lukas asked.

"That's not fair."

"It doesn't answer my question."

"So let me answer it with a question. Who do you think is going to pay *your* salary? Do you think you'll pass the hat at some émigré lecture and live from that? They don't have anything themselves. The only ones who do are the governments."

"But why the British?" asked Lukas.

"Because they know the territory. I understand you saw the boat."

"I did."

"How would you like to go for a ride on it?"

"How soon?"

"Very soon."

"I'm not ready yet, and I'm not going to work for the British and save my country in my spare time. I wasn't sent out to get crumbs like this. And neither were you."

"You expected to rouse the West to help you? Is that it? You mean what I've been doing out here isn't good enough? You just got here. You barely understand the place. I know the landscape and I represent the partisans out here. You might be missing a very good opportunity."

"I'll take that chance."

Lozorius was furious. He gathered up his coat, hat and gloves, but he did not put them on. He stepped out through the door and slammed it behind him.

FOURTEEN

KEMPTEN DISPLACED PERSON'S CAMP, BAVARIA APRIL 1948

WHEN LUCAS STEPPED out into the yard that night, he could smell the late thaw coming on, finally sense the drip of melting water under the remaining snow-banks. He was glad to get some air after the intensely smoky meeting with the émigré Lithuanian government followed by a talk to the hundreds of persons who lived in the camp. He was getting used to speaking in front of audiences.

The place had been intensely cold during the first part of the meeting, but it heated up with all the bodies in the room. Three hundred people sat on chairs and as many again stood at the back or on the sides. Some of the seated women had children on their laps, and most of those who stood were young men, many around his age. They had all been eager to hear what he had to say about the partisan resistance in Lithuania, and that was gratifying. But the most pressing questions were ones he could not answer, requests for news of the relatives the refugees had left behind.

For all their interest in what Lukas had to say, after sitting in DP camps for four years the young men and women, the greybeard teachers, the low-level bureaucrats and farmers were all looking out to their own futures in the West. They missed their homes, but they were realists. They were willing enough to help out, but they had no money, no jobs and no influence. The way back was closed to them, and their contributions in cash barely covered his travel expenses. If they had one fear, it was that the Allies would return to their policy of repatriation. The ones who'd gone back willingly or unwillingly had been imprisoned, deported to Siberia or killed.

Lukas had been surprised to learn about the subtleties of the West, both among the foreign governments and among his own people. There were factions within the émigrés, a split between the government-in-exile and the old diplomatic corps, and, for all he knew, factions within the factions. He was mired in complexities here. Everything had been much simpler back in the bunkers.

And, as Lozorius had predicted, the Lithuanian government-in-exile did not have any money of its own. Lukas was a kind of trophy to them, a fundraiser on tour through the camps of Germany, scratching together loose change. Now there was talk about sending him to America for a lecture series—that was where the real money lay—but the American government was sticky about its visas and in no rush to let him in.

Not yet.

Things were changing slightly. There had been a Communist coup in Czechoslovakia, and so the Americans were far less enthusiastic about their old allies, the Reds. But would they actually do anything? It was hard to tell. They seemed to worry most about Reds in the State Department while not worrying about the Reds anywhere else.

Where did all this put Lukas? He was unsure. As he had toured the Bavarian town of Kempten earlier that day, medieval buildings unbombed, pushed up against the mountains, he had been astonished by the beauty of the place, and then felt guilty for his enjoyment of this moment, for being able to walk around as a tourist while Lakstingala and Flint waited for him to bring help to them.

Maybe Lozorius was right. Maybe he should have taken the British offer. And yet the British offer rankled.

His feelings were becoming unpredictable, powerful and strange. Back home his feelings had been pure and straightforward. But ever since he had left Lithuania, and in particular after he left Sweden, his emotions had become unstable. Now that he was living free of danger, he felt worse than he ever had in Lithuania.

"Excuse me."

A young woman had stepped out of the darkness of the camp courtyard, someone whose face he remembered from the audience at his talk.

"You were a neighbour of mine back in Lithuania," she said.

He looked at her more closely. She was younger than him, around twenty-two he guessed, with light brown hair, a high forehead and high cheekbones. He did not remember her.

"Are you from Rumsiskes?" he asked.

"No, Kaunas. My parents had a house on the same street as the university residence, and I would see you and the other students going to lectures when you were in your first year. My sister and I were still schoolgirls and we used to admire you all from a distance."

"Admire us? What for?"

"Because you were older and seemed so sure of yourselves. We didn't even know what we wanted to do yet, and there you were, you and your friends, sailing along on the journey of life."

That period seemed utterly remote to him now. "What's your name?" Lukas asked.

"Monika, but sometimes they call me Monique, since I live in France."

Lukas had been approached like this many times in the last few weeks, and although it was flattering to have admirers, they made him feel awkward. They considered him many things: a hero, the embodiment of their anger, and a symbol of the life of resistance that they had not chosen because they had fled. He felt like a fraud in all these roles and he longed sometimes for the old friends who knew him from before. And yet that person was gone.

In the eyes of the young people in particular, those his age, he seemed to represent what might have been. They were bored, these DP camp residents, over three years in barracks, some of them, caught between worlds and still unsure of the future. Some of the teenagers who had been schoolchildren when their parents fled now wanted to go back with him to fight.

The poor darlings. No one needed teenagers in the partisan fight, and in any case there was no easy way to get back there.

"I wonder," said Monika, "if you have any information about those who were deported to Siberia in 1940."

"Not in particular. None of them ever came back as far as I know, and a lot more followed them." He hated to disappoint Monika, but there was no use in raising false hopes.

She nodded sadly. "I wanted you to know that I found your talk very moving. I'm very impressed by everything you've done."

"Thank you very much."

She hesitated and then went on. "I don't mean to be unfriendly when I ask this—I didn't want to say anything during question period—but do you think it's right to continue fighting?"

"What do you propose instead?"

"A whole generation is being cut down. Who will be left in the country in the long run if all of them are killed? Wouldn't passive resistance be better than fighting?"

"You're not the first person to say that."

"I never claimed I was original. I was just wondering."

"It's the line that the Chekists try to sell. They keep apologizing for the 'excesses' and telling us we should lay down our arms if we really love our country."

She reddened. "So you think I'm a Chekist too?"

"I didn't say that. I'm sure your ideas are sincere."

"But naive?"

"Completely. If you repeat the party line of the Cheka, then you're helping them whether you know it or not. You must never become confused about your enemies."

"Maybe it's no longer a time to kill. Maybe it's a time to heal."

"Are you a Catholic?"

"I'm not really all that religious. In my own way I'm a doubter. It's the more honest reaction, don't you think? Because if you are a true believer, your cause is assured. It gives you peace of mind."

"What a ridiculous statement. I've had no peace of mind for years. I've watched my generation die out in the forests in order to save those behind us. Don't make me seem like a simpleton."

She was going to respond, but the door was thrown open and two men came out. "Lukas," one said, "you can flirt all you want later. But now you have to come back inside and answer more questions."

Regretting his sharpness, he turned to offer softer words, but Monika had slipped away.

Lukas spent the following morning in a meeting with the émigré government, establishing the groundwork for their relationship with the partisans. There was a shortage of coal in the camp and so the room was very cold, all of them working at the table in their coats and hats, the recording secretary wearing gloves with the fingers cut out. Twenty men representing the various pre-war political parties worked together uneasily, intensely competitive among themselves.

All the discussions about future governments of Lithuania had an air of unreality about them, of detachment from anything that might happen any time soon. Lukas felt ungrounded, as if he were floating in a sea of words.

When the morning meetings ended and Lukas was eating canned corned beef sandwiches with the others, he looked up from his long table in the cafeteria and saw Monika talking by the exit door with another woman her age, a similar-looking woman who must have been her sister. Both had light brown hair and something French about them, a hint of style in the way they wore their scarves.

He had enjoyed the strange meat sandwich. It was a little gelatinous and pleasantly salty. He was surprised by many of the foods he found in Germany, the powdered milk and cornbread and the various tinned foods. American cigarettes were a novelty too, for both their taste and their ability to function as alternate currency.

A priest from the émigré government was explaining that it would take time for the Pope to respond to the letter from the partisans, but Lukas was only listening with half an ear. He excused himself and walked over to Monika.

"How are you today?" he asked.

No emotion of any kind showed on her face. "I'm as fine as I was yesterday. This is my sister, Anne." She was maybe a year older than Monika and looked vaguely familiar, another one of the girls from the street of his university residence.

"I thought I might have offended you," said Lukas.

"You seem to find women's opinions unserious."

"I take women very seriously."

"Do you? It didn't sound like it."

"Women in the underground were everything from couriers to machine gunners. We couldn't have got by without them."

Suddenly he could not speak anymore. The talk of women in the underground made him think of Elena. Her image rose up in his mind so strongly that he could almost see her, almost believe that if he looked across the room she would be sitting there with the others, wondering why he was talking to this woman.

Lukas stopped speaking and looked up at Monika in panic, afraid he might begin to weep in public, in the middle of a crowd. He excused himself. He tore down the steps of the cafeteria to the ground floor, conscious of the clatter of his shoes and the well-wishers who were trying to say things to him as he ran past them on the steps.

As the hero of the resistance, he was the centre of attention. People looked at him, trying to understand the meaning of this sudden flight. Even out in the yard he could not contain himself, and he walked away from the camp into the town, and then beyond it onto a road in the countryside that led from the plain up toward the nearby mountains.

He walked fast, hoping that if he moved quickly he might even be able to escape from himself.

Most of the snow was gone from the road and the fields, though there were still dirty banks at the roadside and against the fence rails; icy water ran in the ditches from the melt higher up on the peaks. In places there were pools of water on the dirt road and he had to step carefully around them to avoid sinking into the muck. No automobile or cart hazarded the mud on this particular road, and so he was alone. Even the fields were mostly empty, with only some faraway cows nudging the earth to look for grass shoots, their bells plinking irregularly in the distance.

He kept walking until he felt his shoulders stop shaking and the tears dried from his face. He did not understand how this could be happening to him. He faced losses no worse than many other people had suffered, and they had seemed to survive. What right did he have to be overcome in this way? The whole room he had spoken to, the whole DP camp, had stories of loss; it was the responsibility of every man and woman to keep up morale, not to let depression get to them. Not everyone could. Some were taken away to psychiatric hospitals, and others hanged themselves in the night. Still others walked around with smitten looks, or went on drinking binges that lasted for days.

To fall into despair was to become a casualty of one kind or another, a victim of Red success, and he was damned if he would let himself become one. But he did not know how to stop these unbearable emotions from washing over him.

He walked for a long time. The April sun felt warm on his face, although the angle was beginning to change and the colour of the fields around him yellowed in the late afternoon light. It was time to turn around. When he did so, he saw a distant figure approaching along the road. He feared it might be Monika, and his fears were confirmed when she was close enough to be made out. There was no way to avoid her.

She had tied her hair back in a scarf, though a strand of it showed on her forehead. There was a thick streak of dirt on her coat and on the sleeve as well.

He spoke out first. "You've fallen in the mud. I'm very sorry."

"It's nothing." She was searching his eyes and put her hands out toward him as soon as she was close enough. He took them in his, startled at her sudden proximity.

"I must have embarrassed you back at the cafeteria," Lukas said.

"No, I'm the one who's at fault. I was making fun of you in a way, I suppose, and you shouldn't make fun of some things."

"It's not that. You triggered a very strong memory in me. I've had some losses, you know. Not more than anyone else, but still."

"Yes, I know about your wife."

He was stunned. "How can you know about her? I didn't think anyone knew about her." He had to hold himself back or the tears would well up again.

"Word gets out."

Now Lukas was mortified. All this time, while he had been on his lecture tour talking about the suffering of the people left behind, the audience must have known about Elena. The sympathy they had lavished upon him was therefore partially due to his own story. This public knowledge of the grief he had held back from himself was completely unbearable. Where he came from, a man did not parade his feelings. There were too many feelings to be had during the war, and the agony of one person did not deserve precedence over the agony of others.

Monika let go of his hands and slipped her arm through his, as if they were old friends. "May I walk back with you?" she asked.

"Of course. I promise I won't break down like that again." He was not actually sure he could keep his promise.

"It wouldn't matter to me if you did."

They began to walk back toward the town.

"Tell me about where you grew up," said Lukas. He wanted her to talk as much as possible in order not to have to talk himself.

"I was a city girl, growing up in Kaunas with my sister. My father was in the ministry of education, but his parents and my mother's parents both came from farm families. It's funny, but when I think of Lithuania, I don't think of the city where I spent most of my time. I think of the two farms where we spent the summers. One was a combination farm and mill with a great millpond where we swam all summer long and our grandparents spoiled us. We didn't have to do anything at all. We were terrible. We'd stay up late, flirting with the farmhands, and then we'd sleep in in the mornings while they had to get up at dawn to go to work."

"And your parents?"

"My father was taken in the first round of deportations in 1940. They would have taken my mother and us too, but we were vacationing at the farm while he had stayed behind to work in town. He never actually said anything, but I suspect he knew what was coming because he sent us off to the countryside before school was out."

The Reds had taken many thousands of people right up to the first weeks of June 1941 and shipped them off to the North. When the Germans attacked, the Reds took some of their remaining prisoners with them as they retreated, but many were executed. For all the rush to retreat, some of those the Reds killed were tortured first and their mangled bodies left behind in heaps as lessons to the Lithuanians about anyone who chose to be anti-Soviet. Many of the Jews were immediately massacred by collaborators and Nazis when the Germans came a week later, and most of the rest were killed afterward.

But the fate of many others, including those taken in the first Red deportations, was unclear. They were simply gone. Monika's father might have died in the cattle cars, or made it to Siberia or the Komi Republic and died there, or survived and be working in a labour camp with no chance of communication. Thus all losses that were indefinite provided seeds of hope. Or of despair, the result of hope that could not be sustained.

"And how did you get to Paris?" asked Lukas.

"My uncle was the military attaché in Paris before the war and he stayed there. He took us in quite early, at the beginning of 1944. We were lucky to be there to see the Liberation. Since then, my mother gives piano lessons and my sister and I have given up our restaurant jobs, but we're looking for something better now."

"How is life in Paris?"

"Most people would prefer to go to America. Except for the artists and philosophers—they would prefer to stay in Paris."

"What would you prefer?"

"My situation is very particular. I can't leave my mother alone and I don't know what other country will want to take a middle-aged widow, if she is a widow. And she doesn't want to go anywhere in case my father does show up somehow. I won't leave her alone to live on bread and marmalade in some freezing seventh-storey room. I think I'll have to make my life in France, unless some other opportunity opens up. I'd rather go home, but I'm beginning to think that will never happen."

They had walked back into the town now. It was late afternoon and the shadows covered the narrow street entirely. It was pleasant walking with Monika. Being with her was like being on a vacation from himself. They were still some distance from the DP camp gates when a young man in eyeglasses, a functionary with the exile government, rushed up to them. Monika let go of his arm, which she had been holding all this time, and stood a little apart from him.

"There is a man who needs to see you at the camp director's office."

Lukas turned to Monika. "Thank you for coming out to look for me."

"Do you think you could make it to Paris to speak to the refugees there?" she asked.

"Who doesn't want to see Paris? And besides, I'd do it for you."

"How will we get in touch?"

"The meeting is very important," the functionary said, pushing his eyeglasses up by the crossbar and peering through them like a fish through a glass bowl.

"Wait for me by the steps to the office," Lukas said to him. "I'll meet you there."

The functionary seemed disappointed in Lukas, but he did as he was told. Lukas turned back to Monika and took her hands in his.

"You've lifted my spirits in a way I haven't had them lifted for a long time. How much longer are you in the camp?"

"We leave by train this evening. Our papers were only for a short visit, to hear you speak. But I can write down my address if you like."

She took a piece of paper from her handbag and wrote out the address. Lukas looked at it carefully and made sure he understood it before folding the paper and putting it in his wallet beside his passport. He had barely finished doing that when she stood up on her toes and kissed him quickly, once on each cheek, in the French manner. He did not quite know how to respond, so he squeezed her hands and turned to go to the director's office.

Zoly was waiting for him, smoking a cigarette while sitting alone at a table. He smiled warmly, set the cigarette in the ashtray and rose to shake Lukas's hand.

"Congratulations," said Zoly. "Everyone loves what you're doing and the money to the émigré associations has been pouring in since you started these talks. And the spring seems right upon you here. Back in Stockholm, it's still the dead of winter."

"When did you get in?"

"Just now."

"Staying long?"

"Not really. A very short time, actually. It all depends on you. Do you feel like going for a walk?"

"I just got back from one. I've been on the road for a couple of hours."

"It makes me a bit nervous to talk here. Maybe we could walk in the street."

Lukas went out with him, back into the town he had just passed through. He looked around for Monika but saw no sign of her.

"So what's this all about?" he asked.

"Lozorius is going back into Lithuania and he wants to know if you'll go with him."

"When?"

"In two weeks. You'd need to come back with me in the car right now. There's a little training you'll need first."

"This is all so sudden."

"Yes, it is, but you've done everything you were supposed to, haven't you? The letter to the Pope will do its work, or not, who knows, but you can't speed that sort of thing along. Actually, the Vatican is still wondering what to do about Martin Luther, so I don't think there's any chance an answer will come soon."

"What kind of support does Lozorius have?"

"What do you mean by support? Technical support? He'll get transportation and radios and ciphers and all that sort of thing."

"I meant long-term support. What are the British promising to give the partisans?"

"They make no promises, Lukas. They ask for the partisans to do a few things for them. Oh, and one more thing."

"What's that?"

"Lozorius would be in charge of the operation. He wanted me to tell you that unless you agreed to that, he would need to withdraw the offer to bring you along."

"He can be in charge until we get into the country, but I have a certain position there. I report to my superior officer, Flint."

"What's his real name?"

"That's an odd question, Zoly. Why would you want to know that?"

"Because Lozorius or some of the others might know him."

"Others? What others?"

"I'm not at liberty to say."

"This is beginning to sound stranger and stranger. How soon would I have to go?"

"Immediately."

"Then I think my answer will have to be no."

They spoke briefly of other things as they walked. Lukas waited for Zoly to insist, but he did not do that. They returned to the camp so Lukas could write a letter to Flint to be taken in by Lozorius.

Zoly was pacing out in the hall, and Lukas found it hard to concentrate on the letter he was writing. There was so much to say in a very short time. Also, he needed to provide a general picture of the situation in the West without giving away any secrets. He needed to warn Flint that Lozorius was acting on his own, without the support of the émigré government and in the pocket of the British. He had to write everything in a manner that would take into account the danger of Lozorius's being killed or the letter falling into the wrong hands.

And all of this he needed to do while wondering why Zoly had framed the offer in a way that forced Lukas to turn it down.

PARIS

MAY 1948

O UTSIDE THE WINDOW, the plane trees along the Seine had just burst into full leaf, their green still fresh and vivid because the dust of the city had not yet descended on them. On a quiet Sunday such as this, Lukas felt as if he might be in the countryside rather than the city. Flashes of light came through the leaves, reflections from the barges that sailed silently by on the river.

Having paused in the delivery of his speech to a school auditorium full of émigrés, Lukas now looked back at the men and women before him. He had spoken in public often enough and he knew he held the audience in thrall with his stories of the resistance against murderous odds back home.

He had been a fighter transformed into an emissary, and now he had become a storyteller, a role he did not like to think about too much. He knew what he did was important, but it was so much less vital, somehow, than what he had been doing before. Yet what he did now was attractive too, holding the attention of a crowd, even though they were far more varied than the DP camp inhabitants of Germany.

There were émigrés who had come here before the war, sympathizers of the Front Populaire who had deplored the excesses of the Reds in Lithuania but could not quite bring themselves to denounce them. There were also French Foreign Legionnaires on leave from Indochina, young men who had wagered their lives for a few more years of fighting in the hope of gaining French citizenship. Many young women had joined convents in France before the war, and so there were at least thirty women in nuns' habits. The remnants of the pre-war diplomatic corps were there too, including Monika's uncle, a distinguished gentleman with close-cropped white hair and a ramrod-straight back, a man who had taken a special interest in Lukas during the reception beforehand. There were labourers from the Renault plant and students, adventurers down on their luck and former bureaucrats who now worked as doormen. They were the flotsam of the war, human wreckage cast up upon this shore, yet so much luckier than the ones they left behind. They did not get along with one another all that well in spite of their shared history, but they were kind to him and generous within their means.

After the talk was over, Lukas lunched with them at long tables in the basement of the school. He was peppered by questions all through the meal, often from halfway across the room. Once the lunch began to wind down, a few of the legionnaires took him away over the protestations of the others and marched him up the street for a few beers on the rue St-Antoine, just west of the Bastille.

On his way out with them, he looked at Monika, who had been helping to serve the meal and was now gathering up dishes. She had an apron over her Sunday blouse—there had been an early Mass before his talk—and wore a pale charcoal skirt that was very tight at the hips and went to mid-calf. He could not stop looking at her. She nodded understandingly when she saw him with the legionnaires, signalling that he should meet her back by the kitchen door in an hour.

Except that it was almost impossible to get away, as military courtesy dictated that a man should drink as long as drink was being offered. Lukas was honoured among the legionnaires for his experience in battle; they had seen a few battles of their own. They suggested he watch out for the Reds among the Paris Lithuanians, and if any of them should prove to be trouble, Lukas could expect a few legionnaires with machine pistols to help him out. All he had to do was say the word.

It was good to drink with these men, who were straightforward in the manner of the partisans back home. The soldiers discussed the virtues of their way of life in the foreign legion, an option, they suggested, for someone with his experience, someone who might be able to lead men if he polished up his French. There were careers to be made in French Indochina or Algeria if one could avoid getting killed.

Even though a full two hours had passed since they entered the café, the men were not happy at first when he wanted to leave them. They had intended to drink with him all night. But they had become French in one way: when he said a woman was waiting for him, they understood immediately and released him from any further obligation.

Lukas lurched back down the rue St-Paul but did not find Monika at the kitchen door of the school. The whole building was locked up. He walked out guiltily to the rue Sully, where he found her on a bench near the metro station. She had a book on her lap but was looking at the trees that lined the river.

"I'm sorry," said Lukas. "It was very hard to get away."

"That's all right. I expected as much and I was enjoying the day." She looked at him as he flopped into place beside her. "Did the legionnaires do you in with their beers?"

"I'm a little drunk," he admitted.

"Maybe we should go for a walk. It might clear your head."

"Good idea. Just let me smoke a cigarette first."

"I don't remember you smoking when I saw you in Germany."

"No. I smoked sporadically back home. I've taken it up again here. I think it helps me to relax and reflect, and it helps to pass the time."

"I thought you were frightfully busy."

"I am, but it's a strange kind of busyness. Back in Lithuania, even though I handled the newspapers, I was in constant movement when the weather permitted it. Here, I'm sitting all the time. It makes me restless. Sometimes I feel as if I'm going to explode."

"You just need exercise. Come on, let's walk. It will sober you up, too."

Monika was slightly maternal in this way, taking care of him, and he enjoyed being in her care more than he liked to admit. It was too soon to permit himself these types of feelings.

He butted the cigarette, rose, felt a little dizzy from the beer and then steadied himself.

They crossed the street and walked along the quay of the right bank, passing the bookstalls in the dappled light. The quay was full of people doing the same as they were. It all appeared so normal, so pleasant, as if the war had never happened. None of the buildings had any bomb damage. To Lukas it seemed both wonderful and slightly unjust that one place should be so lucky. Cities as well as people had destinies, and Paris was one of the lucky ones.

"What was it like when you arrived here?" Lukas asked.

"It was all excitement and light, even though the war was still on, but I don't think about it very much anymore. When I was young I always wanted to visit Paris because my uncle was here and he seemed so sophisticated. He brought us Eiffel Tower souvenirs, and I kept one on my bookcase all through school. When I first got here I wanted to drink in every moment, but now it's fallen into the background. Sometimes life here is very hard, for all the beautiful buildings."

"Paris was the dream of a whole different class from the one I grew up in," said Lukas. "I came from a farm, and Kaunas was already as big a dream as I ever imagined."

"It's important not to feel intimidated by Paris."

"How is it possible not to be intimidated? Just look at this place."

"Places aren't as important as the people who live in them."

"That's right, but the two are linked. The people grow out of the place. They belong to it."

"If that were true, no one would ever migrate. The Indians would still rule America."

Lukas laughed. "I know I don't make much sense, but some people have a stronger affinity to the land than others."

"Are you homesick?"

"A little, but not as much as you'd think. I feel a sense of responsibility. I'm like a soldier whose leave has ended but who can't get back to his unit."

"But you're in Paris—you should enjoy yourself a little."

"I think I'm doing that. What's your life like here?"

"I live with my mother and sister. I'm going to school at the Alliance Française in the evening to improve my French, and I have a new job in a pharmaceutical laboratory as a cleaner, rinsing the test tubes. I've applied to study nursing, and for that my French must be impeccable."

"What do you like best about living here?"

"The slowness of things. Where we come from, the men drink vodka in shots, and once you sit down to eat you fall upon the food all at once. But everything in Paris is about lingering, about squeezing pleasure out of every moment. People sip their wine. The food comes in a stately procession, even if there isn't very much of it and it isn't very good. I like the way a cup of coffee can last an afternoon."

"The Latin temperament. It's all a bit new to me."

She caught the undertone, the northerner's belief that the Latin's way of life was decadent. "I used to think that the Germans were industrious, but now I wonder what good it did them and who cares about their industry. I'm not talking about laziness. Look, the working people in this city put in long hours. I work full-time and study nights to make some kind of life for my mother and myself. But my free time is very sweet, especially now, when the weather is fine."

They walked for a long time, past the islands in the Seine and the Louvre, and were coming up to the Tuileries park.

"I could go for one of those afternoon-long cups of coffee you talked about," said Lukas.

"The café in the park here is very expensive. Maybe we should go to some student place by the École des Beaux-Arts, across the river."

"The legionnaires were stuffing francs into my pocket. I think we can afford a cup of coffee in a fine setting, just this once."

The scene in the park was like something out of a painting, the French children sailing boats in the fountain, the older couples walking in their stately manner, arm in arm, the lovers passing time on the benches. Lukas found it, as Monika had said, very pleasant. The café in the shade of the trees was agreeable too, with a waiter in a white apron who brought them the two cups of coffee with all the flourishes. The cost was the same as two meals in a workers' restaurant, but some expenses were worth it.

"How is your head now?" Monika asked.

"Clearing at last."

"And what do you plan to do next?"

He didn't know.

He had passed up the chance to go back to Lithuania with Lozorius and was feeling a little sorry now that he had. The émigré government was supposed to be approaching the Americans about supporting his return to Lithuania, but he didn't know anything about that. His lecture tour to America itself had been cancelled because he could not get a visa. There was no way to get in touch with the partisans in Lithuania except through a letter drop in Poland, and that avenue of communication worked very slowly. He had heard nothing from Lithuania since his arrival in Sweden. If he chose to go back to Stockholm, he would need to renew his residency papers there as they were only issued for three months at a time.

"I'm stateless, with two more talks to give this week and no plans after that. In the long run I'll go back to Lithuania, but I don't know what I'll be doing a week from now."

"You could stay here for a while longer."

Monika was studying the children with their sailboats in the fountain and he looked at her in profile—the fineness of her chin, the fullness of her lips. She was like a part of the city, a human manifestation of ease and beauty. How was it possible that a city made a woman even more beautiful in this way? The French had the best sense of *douceur de vivre*, the sweetness of life.

"I would like to stay here, but I don't know how it would be possible."

"Remember when I said my uncle was in the diplomatic corps before the war? He still knows some people here. He told me you made a good impression on him and he asked me to speak to you about something."

She had become very still. His head was totally clear now and he felt as if he perceived her more intensely than ever before.

"The Deuxième Bureau might be interested in you, and the French have a tradition of helping refugees. I could speak to him if you think you might like to stay here." The Deuxième Bureau had been the name of the French military intelligence before the war, now changed to the SDECE.

Lukas weighed the proposition. It did not take long to come to a conclusion. He was marooned, and who would have guessed that exile so far from home could be so good as this?

"I think I would like it very much if you spoke to him," he said.

There was an awkward moment. He lighted a cigarette and smoked it, and they made a couple of attempts at conversation, but they could not find it in themselves to spend what remained of the afternoon over their cups of coffee, so Lukas paid the bill.

"Do you still have time to walk?" Lukas asked.

"I do."

They crossed the Seine at the Pont des Arts and began to walk along the narrow sidewalk toward the boulevard St-Germain. At one especially tight spot a car was coming, and he fell behind her. The street was empty and the shadows were already beginning to lengthen. As he stepped back, his hand brushed hers, and thinking it was a sign of some kind, after the car passed, Monika turned around to look and see what he wanted. He was right up close to her, not having expected her to turn, and in this proximity it seemed as if the right thing to do was to kiss her.

She did not seem startled, although he had surprised himself. The touch of her lips was so pleasant that he wanted to kiss her again. She did not seem startled the second time either.

SIXTEEN

PARIS

JULY 1948

*L*UKAS LINGERED in Paris, sleeping in a Lithuanian radio repairman's shop by night and hoarding his dwindling cash reserves. Monika urged him to be patient, as her uncle tried to get him a meeting with someone from the SDECE.

The world that her uncle operated in, one of back-channel French contacts, moved very slowly. And even after it began to move, it sputtered to a stop again because few seemed to be very interested in Lithuania, let alone the Lithuanian partisans. And those who were interested had their own reasons. The French, it turned out, were not all that different from the British.

Wheels turned within wheels in France: the Communists had been important in the French underground, and they resented the concept that "resistance" could be attributed to anyone but them, or that the enemy could be anyone but the Nazis, as they called them here, to distinguish them from the Germans. It was confusing as well to the French that the crime of collaboration could be extended to those such as slayers, who worked for the Reds. Weren't the Reds anti-fascists? If so, Lukas had to be an anti-anti-fascist, which made him a fascist.

And who could tell, as far as the French were concerned, which of these émigrés from the East was a former ally of the Germans? Hadn't some of the Lithuanians greeted the Germans with flowers in 1941? It would have been preferable if they'd greeted the Red Army with flowers.

Already a kind of amnesia about Eastern Europe was setting in. One forgot about the place altogether, or muddled it so that Ukrainians, Estonians and Byelorussians were all the same, no more than renegade Russians. And to be Russian was to be Soviet. Anyone who opposed them was an old-fashioned white, a reactionary of the kind that filled Paris back in the twenties.

Lukas was confused by French politics and perplexed by this hostility to his nationality. People in France sometimes seemed angry with him because he insisted that his people existed. As one man in a café said to him, "All of you people from nowhere insist on your nationality more than anyone I know." Lukas's people were an inconvenient people.

Until they became convenient.

Forces that were as far removed from Lukas as the stars needed to align in his favour, and on June 24, 1948, they did. The Soviets closed down road entry to West Berlin to the British, French and Americans. The Soviets intended to starve them out, but the Allies began an airlift of food and fuel into the city. The operation was chaotic at first, with plane crashes, fires, and logjams of bread, gasoline and small-arms ammunition. To have someone from behind Soviet lines might be a good thing after all, and so Lukas became useful and the French noticed that he existed.

The transformation of his fate happened very quickly. Where initially his interviews had started late, making the point that he was an afterthought, or were cancelled altogether, making the point that he was expendable, suddenly higher officials in more pleasant offices were meeting him on time. The gnomes who peopled these offices began to consider him useful.

Soon after the airlift to Berlin began, the French government gave Lukas a visa, a generous salary and a room in a small residential hotel off the boulevard Montparnasse. Since his French was not particularly good, they registered him in a course at the Alliance Française on the boulevard Raspail, and there he spent four hours each morning working on his grammar, his future *imparfait*. He was promised further training in ciphers, radio, Morse code and skydiving, but those courses would come only after his French was good enough.

There had been a great rush to sign him up, so much so that he thought he might be back in Lithuania within weeks, and then the gnomes disappeared and there seemed to be no hurry at all. The bureaucrats had put him in a drawer and they would open it when they needed him. Every week an envelope with cash awaited him at his hotel desk, and his room and his courses were paid for. So he began his French domestic life; he had not lived so normally since before the war.

Late one afternoon, Lukas walked out and strolled along the street before the shop windows, studying the tins of food in the displays, the incredible variety of items he had never imagined. Prunes in Armagnac were familiar enough, but chestnuts remained a romantic mystery to him. They fascinated him because a childhood poem had mentioned the scent of chestnuts roasting in the streets of Italy. The Jambon de Bayonne, the dried ham hanging in the *charcuterie* window, fascinated him as well, for the meat was not smoked and he did not see how it was possible for meat to dry without going bad unless it spent some time in a chimney. He had never seen sea urchins or oysters, eaten asparagus or artichokes. Even the horse butcher provided him with a kind of dark fascination.

He walked through the Luxembourg Gardens. It seemed that everything cost money in Paris, but the park was free and the exotic palm tree in front of the palace by the fountain was a reminder of the unlikelihood of his existence in France. From there he made his way down the boulevard St-Michel and across the Seine toward the Bastille, to the small apartment shared by Monika, her mother and her sister in the Marais district, a decidedly less exotic part of Paris, the former Jewish neighbourhood now filled with working people and immigrants from Eastern Europe.

Dinner was always rushed. Monika's cheerful mother hurried them along through a light meal because she would soon have piano students in the apartment all evening. They ate bread and butter, and a bowl of vegetable soup on the side—not cabbage soup, because it made the apartment smell bad and some of the students did not like it. Lukas brought slices of ham to put on their bread.

Monika's sister, Anne, was a university student studying chemistry and working in the evenings as a receptionist at a clinic, and she was always in a rush, like the other two. Lukas divined that one of the young medical students at the clinic was interested in her, and she returned his attentions.

After dinner, Lukas rode back across town with Monika on the metro, and this trip to the Alliance for her evening classes was filled with talk of their day. He had a few questions about French grammar—such as why they needed two past tenses, the *imparfait* and the *passé composé*. Wouldn't it have made more sense to have only one? And why one set of verb past tenses for speech and another for writing?

She laughed at him then and asked him if he knew how strange their own language was—how it had two plurals, one for numbers from two to nine and another for ten and above; how it did not distinguish between a hand and its arm, a foot and its leg; how it had no word for "bidet."

Monika had lived long enough in Paris and her uncle long enough in France that the place seemed ordinary to her, whereas to Lukas it was still exceedingly exotic. Monika was his guide in this world, and the possessor of a larger constellation of friends, a group of Lithuanian castaways. All but the ones who had been raised in

France were in transition, and had been for years, dreaming of America, Canada and Australia.

Monika kissed him in the corridor of the Alliance before she went into class. They kissed often these days, whenever they could. He settled in to wait for her in the Alliance student café. He was happy to have spent time with her and her family, happy to expect her in two hours, and glad for the book, Saint-Exupéry's *Vol de Nuit*, to practise his French.

Therefore he was surprised to feel his mood shifting as he waited for Monika in the Alliance café. She was only in class for two hours, but quickly the shadows in the corridor began to grow long. As his mood thickened, he could no longer read. He tried to write, but there was something about the shadows that made him gloomy. This happened sometimes, more frequently than he liked to admit. The memories rose in him and troubled him.

It crossed his mind that since he never saw the body, maybe Vincentas had just been wounded and captured after all. They would have tortured him if he survived, maybe even shot him after they had squeezed whatever they could get from him. On the other hand Vincentas might have been deported to Siberia and still be alive there. Which would be the worse fate, to be alive in Siberia or dead? Probably alive, because one died alone, whereas if one survived, he took others to their deaths with his information.

Lukas heard laughter from the courtyard outside the café, from young people talking. He envied them their lightheartedness. He could not seem to regain his own lightheartedness, the contentedness of an hour ago. Where had it gone?

And so he brooded for the two hours she was in her class. When she came out, she looked at him and saw immediately that something was wrong.

"What is it?" she asked.

"I wonder if you know how hard things can be for me sometimes."

"I think I know." She studied him carefully. He did not ordinarily speak like this.

"And yet my suffering has brought me to you, for which I'm grateful."

He didn't go on, but she could tell there was more to say, so she waited. The corridor had emptied of students and the guardian would be skulking nearby somewhere, waiting to lock up and go home.

"But if it was my fate to be brought to you, why did so many have to die to get me here?"

It was an impossible question. Europe was full of people who could ask that same question, but they must not ask it; they were in danger of getting lost among the ghosts if they did.

PARIS

SEPTEMBER 1949

T HE RUE DES LIONS ST-PAUL was an exceptionally quiet street in the Marais district of Paris, not far from where Lukas had first spoken to the émigré community almost a year and a half earlier. Between the passage of schoolchildren eastward in the morning and westward in the afternoon, no more than a dozen pedestrians passed below Lukas's second-storey study. When they did come, he could tell by the clicking of their heels on the narrow sidewalk.

Since the street window faced north, it did not receive much light anyway, and so, having finished his work for the day, Lukas pulled shut the shutters and locked them. The only other windows in the apartment faced the courtyard, where children were sometimes permitted to play if they did not get too loud and irritating to the concierge. The concierge or her husband was almost always at the window in the passageway downstairs.

A little under a year before, Lukas and Monika had been married just around the corner, in the massive Église St-Paul–St-Louis. They had been lucky to get this apartment, a place once rented by Monika's uncle but vacated when he moved to America at the beginning of 1949. The entire émigré government-in-exile had moved to

America, and as many DP camp residents as could were flying away to the U.S.A., Canada, Australia and even New Zealand. Like birds restless for migration, once the first ones took flight, the rest of the flock followed.

But not all. Lukas and Monika were still in Paris with no plans to go anywhere else, at least for now. Monika had to finish her studies and Lukas was not quite ready to abandon Europe.

A sense of unease had come over him once the weather became fine the previous spring, and it grew all that summer. The world was changing again, but it was hard to tell how it would all turn out. The Reds won in China and Mao Zedong came to power. The Soviets exploded their first atomic bomb, helped by Red spies in America who had shown them how to do it. Nobody talked anymore about what good allies the Soviets had been during the war. Maybe the climate for the Lithuanian partisans was getting better, but now that Lukas had been gone for close to two years it was hard to know what their situation might be. World events seemed farther away now. Like anyone else, Lukas thought of his day-to-day life. He had no cause for unease, unless he was unaccustomed to so much stability and happiness. He had put on weight and his clothing was too tight.

Over the past half decade Lukas had never lived in one place for any length of time, and now that he had been living in the apartment for eight months he felt strangely vulnerable, as if he were back at war and his tranquility in the apartment were a trap. Anyone who looked for him would find a sitting target rather than a moving one. Yet who would be looking for him now that he was a private citizen?

Monika was a full-time student in nursing, very busy. The émigré government had asked Lukas to write a book about the partisans, was paying him a little to do it, and he was working away slowly on that, writing for at least the fourth time the story of what he had done after the war. Since he worked at home, he was the one who went out to buy food for dinner after the stores reopened in the late afternoon, and he was the one to clean the place because he was there anyway and Monika was always studying.

This day, Lukas took his shopping basket, stepped out and went down the steps and out into the courtyard and then onto the street, as usual.

If anyone worried him, it should have been the French. Before moving to America, Monika's uncle had come to explain that the government was filled with Reds and the SDECE was therefore insecure, even dangerous. Sharing information with them was as good as betraying his comrades back in Lithuania. Thus the man who got Lukas into the French secret service in the first place now convinced him to get out. It was an abrupt turn. Dizzying.

They had not taken kindly to Lukas's withdrawal in January 1949, threatening him, insisting that he would be expelled from the country. But since Monika was permitted to live in France and she and Lukas had been married the previous fall, the authorities had no grounds for expulsion. True, Lukas's residency paperwork was laborious, but it was hard to tell if this was due merely to bureaucracy or to the active mischief of his vindictive SDECE handlers.

Lukas was free of them now, but he was barely employed and did not know what to do with the rest of his life. For the time being he scratched away at his memoirs.

He walked up to the rue St-Antoine, where the street was filling with children let out from school and women buying their supplies for dinner. He walked on the sidewalk, between the fruit and vegetable carts on the street and the food stalls of the shops, as women shouted out encouragement to buy their goods. He did not like to be out in crowds like this, where he could not keep track of who was behind him.

And yet what did he have to be afraid of here, in Paris? The French would not kill him. The Soviets might have tried something like that right after the war, if he had been operating somewhere like Berlin or Vienna, but they would do nothing here. He was too small a fish. They might not even know he existed. And yet his old partisan sixth sense told him to be wary.

Lukas stopped to buy beets. Fresh beets in late summer were a gift and he felt a need for borscht, the food of his homeland. Paris had everything, they said, and that was somewhat true, but it still was not home. That place needed to be evoked in other ways.

Lukas felt disconnected, adrift in life. The English had wanted him so badly, but he had turned them down. Now he was a little sorry he had. He had turned down the French as well. With the émigré government in America, he felt like an anachronism, someone who stayed on in school after all the others had left.

Paris could never be home for simple reasons. It did not have sour cream, for one, which was slightly annoying because it was an essential ingredient of proper borscht. France had *crème fraîche* but it tasted different. Lukas would need to buy unpasteurized cream and sour it himself, but that would take overnight and would not be ready in time for this evening's dinner. It didn't matter. He could make a large pot of borscht today, enough for two days, and eat it properly on the second day.

Aside from his memoir writing, he was unemployed and just scraping by. They could not afford much cheese or meat, but there were certain cuts the French did not value, in particular spare ribs, and so they were cheap and he could boil them in the soup.

Baguettes were delicious propositions, but sometimes Lukas missed the taste of the bread of his homeland, so he cut across the rue St-Antoine and went up the side streets where there were some Jewish shops that carried dark rye bread. Borscht and baguette would have been unthinkable. Finally, on the way back to his street, he stopped to buy a litre of everyday wine, a *vin gris* that Monika liked.

Back at the apartment, Lukas opened the bottle and poured his first glass as he put the beets on to boil. An hour later he poured off the hot red water, watching carefully to make sure he did not drip it on his shirt, and then peeled the beets, slipping their skins off, and grated them. He put the grated beets into the pot, ran cold water over his fingertips to lighten the stubborn stains, and then cut the slab of ribs into pairs and immersed them in the pot, adding chopped carrots and onions as well. He waited until the pot came to a boil, took the bottle of wine and a glass, and went to sit by the courtyard window to watch the children play down below before their parents called them in for dinner.

Two girls and a boy played quietly down there, either so terrorized by the concierge that they did not shout and run, or so much products of generation upon generation of Parisian children that they took their confinement in stride. Even in the parks the children barely seemed to run about. They were like prematurely old men, standing with arms crossed as they talked to one another.

After an hour, Lukas went to check on his borscht, found it to his liking, and turned off the pot and set it aside and peeled potatoes and put them on the burner. He set the small table and brought over the wine bottle, then saw that only a glass remained in it. He finished that glass, turned the potatoes down to simmer, and went back outside to the wine merchant to get another bottle.

He met Monika coming down the street from her classes at the institute, a satchel in one hand. Her hair was pinned back, the way she kept it during the day for her studies, exposing her face, which was light gold in the late afternoon sunlight. She had slightly thick lips, soft lips, which turned up in a smile as soon as she saw him. She waved with her free hand.

He embraced her as soon as he was close enough, and when he was about to withdraw she used her free hand to hold the back of his head and prolong the kiss.

"That's very affectionate," he said.

"I've been thinking about you all day." It was like this sometimes, either one or the other overcome with need and on the prowl.

"The potatoes are simmering on the stove. Keep an eye on them and I'll be right back. I'm just going to get another bottle of wine."

"I can't drink tonight anyway, I need to study. Why don't you come back with me now and we'll have a little fun before dinner?"

"What a good offer," said Lukas. "But let me pick up the wine in case you change your mind."

"Aren't we a little early in our marriage for wine to take priority?"

He was slightly irritated and about to say something, but when he looked at her he realized she was right. He kissed her on the neck, drew her free arm through his and walked back to the apartment, listening to what she said about her day while thinking that he should look for a job soon. It was not good to put so much time into the preparation of dinner.

He had just closed the door behind him when he turned to see that she had set down her bag, hung up her jacket, and was pulling the pins out of her hair. "You look like you're in a rush," he said.

"I'm hungry for you."

He reached around her waist, pulled her close to kiss her and then undid the clasp at the back of her skirt as well as the button below it. Her skirt dropped to the floor and she began to laugh.

"You said you were in a hurry," said Lukas.

"But I thought we might make it to the bedroom first."

"No time for that, *madame*. Hands up." She raised her hands and he took her sweater and peeled it up from the bottom and then threw it behind her, over her head.

Someone knocked at the door.

Monika's face lit up with mock panic and she smothered a laugh, and then began to gather up her discarded clothing.

"Who is it?" Lukas asked through the door.

"It's Anne."

"I'll be right there." He waited a moment until Monika was out of the hall and then opened the door. Anne was standing outside with a large jar in the crook of one elbow and her briefcase in her other hand. She wore eyeglasses now and looked very serious as a result. She kissed him on each cheek. "It's bad luck to greet someone across a threshold."

"Only in Lithuania," said Anne. "And since we're in Paris, we don't have to worry."

"What have you got in your hand?"

"Mother pickled some cucumbers and sent me over with them."

"Will you stay for dinner? It's almost ready."

"I think I will. I might stay here to study after that. Mother has piano students all evening and I want to get in a little reading before classes begin next week."

"You're always welcome here," said Lukas, his heart sinking a little.

Monika came back in and the sisters kissed, and then they all went into the kitchen to eat. Anne tried yet again to convince Monika to give up her studies in nursing in favour of medicine, but Monika declined. Nursing was faster. She wanted to get on with her life.

After they had eaten, to Lukas's embarrassment, Monika told Anne to go for a walk for half an hour, which Anne agreed to do if they spotted her the money for a cup of coffee in a café. The sisters were practical and unashamed about their sexual needs, while Lukas still felt a little like the overmodest country boy.

He was washing dishes when Anne came back, and the sisters set up on opposite sides of the table to do their work. They were a serious pair, barely talking to one another. Lukas left the wet dishes to air-dry on the counter and took a book to the living room. The evening passed quietly, and when it grew late he and Monika walked Anne back to her mother's apartment. The evening was getting cool as they returned. Lukas asked Monika if she would like to go for a drink before going to bed, but she was tired and they didn't really have the money to drink in cafés. She encouraged him to go ahead. He walked her back to their place and then returned to the rue St-Antoine for a drink.

He went into a workers' café just off the main street. It was full of men in blue smocks, some of whom worked odd hours for the city and some of whom had been drinking here since they finished work a few hours ago. Their wives would not be too happy to see them when they finally came in. The place was thick with smoke and talk in various languages; many of the workers were Polish or Italian.

Lukas ordered a glass of beer and a shot of Calvados, the cheapest of the liquors, and then drank both down quickly and ordered another beer. It was only after he felt the welcome rush of relaxation that he turned around with his back to the bar in order to look across the tables and onto the street beyond the windows.

Zoly was sitting at a table by the window with a glass of wine in front of him, his arms crossed as he watched Lukas. Zoly was in a suit and tie, and his hat was on a chair beside him. He was smoking a cigarette—ever the man of the world, even here, in a working-class bar.

H E FELT oddly vindicated by the sight of Zoly. Lukas's unease, the prickly sensation at the back of his neck, had been warranted. He finished his glass of beer because the waiter would not permit him to take it to a table, where he would be expected to order again at a higher price. He then walked across the short distance and pulled out the chair across from Zoly and sat down.

"Surprised?" Zoly asked.

"I've smelt you around for the last little while, like a piece of dog turd deep within the treads of my boots."

"Your rough language is true to your country roots, I see," said Zoly. He called over the waiter and ordered another Calvados and beer for Lukas. He butted one cigarette, took another from the pack, but seemed in no hurry to light it, first studying the street outside.

Lukas could feel the alcohol as he had intended to, to help bring on sleep. He enjoyed the slight intoxication and would have liked to drink the Calvados in front of him, but he didn't touch it, and when Zoly finally did light his next cigarette and proposed a toast, Lukas just sipped at his beer.

"Let's catch up," said Zoly. "I'm a little insulted that you didn't invite me to your wedding."

"It wasn't much of a party—just family and a few close friends."

"Belated congratulations."

"Thanks."

"And how is the life of the *bourgeois gentilhomme* agreeing with you?"

"The married part of my life is quite wonderful, but I'm under-employed. I'm finishing off a book about the partisans for the government-in-exile, but there isn't much money in that. It's not easy to find work in France."

"I imagine not, but you always seemed a little above making a living, if I might say so. You brushed us off, and the French as well, I understand, as if you didn't need to earn your way through life. You must have been saving yourself for your wife."

"For the Americans, actually."

"But they never came to call."

"I'm not at liberty to say." There wasn't much point in being evasive, but Lukas did it out of pride. If Zoly knew he had been with the French and left them, he knew just as well that Lukas was not working for the Americans.

Zoly smiled ruefully. "You're bored to tears, Lukas. This isn't the life for you."

It was a kind of insult, but a relief as well. Lukas took the shot of Calvados in his hand and finished it. He regretted his weakness when he looked up and saw Zoly's faint smile. "You've travelled to Paris to tell me how I should live?"

"Coming into this place for nightcaps every evening? You may not be an alcoholic yet, but you will be soon enough at this rate. You can't even afford these drinks. You'd be better off drinking at home alone after Monika goes to sleep."

Her name on his lips sounded a little dirty. "Have you come to make me an offer?"

"I have."

"What is it?"

"Let's go for a walk. I'm uncomfortable talking in this place."

"What for? You made a spectacle of yourself in the window. If anyone was looking for you, they could have seen you easily enough."

"Yes. I wanted the French to see me if they were watching, but I'm not so eager for them to hear me. The Americans either, if they're bothering, which I doubt. Maybe even the Soviets are here. This whole crowd could be made up of spies, for all we know. You can finish your beer before we go out, if you like."

Lukas stood up to go without touching his glass, but he regretted the beer he was leaving behind and then was embarrassed by the regret. They walked out. It was a cool night but the streets were somewhat full. They walked in the direction of the Bastille.

"Do you have any news?" Lukas asked.

"Odds and ends. More important, we finally have some interested parties. The Russian bomb and the Chinese Communists have excited the Americans to look for traitors among themselves. There are plenty enough of those, but they'll never find them all. The British are better off because of their class system. The upper classes are all playing for the same team and they'll never betray it. We have a very good relationship with the Americans, actually. We do many things together."

"What about the partisans in Lithuania? Is there a central command structure now? Have the British provided arms and radio contact?"

"You want to know an awful lot for a man who's no longer in the game. I can say some things are very bad, but there's always hope they'll get better."

Lukas was exasperated. "All right, then, you don't have to tell me anything except for this. Why are you wasting my time? If you want something, tell me what it is."

"We were just wondering if you'd like to make a return visit for us."

"To Lithuania?"

"Obviously."

"What for?"

"There are a couple of pieces of equipment that have broken down. We need someone to bring in replacements."

"The last time around you wanted me to assist Lozorius. Now you just want a courier."

"More than a courier. Someone we can trust."

"There must be others besides me who could do this."

"There are. We have young volunteers, but no one who is known inside Lithuania. Besides, there's another reason."

"What's that?"

"Lozorius asked for you by name."

"He's still in Lithuania?"

"Yes."

They had come to the end of the rue St-Antoine where it met the vast traffic circle at the Bastille, a major hub that gathered up the cars and redistributed them.

It was oddly heartening to know that Lozorius had asked for him by name, but Lukas fought down the satisfaction of it. Charismatic types were appealing but could not really be trusted. They put you in danger. Unfortunately, knowing this did not diminish their appeal.

"Have you ever seen the column at the centre of this square?" Zoly asked.

"Not up close."

"Let's take a look."

Lukas followed Zoly through the thin night traffic out to the column, which did not look like much at all in the dark. Zoly stopped to talk there.

"Well?" he asked. "Do you think you would consider going in again?"

"For Lozorius's sake?"

"For the sakes of your colleagues. Say, Flint?"

"Do you know if he's still alive?"

"I don't know that he's dead." Zoly was watching the people who were standing around the column, mostly boulevardier types looking for action on the street.

"I do feel a sense of loyalty to them."

"So you should. You took an oath to follow orders."

"But I also took an oath before my wife. Who's to say which oath is more important?"

"The one that came first."

"You're talking like a lawyer. I did what I could. I tried hard to get back on my own terms in the first year. Now my life has moved on."

"Lucky you. And what do you intend to do with this glorious freedom of yours? You studied to be a teacher back in Lithuania, and in literature. Lithuanian literature! Don't make me laugh. The only type more useless than you out here is a Lithuanian lawyer. There is no life for you unless you join the army or get a factory job. I can't see you in either one, somehow. Besides, what's more important than your country?"

"I don't need to establish my patriotic credentials with anyone, least of all you. I was in Lithuania during all three occupations and I lived underground in bunkers for months at a time. I've killed more men than most soldiers, and many times I've come close to being killed myself. And meanwhile, what are you? A former diplomat. One of the grey men who takes a paycheque from the British and a pat on the head from the Swedes and tells himself he's doing it for his country."

A gang of five singing youths with arms over one another's shoulders walked up to the column. Zoly touched Lukas on the elbow. They walked on. He didn't seem to be upset by what Lukas had said. They strolled up the boulevard Beaumarchais.

"I don't suppose money would interest you, would it?" asked Zoly. "Not that there's all that much, but I know Monika isn't working while she's in school. If you went away, she could use something to help pay the bills."

"If I went away, she certainly could use money. But that's not the point, is it? Since I'm not going away, the question is academic."

"Anyway, she's a resourceful woman. Did you ever wonder how Monika came to see you speak?"

"You mean back in Germany, the first time we met?"

"Yes, I do. There were no other people there from France. There were no visitors from Italy. There were no people from any country but Germany, hardly anyone from another occupation zone. How do you think she ever got the travel documents to visit the camp in the first place?"

"She said she wanted to hear me speak."

"And I don't blame her. You were a very big star, the partisan hero. You made Lozorius a little jealous, you know. I think that's why he went back into Lithuania so quickly. He didn't really want you outshining him."

"And that's why you insisted that I report to him if I went back in then, right? To discourage me?"

"Oh yes. He had a need to be in charge. He must be in trouble if he's asked for you now."

"What kind of trouble could he be in?"

"I can't really go into much detail until you commit."

"But it doesn't sound like I'm going to do that, does it?"

The street became seedier as the boulevard Beaumarchais changed to the boulevard du Temple and they drew closer to the Place de la République. Prostitutes called out to them from the other side of the street.

"There is one bit of information that Lozorius passed on that I think you should have, no matter what you choose to do."

"What's that?"

"It's about your wife."

"What about her?"

"Your first wife."

"Yes?"

"Elena is alive."

It took Lukas a few moments to understand what Zoly had said.

"Alive? Alive where?"

"Not in Siberia. Elena is in Lithuania. She was very badly wounded and put in a prison hospital."

"Is she in prison, then?"

"Flint broke her out. She's in Lithuania, and she's free, but she's in hiding."

Lukas stopped and looked at Zoly. They were almost at the Place de la République.

"When did you find out about this?"

"A couple of weeks ago, but I couldn't get here any sooner."

Lukas slapped Zoly across the face, so hard that his gold-rimmed eyeglasses and the cigarette he was about to raise to his lips went flying. After a moment's shock Zoly tried to say something, but Lukas slapped him again. He was going to do it a third time but Zoly raised his hands to protect himself, and Lukas took him by the lapels and pushed him back against a tree and then pulled him down to the earth.

"Tell me everything you know."

"That's about all of it."

"Who told this to you?"

"Lozorius."

"How did he get word out?"

"It was in his last radio transmission."

"What else did he say?"

"Just that he needed you and that your wife was still alive. He said the set was damaged by water. It wouldn't work properly."

"Any more transmissions?"

"Two garbled ones."

"Is it really him?"

"The radio operator on this end says it's him. He can tell. Each person develops his own style on the telegraph key and Lozorius has his. It can't be copied."

"Has he been captured and turned? Is it a trap?"

"We don't know."

"So it could be a lie."

"Anything is possible. We don't know."

Lukas slapped him again.

"Why are you hitting me now? What was that for?"

"For lying to me."

"Do you hit everyone who lies to you?" Zoly asked. He rose when Lukas released him and retrieved his eyeglasses, and once they were back on, a little crooked, he looked for the cigarette that had been knocked from his hand. He picked it up from the sidewalk, reached into his breast pocket for a box of matches and lit it. He looked up at Lukas. "It might be time to reconsider the various vows you've taken."

NINETEEN

THEY SAT IN CHAIRS across from one another, a half-empty bottle of wine between them, but Lukas's glass was untouched. The window to the courtyard was open and he could hear the children murmuring outside in the cobblestoned yard. What did children that age have to talk about so intensely and so quietly?

Secrets, probably, and confidences. From the very beginning one veiled and unveiled truths, and reality changed accordingly.

Lukas wanted the wine in the glass on the table before him, but he was resisting it. Already the luxury of wine seemed to belong to another world, a kind of dream world he had been living in until Zoly reappeared.

Lukas thought about things he had not thought about for a long time. Whether Flint and Lakstingala were still alive. Whether there was any news of his parents. Above all, how it was possible that Elena was still alive when Flint had seen her body lying on the earth outside the bunker.

What the Reds must have done to her after they took her to prison did not bear much thought, but he couldn't help thinking about it. His one consolation was that they would not have tortured her if she was hurt badly. They would have tried to heal her first and only then begun to break her down again. And if they knew her as the killer at the engagement party in Marijampole, she could not have expected much mercy.

But maybe Flint had got her out in time.

One of the courtyard children cried out in pain. She had fallen and was sobbing as her friends tried to soothe her. He would have liked to have children sometime, to live in a time when children were possible.

Monika's face was tear-stained, but she had calmed a little since the conversation had begun an hour ago. He started again.

"My duty is to my first wife. I have to go back to her. I made promises to others before I made promises to you."

"Your first wife," Monika said bitterly. "You're making poetry out of my grief."

Monika thought Lukas was referring to Lithuania as his first wife, making a metaphor, but he didn't correct her. Lukas felt protective of Elena now, not wanting to talk about their lives together in the presence of another woman, not even this one. He was putting distance between them and already she was looking stranger and stranger to him, like someone from an accidental moment in his life.

Although he knew he had to make himself hard, Monika was still the woman who had come to him in the countryside in Bavaria, the one who had made life possible in the first confusing months in France. He loved her, but could not let this feeling dominate his thoughts. He had to drive her from his heart, but the necessity of the task did not make it any easier.

Lukas had not told Monika everything that Zoly had said, just that there was a new offer from the British for him to go into Lithuania and he was accepting it.

Monika reached for her glass and drank it down but did not refill it. "We've only begun our life together here," she said. "We were on the way to building something. And now you want to throw it all away on some kind of adventure. You could have studied anything you wanted after you finished writing that book. Medicine, architecture. If the military appeals to you so much, you could have applied to French officers' school."

"I didn't say I wasn't returning." Elena might be dead after all. Zoly might be lying to get him back inside to help Lozorius.

"Don't try to soften what you're saying. What are the odds, really? You might get killed on the way in, or you might get killed while you're there. You'll almost certainly never make it out again. It's not called the Iron Curtain for nothing."

"It's risky, all right, but not impossible. I made it out once before. I could be back in a year."

"It's like going to the land of the dead. Think what you're giving up. Do you love me so little?"

"I love you so much."

"This makes no sense at all. You're just a soldier who's finding it hard to adjust to civilian life. You need to give it a little more time. You're bored now, sitting at a desk and writing that book, and worse, in the writing you're thinking about the past all the time, reliving your old battles. But you wouldn't have to sit at a desk all day if you didn't want to. You could be something else—a builder, a farmer like your father—I don't know, a pilot." Lukas said nothing to this. "Help me. I'm looking for the words that will make you stay."

"You won't find them. You knew this day might come. What did you think the SDECE was training me for?"

"That was all over. You quit all that. This strange idea of duty is going to undo both of us. What about your duty to me?"

Lukas looked out of the window and reached over for his glass of wine, but stopped himself. He was going to refill Monika's glass and looked to her to see if she wanted more wine, but she shook her head furiously.

"Tell me this," Lukas said. "How is it that you and Anne went to hear me speak in Germany?"

"We had heard all about you. We were homesick and wanted to hear about Lithuania."

"Yes, but no one else came from another country. We barely had people from other occupation zones of Germany, let alone France."

"Where are you going with this? Why does it matter now?"

He would not let it go. "How did you get the right to go to Germany?"

"Anne and I applied for a visa. I don't know. I can't remember."

"No one would ever have issued you a visa just like that, because you asked for it. Travel was restricted. Your uncle must have helped. Did he?"

"I suppose he did."

"Or did he come up with the idea in the first place? Was he asking you to do a favour for him, for the SDECE? Were you supposed to lure me to France so they could make me an offer and keep me here?"

"Maybe it was something like that. But I had no idea I would fall in love with you. I've never been false to you."

"When I walked away from you that morning in Germany, you followed me out into the countryside. You convinced me to come to Paris. I'm not saying you lied. I'm saying things got out of hand. You brought me out of Germany for your uncle and the French secret service, and when you discovered you liked me, you asked if you could keep me. Your uncle managed it all for you as a going-away gift before he left for America."

"So what are you accusing me of? Loving you too much?"

"I'm not accusing you of anything. You did what you believed was right. I'm doing the same thing."

"But it's not right to choose death. Think how miserable I'll be as your widow. The Reds will kill you. Yes they will, don't deny it, and it would be better for me to die rather than to lose you. Your absence will be a wound that never heals. Take pity on me and don't make me a widow."

"I can't shrink away from this now. I could never live with my-self. I'd die of shame."

"Shame before whom?"

"Both the living and the dead. My heart tells me to go back."

"Then your heart has no place for me."

"It does have a place for you, but not the way things are now. We could make a life here. People have left their homes since the beginning of time, and some have made better lives for themselves. But I can't stand the thought of being torn away from my country to be some kind of vagabond in the West. I feel worthless here. I don't care how rich these countries are—they'll never be mine. And I'll never be respected here. I'll be some kind of foreigner, a migrant, a hobo picking his way through the rich scrap heap of Western Europe or America. My dignity doesn't allow it."

She said nothing. Lukas stood and went to her, but she turned away from him. He nevertheless crouched beside her chair and caressed her hair and tried to wipe her cheeks.

"I won't let anyone kill me so easily," said Lukas. "I'll be careful. But we live in certain times and the times shape us in certain ways. I have to be what my time tells me to be."

"Why are you invoking fate? Think of all those people who did their duty during the war and died for their trouble. Nobody believes in duty anymore. People matter now."

"There are many things people don't believe in anymore, but that doesn't make them any less true. No one escapes his time, whether he's brave or a coward. No woman either."

She refused to look at him. He knew he couldn't console her, so he stood and walked to the window to watch the children playing in the courtyard.

"Zoly promised to stay in touch with you and to help you with money. If you can, wait for me, but only for a while. If you hear nothing for too long, make another life for yourself."

She didn't answer.

PART THREE

TWENTY

OFF PALANGA, LITHUANIAN SOVIET SOCIALIST REPUBLIC NOVEMBER 29, 1949

*T*HE WIPERS on the window at the bridge irritably slapped at the constant spray off the Baltic Sea. As the E-boat dipped and then rode up on the swell, Lukas made out on the right the glow from the Lithuanian resort of Palanga. A lighthouse blinked on the left, from the Latvian side.

"Is this the departure point?" Lukas asked.

The German captain pulled the pipe from between his teeth where he had held it for the last hour, long after it had gone out. "Still too far offshore. I'll come in closer, but you'd better go out to the raft now. And don't slip off the deck—we haven't got the time to go looking for you. Check to make sure the raft's inflated all right. You'll be on your own as soon as you touch the water."

Lukas nodded to his two men, but neither one seemed all that enthusiastic now that they were so close. Rudis took a couple more puffs on his cigarette before dropping it at his feet without bothering to butt it. He adjusted his black cap so that each curl of blond hair was tucked beneath the cloth. He did not like to show loose strands. It was the sort of casual insolence that no partisan leader would stand for, but Lukas did not have much choice.

He didn't like either of his two recruits, but it had been important to get out before the winter in order to make the crossing of the
Baltic, and there had been no time for a proper personnel search or
training. Lukas had found Rudis waiting on tables in a restaurant.
He had deserted from the Wehrmacht in Norway during the war
and walked into Sweden. It was not much of a job history, but it did
show he knew how to survive. He had been in Stockholm for five
years and was still waiting on tables—no ambition to do anything
but pick up women with his beautiful hair. To his credit, Rudis was
good with a radio and could tap out Morse code at record speed
once he had practised for a few days.

The other man, Shimkus, had been a sailor who could not see
past his next shore leave. He was lean and agile, happy with a beer
and a smoke, and might have been in it for the money—it was hard
to tell. Shimkus smiled easily, though it was unclear if he did it from
a sunny disposition or a mind free of excess thought.

Everything would be all right if the letter Lukas had sent through
an old drop box in Poland made it to its destination.

The Americans were involved in the mission now, along with the
Swedes and the British, and as a result Lukas, Rudis and Shimkus
were carrying too much materiel: a radio each, MP-44 assault rifles,
Walther pistols, ammunition, twenty thousand rubles, a thousand
dollars, sleeping pills, cyanide, amphetamines, grenades, penicillin,
morphine, aspirin, topographical maps, long folding knives almost
as big as bayonets when opened, compasses and secret pencils that
wrote in invisible graphite.

Dunlop had needed Lukas to run the mission, but having been
spurned by him once, he was not entirely happy to have him back.
"The only reason you returned is because of your Lithuanian wife,"
he said, as if accusing Lukas of a crime.

They had trained out of a summer house on a fjord south of
Stockholm, empty now that the summer was over. Dunlop still drank
heavily, but his enthusiasm for it had evaporated. He had lost maybe

thirty pounds, not so much that he was thin but enough that his skin looked slack.

"I disapprove of personal motivation," he continued.

Lukas was practising with the secret pencil, drawing it flat against the sheet one way and then another, and then laying a sheet on top to write the invisible letters. "You're the one who passed on the message from Lozorius to me. If you didn't want me, why did you tell me Elena was alive?"

Dunlop had no answer to this. He was very drunk. "Personal motivation is fickle, like love."

Lukas looked at him closely to see if Dunlop was making a disparaging remark about his two wives. "In the end, personal motivation is all there is. The best causes are the small, personal ones."

"I wouldn't call those causes. I'd call them grudges. If everyone thought like you, we never would have defeated the Nazis. If everyone thinks like you, we'll never defeat the Reds."

"If everyone thought like me, we wouldn't have either of those two to begin with."

By midnight, the E-boat was fifteen-hundred metres from the beach, and the captain gave the order to launch the rubber dinghy. The offshore wind slowed them, but at least it would muffle the noise from the E-boat. Lukas worked the paddle hard, and when he first thought to look back for the E-boat, fifteen minutes had passed and it was already gone. It took two more hours to cover the distance.

The rubber boat was very heavy, so they cut it up at the water's edge and then pulled the pieces a hundred metres up the beach, where they hid them in the underbrush. Then they shouldered their fifty-kilo packs and, taking a compass reading, headed inland due east, avoiding farmhouses and crossing meadows where the grass stood bristling with frost. Three kilometres inland they found a forest with a cutline, as marked on their map, and they were deeply into it when dawn began to come up. They went in among some bushes to hide themselves during daylight.

Shimkus and Rudis fell asleep with their heads on their packs and Lukas took first watch. Even though it was November and the air was damp and cold, it felt good to be back. For all the freedom of France and Sweden, he had been a foreigner there. Now he was home.

Working in the Swedish summer house with Zoly, Lukas had analyzed Lozorius's messages out of Lithuania again and again. Why had the man called for Lukas in particular to return to Lithuania? Why not any agents the English could find? There were several possibilities, some better than others. Maybe Lozorius trusted Lukas the way he trusted no one else. Maybe, on the other hand, he wanted to entrap the most prominent representative of the Lithuanian partisans abroad. Some of the Ukrainian partisan spokesmen in Western Europe had already gone missing, and the same was true of the Estonian and Latvian partisans.

"What else has he been telling you in his radio broadcasts?" Lukas had asked Zoly.

"He writes that the underground has got weaker. The central control structure has collapsed and the local units barely have any contact with one another anymore. The senior partisans are mostly dead and the new ones aren't educated. They can't run the propaganda newspapers that they used to."

This information was troubling to Lukas. He was relying on old ties to help him once he got back in. "How did the English like to hear that?"

"I keep telling you, they're Brits, not English."

"They can't tell *us* apart. Why should I bother?"

"Anyway, the Brits didn't like Lozorius's news at all, and they're not the only ones. The Americans believe Lozorius may have been captured and turned."

"On what grounds?"

"First, because you and others told them there was a whole, solid underground network in place in the Baltics and his news sounds pessimistic, the kind of thing the Reds might want us to believe. The Americans hate pessimism. Next, they believe that the Reds, having developed an atomic bomb, are more confident and beginning to mass troops for an offensive against Western Europe in the spring. But Lozorius says nothing about massed troops or materiel transports heading west. Therefore, he sounds suspicious."

Lukas was sitting with Zoly at a table at a window that overlooked the front yard of the house and the sea beyond it. Shimkus and Rudis were being trained for hand-to-hand combat by an Asian Swede. The three looked like sportsmen practising wrestling. The whole session had an air of unreality to it, as if they were playing a game.

"Maybe Lozorius is pinned down in his bunker and doesn't know anything," said Lukas.

"Maybe. Or maybe he's sending disinformation." Zoly said it dispassionately enough, as if he had never known the man in all his charisma. He stood up and took the full ashtray from the table and tossed it on the cinders in the cold fireplace. When he returned to the table, he lit up again.

"If what you say is true, they're asking me to walk into a trap," said Lukas.

Zoly shrugged. "You have to be prepared for whatever reality you find there."

"Or maybe what Lozorius is saying is true, he has not been turned, and the Americans just don't want to hear it."

"That's also possible."

"If they don't want to hear it from him, they won't want to hear it from me. I wouldn't want to be stranded in the country because they doubted me."

"I've promised to get you out of there once you've contacted Lozorius and collected some information."

"You'll have to do better than promise. I have no intention of dying. I'm going in there to get my wife out, and you have to help me."

"I said I would."

"If it means rowing a dinghy yourself to pick us up, I expect you to do it."

"I'll do everything I can."

"You have to do the impossible, Zoly. And if I don't make it out, you have to watch over Monika and watch over Elena. Get Monika a pension or something."

"What am I supposed to do for Elena from here?"

"I don't know. Send Elena Red Cross packages, if they're permitted."

"I promise I'll do the best I can!" said Zoly, throwing up his hands. "Just remember this: the Brits, Americans and Swedes are going to a lot of trouble putting you in there. Remember that you owe something to them. Get some intelligence. Set up a conduit for information. They want to know about troop movements and missile bases. Don't be quite the high-minded soul you were when you first came out. Help them and you'll make it easier for me to help you."

"All right. There is just one more possibility I'd like to explore."

"What's that?"

"The possibility that Dunlop has made it all up."

Zoly stood and walked into the kitchen to put a kettle on the stove. He came back to lean on the door jamb as he waited for the kettle to boil. "I thought of that too. So I asked to listen in on a recording of Lozorius's transmission. Dunlop didn't let me do that. He said there was no recording. But there was a transcript. I looked at that."

"Well?"

"Lozorius does say that your wife is alive, but not much more than that. Maybe he doesn't want to betray her accidentally."

"So you're satisfied what he said is true?"

"True?" Zoly laughed. "I saw the transcript, but I can't prove that he sent it, or that he was telling the truth if he did. The Brits or the Americans might be luring you in to go and test whether Lozorius has been turned. On the other hand, he might be intending to lure you in so the Cheka can take you as a prize. Or it could all be true. Even if it is true, Elena might be under some kind of pressure of her own, something we're unaware of. We can't be sure of anything."

Too restless to sit still as the other men slept, Lukas walked cautiously along the forest cutline to the point where it ended a kilometre farther along, and there he looked out to where a few farmhouses stood among the autumn fields. The first one, a thatched-roof wooden home, belonged to a man named Martinkus, supposedly a friend and contact. Lukas watched from the distance but did not see anything out of the ordinary about the house or the surroundings.

When he made his way back, he found Shimkus poised in a crouch with his rifle at the ready. So much for his easygoing attitude. He had been boiling water over a small fire.

"Where did you go?" Shimkus asked accusingly.

"I wanted to look around."

"Never walk off like that without leaving word."

"Why not?"

"I thought you'd abandoned us."

"I didn't think you were the nervous type."

"I'm not from this part of the country. I'd be lost on my own."

"Is Rudis still asleep?"

"I tried to wake him, but he told me to go to hell."

Shimkus had an aggrieved air, like someone who nurtured his insults. Lukas resolved to keep an eye on this tendency. You could never tell what a man was like until you were with him in the field. Some became better and some became worse.

Of the two radios they had brought, only one worked because the other's batteries had got wet. Rudis was finally woken and came up sullen, but after a cup of tea and a cigarette he was prevailed upon to transmit a signal back to Sweden. They waited for a response but received none.

At dusk, all three of them went to the farmhouse, where Lukas rapped on the window. A middle-aged man came out.

"We're looking for a farmer named Martinkus," said Lukas.

The man looked at their weapons and packs. He did not appear to be afraid, but he did not look too happy either. "He's dead. I married his daughter, but she's lying inside, pregnant and sick."

"We're partisans come in from Sweden," said Rudis. "Someone was supposed to meet us here."

Lukas did not like it that Rudis spoke out on his own.

"I don't know anything about it," said the man, and he turned to go back inside. But Lukas made him take two of them in, leaving Shimkus on guard outside.

The pale, frightened wife was lying on a bench in the kitchen, two small children playing around her. Rudis took off his hat and shook out his golden hair and smiled down on the woman. Lukas was astonished that the man imagined he could work his charm here.

"We mean no harm," said Lukas.

"Then please take what you want and go away."

Lukas wished he could do that, but he could not. He sat down with his knapsack and began to take things out of it. He showed them a Swedish camera, wonderfully miniature. He took out a bar of chocolate and gave it to the children. They held it in their hands, afraid, so he took it back and unwrapped it, breaking off pieces for the woman and the man as well as the children. He showed them the Swedish wrapper.

"We don't have any ties with the partisans," the man said eventually, "but if you tell me where you're camped in the woods I can start looking around and send someone there."

"Don't send anyone. We'll come back tomorrow to find out if you've learned anything."

"Please," said the woman, "don't come to the house. Meet him by the shrine half a kilometre down the road. I don't want people to see you coming here."

They bought eggs, butter and bread from the couple, paying 350 rubles, which seemed high, and then went back to the forest.

"What do you make of that?" asked Rudis.

"They were terrified. They thought we might be *agents provocateurs.*"

"She was a nice-looking lady, though, for all her problems."

For three days they camped out in different spots, warily meeting the farmer each night. Once they bought bacon and another time bread, eggs and butter. Lukas was beginning to think the farmer had found a useful private market, but on the fourth night he said he had someone for them to meet, a partisan.

Lukas asked him to bring the man into a clearing in the forest at dawn. He kept Rudis with him and asked Shimkus to stand a little way inside the forest beyond the clearing in order to cover them in case of complications. An hour before the meeting, Lukas and Shimkus combed the forest around themselves, looking for movement of partisans or interior army agents. They saw nothing.

The man the farmer brought with him was middle-aged, which was a little surprising. Older men did not do well in the partisan movement because the living conditions were so poor. This man had a very straight back and a good, if old, long brown leather coat over his jacket, and he wore a tie as well as a woollen cap. He looked somewhat familiar.

"This is the partisan I told you about," said the farmer. "I've seen him around before. He calls himself Karpis. I hope you two will straighten out whatever you have to say to one another, but I ask just one thing. From here on in, leave me alone. I have a sick, pregnant wife and two children. My problems probably don't interest you, but your problems don't really interest me either." He walked away without so much as a wave.

"You see how it is now," said Karpis. "The people are tired."

"Are you armed?" Lukas asked.

"Just a pistol."

"I'd like to see it."

Karpis pulled a small PPK from a pocket inside his leather coat. "Maybe you and your friend should set down your arms as well."

Lukas and Rudis did as he asked, and Karpis knew enough about them to ask where Shimkus was, but they said he was away. Lukas asked Rudis to sit apart from them as they spoke, but Rudis ignored the order and stayed nearby. It was standard operating procedure: no man should know more than he had to. Rudis's refusal demonstrated his incompetence and his stupidity. Now Karpis would know that Lukas's men did not follow orders.

"The farmer tells me you come from abroad," said Karpis. "How can this be possible?"

"We landed on the beach in a rubber raft."

"Could you show me where you buried it?"

"I don't think so. We don't want to go back there. But look at this." He took out the folder with the American money in it—a thousand American dollars in tens.

"This shows me you're rich, but the money could have come from anywhere. Anything else?"

Lukas showed the miniature camera and a letter he had posted to himself just before leaving Stockholm. The postmark seemed to convince Karpis.

"And what about you?" Lukas asked. "How do I know you're a partisan?"

"You might recognize me, for one thing. I was the mayor of Panevezys before the war."

"Not my part of the country."

"I'm the brother of the late president's wife."

Lukas looked him over. The late president had installed many of his wife's relatives in the government. Poor former mayor. He would have lived the life of striped pants and municipal receptions until the war—a soft life. How did men like that survive now?

"Bring me up to date with the situation in the country," said Lukas.

"We don't carry out many missions anymore. We're hard up for food and we're out of touch with most of the other partisan groups. We just try to survive now. We haven't actually fired on anyone in months. We're down to collecting information and printing up newspapers whenever we can find the ink and the paper."

"It sounds bad."

"It is. What did you come here for? If I had a way out, I'd take it and never come back."

Lukas glanced at Rudis. The man was looking more unhappy than ever, if that was possible. He had even let some of his precious curls slip out from under his cap.

"If you want, we can help you a little," said Karpis. "My men and I can escort you to the frontier of the next partisan district. It's true we've lost touch with them, but we might be able to use some of the old contacts."

"How many men can you spare?"

"There are three of you, right?" asked Karpis.

"That's right."

"Then I could send along four or five escorts. We're short of manpower—I'll come along too."

"Are you sure you want to go yourself?" Lukas asked.

"Don't worry. I look old, but I'm tough."

They agreed to confirm their plans the next day. Then it would take a couple more days to gather up the men, who were scattered in pairs in small bunkers, getting ready to settle in for the winter.

After Karpis left, Shimkus came out of the woods and Lukas told him what Karpis had said. Rudis corrected him twice on details, and Lukas told him to shut up. Rudis sulked.

"There's something I don't like about Karpis," said Lukas.

"What's that?"

"His long leather coat. It's the kind of thing you might wear in the city to cover a revolver in your pocket, but out in the country it doesn't make sense. It would get caught on branches, or all bunched up when you were crawling into a bunker."

"Maybe he just uses it for special occasions," said Shimkus, smiling at his own joke.

"What did you think?" Lukas asked Rudis, trying to mollify him.

"I don't see why he'd lie to us. I think the greater danger comes from the farmer."

They radioed Stockholm again to say they had made contact with a partisan code-named Karpis. Unsure of his own intuition about Karpis, Lukas asked for instructions. Six hours later the reply came in, terse, the exasperation clear even in the brevity of the message: Follow the plan. Use partisan contact to gain access to Lozorius.

Karpis did not return the next day as planned, but all plans were contingent. They changed the placement of their camp and permitted themselves a small fire, which Rudis tended, breaking sticks into shorter and shorter pieces until they could not be made any smaller. Lukas cleaned his gun, sensing Shimkus's eyes on him.

Lukas tried to be calm and methodical for the sake of the two men, but it was hard to keep up appearances. One was too nervous and the other was undisciplined. In his other partisan bands he had relied on the men with him, but these men did not fill him with confidence. And he could not forget Karpis's long coat.

"We could just go across country on our own," said Lukas.

"Why would we want to do that?" asked Shimkus. Rudis just looked at him, his eyes giving away his alarm. Lukas did not press the matter.

That night Lukas offered to take second watch. When Shimkus woke him at one in the morning, he put the strap of the rifle across his shoulder and walked out beyond the perimeter of firelight. He waited there a half-hour until he was sure Shimkus was asleep, and then he came in closer, lifted his knapsack and carried it a little farther away where no one would hear him rustling through it. He unpacked whatever he considered too heavy, leaving the radio and most of his ammunition. He dabbed the soles of his boots with lamp oil. He checked the map in the campfire light, took a compass bearing and walked to the edge of the forest before cutting across country on his own.

When Karpis appeared the next day, he came with five other men dressed in short woollen jackets with turtlenecks underneath and woollen caps on their heads. They carried a variety of sidearms and two types of light automatic rifles—the kind with the banana clip below the barrel and the kind with the round pan above. None of these weapons was of much use because they found Shimkus covering Rudis, who was sitting on the ground, his jacket pulled behind his back pinning his arms, and his hands tied at the wrists for good measure. His hat was askew and his pretty hair spilled down one side of his head. He had a bump on his forehead and was bleeding from it, the blood running down over his eye.

"Thank God you've arrived," said Shimkus.

"Where's the other one?" Karpis asked.

"He took off in the night without any warning."

"Why didn't you go with him?"

"I would have, but he didn't give me a chance. This one wanted to follow after him this morning, but we don't even know what direction he headed in, and he left the radio behind. This one is the radio operator. We can use him."

Karpis swore. "It would have been better to stick with the other one. He's the big fish. Then we would have taken both of them."

Moscow was going to be unhappy about this, and unhappy Moscow put pressure to bear on Vilnius, and they would put pressure on him.

Karpis hated this kind of work. One more prize like Lukas and they might have let him retire, but now he would have to keep this up, risking his neck again and again when he wished he could just sit by the fire once the cold winds blew in.

TWENTY-ONE

LITHUANIAN SOVIET
SOCIALIST REPUBLIC
DECEMBER 1949

IRST THE CEMETARY in the Jewish Pine Forest had been rendered unneeded when most of the Jews were slaughtered in 1941, and now, eight years later, the cemetery was rendered derelict by the absence of their progeny. A stone-and-board fence had surrounded the old cemetery. The fence was a wreck, the boards gone and the graves inside overgrown and untended. The brick gatehouse was burnt out, the roof gone and the windows empty of both glass and frames. There was a small chalked X by the gatehouse entranceway where double doors had once stood. Checking to make sure no one saw him, Lukas took the piece of chalk he had carried from Sweden and put a circle beside the X.

He found a copse of trees and tall grasses and hid his pack, and then carefully made his way to a vantage point where he could see the village of Rumsiskes. From a distance it looked completely unchanged. If he suspended his knowledge for a moment he could imagine going into town to visit the market and some of the Jewish shops. He knew the illusion required distance, and he had no desire actually to descend into the town.

Then he made his way to the other side of the hill to look for the family farm, but could not find it. Unsettled by its absence, he thought he was confused, and checked his bearings again. He went back into the forest and recognized the dune where he had played as a child. Many things were pretty much unchanged, though the trees were taller and the light fell through them in a different way, making them strange. When he went back to look for the farmhouse, it still did not appear. The house, the outbuildings, the fruit trees and the currant bushes were all gone. Even the fences had been torn up. In their place lay plowed land, the furrows crooked in places.

If ever there was a time when he felt his days were as grass, this was it. A wind had descended on the land and all those he had known were gone, and many of their works as well. Unnerved for the first time since his return, Lukas went back to the place where he had stowed his gear and waited through the night.

In the morning, he set himself up in the scrub undergrowth where he could watch the burnt-out gatehouse to the cemetery. A pair of boys came through that day, young vandals who knocked down a couple more headstones. They depressed him, but he could not go out and chastise them. Two more days passed until a shepherd came by, looked over the gatehouse and walked on. He did not have a flock with him but did carry a stick. Lukas shadowed him for a while, and when the man sat down with his back to a tree, still within the Jewish Pine Forest and still at a distance from any houses, Lukas approached him where he sat with his cloak thrown over his head against the cold.

"Did you hear a nightingale?" Lukas asked.

Lakstingala lifted the cloak off his face. "Where?"

"In the copse of trees across from the gatehouse."

Lakstingala looked at him hard, and then rose and threw his arms around Lukas and embraced him tightly. Lukas could feel the rifle under the cloak as well as Lakstingala's thin body.

"I'm glad my letter reached you and I'm pleased to find you alive," said Lukas. For the first time since he had arrived in Lithuania, he was in the company of a man he could trust. But if he had not known it was Lakstingala, he wouldn't have been able to recognize him from a distance. He had always been a small, tough man, but he seemed to have shrunk. Although it was only early winter, his face was pale, his eyes watery.

"I'm the last of the old partisans in our group," said Lakstingala.

"Flint is dead?"

"Yes."

"Tell me how."

"I don't know much. He loaned me to another group of partisans and I barely saw him anymore. They say they took him by ambush last spring when he was out gathering wild strawberries. He didn't even have any weapons and he was dressed as a civilian. The Cheka troops were lying on the forest floor under the ferns, and they rose up and started to fire without any warning. Two others were killed and he was badly wounded, but taken alive.

"They brought in a couple of local farmers to identify him, but the farmers said he was just some berry picker and the Chekists became worried that they'd shot the wrong men. Flint died without saying anything and they buried him nearby, not far from the base where you and I first met. But one of the slayers must have mentioned that he had a French calendar, and the Cheka knew Flint spoke French. The Chekists figured it out. They dug up the body, identified him and then threw the body back out in the Merkine market square."

"The town we held for a day."

"Right. They have an idea of symmetry. His wife came to claim the body, and she and her children were sent to Irkutsk."

Lukas had not even known Flint had a wife or children. He was saddened to hear of his leader's death. "And what about you, my friend? How did you survive so long?"

Lukas looked deeply for the man who had taken him out on his first mission five years earlier, but could not see him. On the other hand, the young man whom Lakstingala had taken out was not there any longer either.

"I was lucky. I broke my leg not long after you left. I stepped in a posthole at night and snapped the bone just above my ankle. It took a very long time to knit properly. Death probably came looking for me then out in the fields, but I was lying in bed and couldn't be found. Death's been looking for me ever since."

"It'll find us all in good time."

Lakstingala looked past Lukas, ever vigilant, watching for movement in the forest. "I don't suppose you're bringing good news in from the West, are you?" he asked.

"No. They've finally become interested in us, but no one is going to fight a war for us."

"Then why did you come back? You could have saved yourself."

"I came back for Elena."

Lakstingala shook his head. "What makes you think she came back to life?"

Lukas told him about Lozorius and his message and the help from the British. Lakstingala had not seen Lozorius for years and did not know where he was, but he might be able to find him. As for Elena, he was less sure.

"The story stinks," said Lakstingala. "For one thing, Flint never told me about it while he was alive. For another, I've heard of people I thought were alive being dead, but not the other way around. Not anymore. And anyway, what good did you think you'd do Elena if you did find her alive? If it's true, you'll open old wounds. By now she thinks you're dead or she knows you got out and hopes to receive a Red Cross package someday. And if she's not dead, she might be in Siberia."

"Why are you so angry?"

"Because it irritates me that you're throwing your life away. Most partisans are like men with cancer—we're doomed. But you had a chance to escape."

"Didn't we all swear to follow orders? Didn't we all swear to fight until the end?"

"Of course we did, but we've reached the end. We reached it some time ago. So many lives destroyed and now you have to throw yours away too."

"I have no intention of throwing my life away. I intend to find Elena and to take her out of here."

"How? Through Poland? All the Lithuanians who lived on that side have been moved away from the border. The Polish partisans have been wiped out and we don't get any help from there anymore. The first Pole who sees you will turn you in or shoot you."

"I can get out the way I came, by boat."

"Maybe. I can't say if that's possible or not."

"If worse comes to worst, I can get false papers and live legally."

"How easy do you think that would be? If it were possible, a lot of others would have done the same thing."

"Lakstingala, my friend, your song is as bad-tempered as ever. I have every intention of finding Lozorius to determine if my wife is alive. You can help me if you like or you can go back to your bunker and stew all winter long."

"Oh, I'm coming along. I have a soft spot for love stories. But don't expect any sympathy from me if it's all a lie."

TWENTY-TWO

*T*HE WEATHER turned against them as Lukas and Lakstingala made their way south to search for Lozorius. It snowed
by night and rained by day, and all across the country the
roads and paths were full of Cheka cars and Cheka troops, as well as
slayer units swarming like bees.

"Is it always like this?" asked Lukas when they had hidden among
thin winter bushes yet again for a couple of hours while water
dripped down their collars.

"Not usually quite this bad. They must know you're here and
they're turning the country upside down."

"I'm hundreds of kilometres away from where we landed."

"Maybe your friends were caught. Maybe Lozorius gave you
away somehow. You're a bit of a legend and word of you must have
got out."

"Legend? I'd rather be invisible."

"Well, a legend helps to raise the morale of the people, but it also
raises the bounty on your head."

The danger passed, and they came out from behind the bushes to
walk through the rain, in one way better than the snow because they
left no tracks, but in another way worse because the mud adhered

to their boots and they had to stop every fifteen minutes to scrape it off.

Partisans had become like wolves whose pelts brought income to bounty hunters in a hungry country.

"Has the number of collaborators risen so high?" Lukas asked.

They were standing among the cows in a barn by night, hoping to borrow a little heat before moving on.

"Collaborators," said Lakstingala ruefully. "What a funny word. We don't use it anymore. You only call someone a collaborator if you've defeated him. If the Germans had won, there wouldn't have been any German collaborators either—the very idea would have seemed odd. Now the Reds are winning, so there can be no Red collaborators. Anyway, as time goes by, more and more of our people have to find a way to survive."

"I never thought you'd have sympathy for traitors."

"I don't, but I need to understand them if I hope to live on. When you were last here it was so much simpler. In those days they simply tried to kill partisans, but now they try to capture us and turn us and send us back to smite our former friends."

"*Smite*? That's an unusual word. It sounds medieval."

"Coined by the Cheka. They call the turned partisans 'smiters.'"

Lukas laughed. "Yet another way of getting us."

"Partisans are the last free people, and it gives me some satisfaction to know we can still irritate the Reds even if we can't defeat them. But every day we have to be more and more wary. They've become subtle in getting co-operation from the farmers. We don't eat with the farmers much anymore, not unless we know them very well."

"Why not?"

"Another one of the new tricks they brought in after you left the country. The Cheka handed out sleeping potions to farmers and told them it was their responsibility to trap us. If partisans came asking for food, the farmers were supposed to put the sleeping potion in it. Some of our people just disappeared that year because the farmers were afraid to make the potion too weak, so they made it too strong. Nineteen forty-eight was the year of sleep, and some of our partisans haven't woken up to this day."

"What farmer would do that?"

"You'd be surprised. One day I went out with a partisan called Anupras to get milk from a certain farmer. We needed to keep shifting around so we weren't asking the same people for food all the time. We were being careful, so I waited for him in the forest when he went to the farmhouse, but he was taking a long time. I went looking and finally found him, wandering along the path, falling down and getting up and then falling again. He'd lost his firearm. I could tell by his eyes that he was drugged, and pretty soon he passed right out. We were on our own, and knowing the Cheka wouldn't be far behind I dragged him off the path as far as I could.

"I laid him in a hollow and took away any identifying papers then covered him with mosses and pine needles. I sprinkled the area with lamp oil and tobacco to confuse the dogs, and then swam across a nearby river to see what would happen from a hiding place on the other side.

"The Chekists arrived soon enough, three cars of men and dogs. They searched high and low, but they didn't find him. Later the next day Anupras woke up and crawled out of his hollow. His face was dirty and his pants were torn. The soldiers were still around, but they were looking for an armed man, and Anupras was not just unarmed but also disoriented, like some sort of village idiot. He wandered around until he came across a farmer who knew him and managed to get him back to the partisans."

"It sounds like some sort of fairy tale."

"More like a horror story. Anupras said he'd had a few glasses of milk. The sleeping potion must have been poured into the milk, but the fat in the milk inhibited the effect of the drug."

"Did you get the farmer?"

"He ran away somewhere, but not to America."

"America? Why do you say that?"

"He was the American farmer. You remember him?"

"He helped to teach me English."

"Well, if you ever run across him again, shoot him."

"What happened to Anupras?"

"He was never the same after that. His mind had been damaged. We managed to get him into a mental institution where they have others like him."

The weather was terrible. When they reached the outskirts of their old district six days later, the duel between rain and snow had settled into a compromise of freezing rain. By then they had been cold and wet for so long that they barely remembered what it meant to be dry.

Lakstingala knew a farmhouse where the owners were friendly, but he hesitated to go there because the farmer was under suspicion of the Cheka, and Lakstingala did not want to get him into trouble or stumble onto a closely watched site.

"It's a risk," he said to Lukas as they stood outside the house of squared logs and thatch, "but we'll die of pneumonia if we don't dry out and warm up for a while, and it doesn't look as if anyone's around. You wait here."

Lakstingala knocked at the door as Lukas squatted among the gooseberry bushes, intensely aware that the cover of bushes was poor in the winter. A young woman with a thick, dark braid met Lakstingala at the door. They spoke for a moment and a man joined them, and then Lakstingala waved Lukas over.

It was a small house, deliciously warm inside, just a vestibule and two rooms. A new baby was in a basket hanging from a beam in the combined sitting room, dining room and kitchen, swinging gently from side to side. The farmer was a young man named Almis, and his wife was Vida. They both knew Lakstingala and took no notice of his regret at bothering them, being distant cousins whose sense of hospitality had not yet been destroyed by the times.

Almis and Vida charmed Lukas, and gave him a whiff of melancholy as well for the life he might have had in a different time. He had vaguely hoped to have children one day, and the sight of the baby, swaddled and with a knitted cap on her head, awoke the old desire in him. But it did not do to have such thoughts. They could only make his heartache worse if he dwelled upon them.

He and Lakstingala went into the other room to change out of their wet clothes. There was a ceramic wall shared by the two rooms, a built-in wood-burning furnace that was warm to the touch. Lukas hung his clothes from nails nearby and then leaned against the tiles for the warmth that radiated through his back. Soon he would turn to warm his other side.

There was a noise outside and shortly after that the door to their room opened and Almis poked his head inside.

"Some slayers just pulled up in the yard in a car."

"How many?" Lakstingala asked.

"Just two. But one of them is a drunkard named Imbrasas who keeps coming here to threaten us and to make eyes at Vida."

"I can deal with them for you, if you want," said Lakstingala.

"No, please. We have a baby in there and Vida's sensitive. They're not here to search the house. They come for alcohol and food and to terrorize us a little. Just be very quiet in here and they might go away after they've eaten and I've given them a little liquor for the road."

Lakstingala nodded. He put a revolver in his pocket and stood by the wall on the other side of the ceramic oven with his assault rifle in his hands at the ready. Lukas prepared himself for a fight as well, crouching behind the door to look through the keyhole into the next room.

The sergeant who came in with his escort was stout, his hat tipped back slightly on his head so the bill pointed up jauntily. His uniform was a little too tight and one button of his tunic was undone over his belly. He carried only a sidearm, but his soldier had a rifle in his hands. Slayers had not dared to travel in pairs in the past, before Lukas had left Lithuania. Back then they had moved in packs. It was a depressing sign of their new-found confidence that the two came as they did, unescorted.

"You can wait in the car," said Imbrasas.

"It's safer if we stay together," said the soldier.

"Afraid?"

"For your safety, yes. This is a lonely place."

"I know what I'm doing. Get out there, and I'll bring you something to make it worth your while."

The baby in the crib cried out once as the driver left, but then settled back to sleep when Vida pushed the cradle and it began to swing from the beam again.

Imbrasas, the slayer who remained behind, had been to the house many times before, sometimes with the troops and sometimes on his own. He kept a flock of farmers like these, small landowners who hadn't been collectivized yet, ones who could be visited in a circuit for food or liquor. He considered himself their protector, for he was important enough as a slayer to hold off others of his kind, and even had a little influence among the lower levels of the Cheka, where he hoped to make a career.

His protected herd of farmers was milked in rotation, with one exception: Almis, or more precisely his wife, Vida. He developed an interest in her that grew to fondness and blossomed into obsession through her pregnancy, and this passion continued to grow after she gave birth. His attraction was foolish, and he knew it and tried to suppress it by any means possible, primarily alcohol.

But the alcohol didn't really help; it merely changed the nature of his fixation. When he drank, Imbrasas began to feel underappreciated for all the help he had given her against the baser elements in the Cheka. Most of the farms in the district had been collectivized already, but not the one belonging to Almis and Vida. If he had been like some of the grosser slayers, he would have had the husband deported and kept Vida for himself.

Imbrasas congratulated himself for not having done so, but the drunker he became the more he began to feel offended that his good works had not been recognized. How the young couple should have known what he had done for them and how they should have paid him back was unclear to him, but the sense of injustice remained in his mind and grew.

Almis went to the pantry and brought out three half-litre bottles of samagonas, one to drink from and two to give away. He cut a piece of smoked pork and wrapped it in a newspaper. He carved off a kilo of bread and brought it in as well. Vida had set out plates and cups and butter. She put fresh kindling into the cookstove and set the kettle on top.

Imbrasas watched this activity with growing impatience. They were behaving as if nothing were wrong, as if they were not aware of their debt to him, or if they were aware of it, they were ignoring it. He was particularly incensed by Vida, who remained silent as her husband talked about the weather and the farm, his animals and the crops, the only safe subjects in a politicized world.

But not safe enough.

The baby sensed Imbrasas's mood better than her parents, and she began first to whimper and then to cry. Vida gave the hanging crib a push so it began to rock gently, and the baby quieted for a moment.

Almis poured out two small glasses of home liquor, and Imbrasas did not even wait for an invitation but drank up. He had been drinking all afternoon. Each man chased the liquor with a piece of bread and a little smoked meat. Almis could see that Imbrasas was following every move his wife made, and he tried to distract the man, but there was nothing much he could do about him because Imbrasas was implacable in his strange silence and brooding eyes.

The baby cried out and would not be stilled, even when Vida pushed the hanging crib again.

Almis poured another glass of liquor and invited Imbrasas to drink. In such circumstances the best strategy was to make the visitor drink a great deal and hope that he became drunk enough to pass out before he did any harm.

As the baby would not stop crying, Vida took her out of the crib and held her in her left arm as she worked at the stove with her right hand. She was all too aware of Imbrasas's silence and her husband's inability to do anything about it.

Vida went to the pantry and brought out a cup of flour, which she poured into a bowl, and then returned to get a cup of milk and two eggs, which she mixed with the flour to make into a batter. She tried to pacify the baby, who was wailing inconsolably now, sensing the tension in the room.

She put a large cast-iron frying pan on the wood stove and a minute later dropped a pat of butter into the pan, where it sizzled and sputtered.

"Comrade Imbrasas," she said, "it's a terribly cold and wet day, and the only way to comfort oneself on a day like this is the way our mothers comforted us when we were small—with crepes. I'll fry up a batch of them and soon you'll see how much better you feel."

Vida was trying her best to help her husband, but she could not read the mind of Imbrasas, who had never been comforted as a child by his alcoholic mother. She had beaten him and starved him and his father had not been much better. Worse, Vida could not know that in his mind the offer of crepes was as good as an insult, a paltry compensation for his heroic efforts to save them from deportation. Here they were, warm and happy when so many others had been sent away, and all she could offer in thanks was a plate of pancakes. Such an insult was unbearable.

"Bourgeois capitalists, the both of you," he spat. "I'll show you comfort."

Imbrasas snatched the baby from Vida's arms and laid her on the sputtering frying pan, holding Vida off with his free hand. Handled roughly and thrown about, the swaddled baby wailed, but not so loudly as she would wail when the heat of the pan burned through to her tender skin.

The fat in the pan sputtered and snapped as it did when a piece of meat was put upon it. Above all this the mother shrieked and the baby wailed, but Imbrasas held Vida off and reached for his sidearm to keep Almis away as he fried the baby on the pan.

Lukas slammed open the door at the first screams, and Imbrasas looked at him in surprise, frozen for a moment. Almis moved quickly. Snatching up a dinner fork from the table, he drove the tines into the neck of Imbrasas before the slayer could get a proper hold of his pistol. Vida snatched the baby off the hot pan.

Imbrasas's face twisted in pain and fury and he reached for his throat to staunch the blood, and Almis grabbed the man's head and pressed his face onto the hot pan, where his cheek sputtered in the grease. Imbrasas screamed, but rather than inciting Almis's pity, the cries excited his anger. He lifted Imbrasas's head by the hair, pulled the pan off the stove and, lifting the stove lid to expose the burning wood beneath, pushed Imbrasas's face into the fire. Imbrasas was down on his knees in a moment, flailing.

"Don't shoot or the soldier outside will hear the gunfire," said Lakstingala.

Lukas took the frying pan from the floor and banged it hard against Imbrasas's head, which was sandwiched between the frying pan and the metal stove. Imbrasas slumped, and Almis released him to fall onto the floor. The room smelled of singed meat and hair.

Almis turned to Lukas and Lakstingala. "Get the other one in the car outside."

Lakstingala nodded and the two men went out.

The soldier in the car had not heard anything from within the house, but he saw them coming and tried to get out of the car to free his rifle. They shot him through the door and the window before he could escape.

Daylight was fading, and no one would come out looking for the dead men that night. Lukas and Lakstingala dragged out Imbrasas's body, fired a few rounds into his neck to make it seem that bullets had killed him, and then put both bodies in the back seat of the car.

"Let us rest for a couple of hours," said Lakstingala, "and then we'll drive far away with the bodies. No one will even know they were here. The rain will wash the tracks away from the lane."

"But what if he told someone where he was going?" asked Vida. She would not let go of the baby. It had been swaddled and had made no direct contact with the frying pan, though the edges of the cloth had been singed, but she had unwound the cloth and swaddled it anew. The baby was strangely quiet now. Vida, on the other hand, was not calm.

"It's unlikely he told anyone he was coming here, but even if he did, we'll drive the car back in the direction he came from for a few kilometres and then set it on fire in the forest. It will look like they were ambushed before they got here. If you're lucky no one will even ask you about them."

"But what if they do?" She turned to her husband. "You'll go to the district committee this week and you'll sign up to join the collective farm."

"My father left this farm to me," said Almis. "I can't just give it away."

"You can and you will. Your father would prefer you alive rather than dead." She turned to Lakstingala. "It hurts me to say this, cousin, but I don't want to see you at our door anymore. One of these days they'll make us talk somehow, and I'd rather not be the one who has to give you up to the Cheka."

"These are the men who saved us!" said Almis. "What about the soldier back in the car? What would we have done about him?"

"I could have killed him myself. In any case, it doesn't matter. The regime wants us to give up our land. We'll do that, and we'll be safe for a while. We'll keep our heads down and wait for better times."

The partisans dried out their clothes as best they could in two hours. Almis scrubbed the floor where Imbrasas had spilled his blood. Then he packaged up the bread and meat that he had portioned out for the dead man. Lakstingala and Lukas took one half-bottle of liquor against the cold, as the rain had not let up outside. Vida went into the next room and did not come out again, even after the men slept for two hours and then rose to take away the car and the bodies.

Almis walked them out sheepishly into the yard. "I'm sorry for what she said."

"It's all right," Lakstingala replied. "But try to keep the spirit of resistance in you even if you do join the collective farm. No one owns your spirit if you don't let them."

"No, but they do put your spirit on a grindstone here. They begin to wear it away."

TWENTY-THREE

WINTER–SPRING 1950

*T*HE REDS IN EASTERN EUROPE were like dike builders, damming up their positions to keep out the news from the West. But they could not prevent seepage from the BBC, from Sweden and even from Poland, a friend whose censorship was not all it could be.

Even within the country, underground news found its own way of flowing, persistent as water, running through the crevices and the cracks, pooling in the low places and building pressure until it burst through to the surface. Sooner or later everyone learned the same thing: the Cheka, the partisans and the farmers all heard that Lukas had done the impossible, had come into the country again.

The Cheka was eager, bordering on hysterical, to seize him, to redirect him to its own purposes. Best of all would be to get him alive in order to send disinformation out to the West, or to make him into a smiter himself, or at the very least to sound the depths of his knowledge. It would be terrible to have to kill him, but better to have him dead than running around the country like some kind of folk hero.

And to the folk he did remain a hero, a kind of invisible man who crossed borders as if they had no meaning, who evaded smiters and slew the slayers and left their bodies in cars that had been riddled with bullet holes.

And yet, for all his renown, the limits of his life were once again the damp walls of a bunker in his old partisan district, a pitifully small burrow with barely enough room for four men, and another bunker a kilometre away with room for two, a kind of citadel in case the first bunker was betrayed. Here he waited as Lakstingala sought contact along the tattered web of remaining partisans, trying to find news that would lead Lukas to Lozorius and through him to Elena.

"I'd like to go with you," said Lukas.

"And so would the Cheka—that way you'd be easier to catch. No, no, you sit tight. The fact that you're here at all is some kind of miracle."

"But what if something happens to you?"

"If I'm ever gone more than a week, find a new place to live. Sniff around the town of Perloja for a partisan named Hawk. I think he's still around."

"I'd heard he died years ago."

"That's not what I heard. You never know."

"I came to look for Elena."

"The way to her is through Lozorius. Nobody I know can find her and I don't want to stir up a hornet's nest by asking too broadly or too quickly."

"I love her."

Lakstingala winced. "I have a wife too. Have you ever heard me talk like that about her?"

"No."

"Exactly."

"So tell me about her. What is she like? How has she managed all these years when the Cheka must know who you are by now?"

"I think something must have happened to you out there in the West. You're not the same anymore. As our world gets more danger-ous, you want to share more information. What's going to happen if one of us gets taken alive? Do you think you'll be able to stay silent under torture?"

"I don't know."

"Exactly. So the less you know about me, the better. It's bad enough I let slip that she existed at all." Lakstingala looked away, and then took out a pouch and rolled himself a cigarette. He lit it and took a couple of puffs and then studied the ember. "As for love, you're not the only human being in this country."

Lakstingala left him alone after that, going out again to forage for information.

Lukas had no radio of his own, no contacts beyond Lakstingala, no farmers he knew of nearby. He felt as if he had fallen asleep with the drugged partisans of 1948 and was awaking now to a place he didn't know anymore.

The winter rain continued without end, working to wear him down with its *drip, drip, drip* through the ceiling of the leaky bunker. The hideaway had been built in an old gravel pit and not much earth was layered over the ceiling. The upper bunk was covered with bowls to catch the drips, but the place was still damp and stank of mildew.

After slinking across the country for weeks, it was hard for Lukas to be still like this, awaiting news from Lakstingala. It was impossible to become used to life in a wet hole. Lukas read a German novel about a couple of artists who forswore their bohemian ways in order to find happiness in working the land and raising a family. The novel helped to pass the time, but when he was finished he realized it had nothing to do with him. It might as well have been science fiction.

He opened up the hatch to the outside and listened to the wind rattling the leafless branches.

Every few days, or sometimes at longer intervals, Lakstingala would return, but he rarely brought any uplifting news, just fragments of stories, scenes disconnected from some bigger narrative. He had seen two young women escaping from the Cheka, running barefoot across frozen fields, their feet bleeding, being pursued by soldiers who fired wildly at them from a distance. No one knew where the women came from or how the story ended. With his own eyes Lakstingala had seen a boy of around seven or eight sitting on a huge sack at the roadside and crying. The child was incapable of speaking through his tears, and Lakstingala could not help him in any way, although he was probably an orphan with no place to call home. Lakstingala left the boy behind and continued his search for Lozorius.

These were the kinds of scenes that excited Lukas's impotent fury. There were perhaps a dozen partisans left in the district, living as he did with mouldy belts holding old bullets that could not be relied on. How much could they do? And yet for all their impotence and dwindling numbers, the partisans occasionally found a recruit who wanted to join them, and Lakstingala brought news of just such a one.

"He claims he knows me?" Lukas asked.

"He never said your name, but he said he was in university in Kaunas at the same time that you were. I thought you might be able to look him over and see if you remember him."

Lukas agreed. He made his way to a barn three kilometres away and waited there as Lakstingala went out to bring in the new man. Lukas kept his assault rifle at the ready. He had checked out the back of the barn and looked out of the window there to familiarize himself with an escape route if he needed it. Then he watched the partially opened doorway from within the darkness and finally saw two men walking across the yard. The first was the new man, and behind him came Lakstingala.

The man was tall and reedy, slightly stooped, and Lukas's first thought was that such a tall man would be no good for life in a bunker. His second thought was that he knew him.

As soon as the two stepped inside the door, Lukas signalled them to stay there and stand in the light.

The man had barely aged since Lukas had known him half a dozen years earlier. He still had the beaklike face and the habit of appearing to be a snob because he kept his nose slightly elevated and therefore seemed to be looking down it. His clothes were a shambles, a wrinkled raincoat and beret, yet somehow a little stylish, something he must have learned on the lap of his artistic mother.

"Well, if it isn't Lithuania's answer to Charles Baudelaire," said Lukas.

The man looked at him as if he were an insolent toad. "Do I know you?"

"We shared a room together when we were students in Kaunas."

"That feels like so long ago."

"We burned each other's student files in the Kaunas library stacks."

"You were reading H.G. Wells," said Rimantas. "It's beginning to come back. You must be Vincentas Petronis."

"That was my brother, you fool. My name is Lukas. Come here and sit down."

Lukas brought him to a bench while Lakstingala stayed by the door to keep watch over the yard.

"You were studying literature the last I heard of you," said Rimantas. "Did you keep that up?"

"No, I went into the forest. You must have known."

"Oh, students were disappearing one after another in those days. I didn't know if you'd run away, been deported or been killed, not that I put much thought into it. I just kept my head down and hoped no one would think of me. I suppose I got lucky."

Lukas now remembered so well the mixture of rueful delight and exasperation that Rimantas used to excite in him, but because the emotions went back so far, to his student life, he enjoyed them more than he used to in the past.

"Why do you want to join the partisans?" he asked.

"I wanted to do something, you know, for my country. I thought I could contribute my talents to the underground press—unsigned, of course."

"The press needs help. We've lost a lot of our writerly types. We could certainly use another one, although you'd probably have to print the paper as well as write it and edit it."

"I'm not very technical, you know, but I'm a good critic and a good writer."

"Tell me a little about your life since I last saw you."

"Well, I finished my studies and wanted to do graduate study, but the university is all about engineers and statisticians now. They don't give a damn for the humanities. They told me I was going to be a teacher in some godforsaken provincial town, but first I had to do my military service. Now, *there* was a comedy. They never did find clothes that fit me, not even shoes. The sergeants were all bullies and it was just terrible what they put me through. By then the war with the Germans was long over, of course, so they didn't have a front to throw me against, and I ended up peeling potatoes in Ukraine, which was dangerous enough in its own way. They have partisans too, you know, and to them anyone in a Red Army uniform is a Red. I'm lucky I didn't get shot. By the time I got back I thought the authorities would have dreamed up something better for me to do, but it doesn't look like it. It's gotten worse. They assigned me to a hamlet on the Byelorussian border, all swamps and illiterate peasants, and I'm to teach in an elementary school. In any case, I'm not going to put up with that. So I came down here, where I have an uncle, and let out the word that I wanted to join the partisans."

Lukas listened to Rimantas with a mixture of annoyance and wonder. It was said that God loved drunkards because he saved them from so many accidents, but if that was true, God must love fools too, because Rimantas should have been imprisoned or deported long ago. To be so unaware and yet survive was a kind of crime.

"Joining the partisans isn't going to make your life any easier than teaching in a provincial school," said Lukas. "You'd have to live in hiding and on the run most of the time. I don't think you're up to that."

"Don't underestimate me. I'm tougher than I look."

"I'm sure that's true, but maybe you could help us while living above ground instead of going underground. How is it that you're not at the school right now?"

"I knew a doctor who sold me a medical condition, but I couldn't afford anything longer than half a year. I'll have to go to Byelorussia by next September."

"Maybe in the meantime you can just help us out."

"What did you have in mind?"

"Well, I know we have a drum copier and some alcohol, but we don't have any stencils or paper. Do you think you could get us some paper?"

"How much?"

"Whatever you can. Maybe a thousand sheets, if possible, even if you can't get the stencils. If worse comes to worst, we'll type out triplicates with carbon paper. Do you think you could do that?"

"To tell you the truth, it's a little disappointing. I was hoping you could assign me to a partisan group where someone like me could be head of propaganda."

"Maybe we should just start with this. But you must be very secretive and tell no one what I've asked."

Rimantas gave him a withering look. "I am not as stupid as I seem."

"I'm sure you're not."

"I know partisans have code names. What's yours?"

"It wouldn't be much of a code name if I told it to you when you already know my real name."

"I see. Well, maybe I could choose a code name of my own."

"Be my guest."

"I'd like to be called Poe."

"Like the Italian river?"

"No, like the American writer, with an *e* on the end. *Poe*. Do you understand?"

"I think I do."

"Do you live here, in this barn? Should I come here when I have the paper you want?"

"No. This is a neutral place. Someone will contact you to check and we'll choose another meeting place."

"It sounds a little like you don't trust me."

"Nothing personal. These are just operating procedures."

"Do you still read poetry?"

"When I can."

"Would you like it if, when I came, I brought some of my poetry?"

"I'd like that very much."

"I've had a few things published in a journal called *Lighthouse*. Have you heard of it?"

"I don't get magazines very often."

"Well, try to see if you can find it. I've always valued your opinion."

Lukas and Lakstingala left soon after Poe made his way down the wet road.

"He sounds like an idiot," said Lakstingala when Lukas explained the conversation they had had.

"He was always eccentric. He's a narcissist. But maybe he can help us."

"Fools are dangerous. They mean no harm but get you killed anyway."

"We can take another look at him later and reassess."

"Just don't let him anywhere near the bunkers. I don't trust him yet and winter is no time to go digging new holes in the earth."

"The ground isn't even frozen."

"No, but it's wet. Every shovelful weighs twice what it would in the summer."

Shortly after Lakstingala left on one of his sorties, it snowed heavily in the night and then a cold front came in. The dripping of the water stopped, but it was impossible to go outside because Lukas's feet would break through the crust of snow and then there would be no way to mask his tracks. Lakstingala would not be coming back any time soon for the same reason.

Lukas opened the trap door and looked out onto the blindingly white snow. He felt pale and grey and would have liked to climb out and bathe himself in sunlight, but it was some consolation to be looking out on the brightness from the passageway, even if it meant that he needed to keep a blanket over his shoulders to protect himself from the cold.

He could see only tree trunks and some open meadow beyond them. There were no houses visible, but somewhere within a few kilometres lay Merkine, the town they had once taken and where his brother had died. And somewhere beyond that, he didn't know where, Elena was apparently living.

He would need to get word out to Žoly somehow, to have a rubber raft come to pick them up at Palanga. But Lukas had no radio, and was not sure a raft would come even if he asked for one. Could he and Elena live somewhere in the country with false documents? Perhaps, but the drunken forger was long gone and Lukas did not know where one got false documents now.

They could give themselves up and hope to have some sort of life if they survived deportation, but Lukas had not heard of anyone coming back. Besides, he had killed too many Reds and would not be pardoned unless he betrayed others, such as Lakstingala. Maybe not even then.

Just as Lakstingala had said some things were not to be talked about, so some things did not bear much thought. This must be the way animals lived, in the here and now. He would wait and see. He would deal with his future as it came at him.

Three days later, the weather warmed and it started to rain. The earth was still frozen, but soon it would warm enough for the roof to begin leaking again. Lukas watched the snow melt with all the interest of a farmer waiting for spring. Anything was better than waiting out the winter in a hole. One day, patches of mud began to show amid the snowbanks, and the following morning, just before dawn, Lakstingala tapped four times on the door twice, their agreed signal. Lukas embraced him as a combination comrade and friend, and even as a kind of uncle who came bearing gifts.

On the tiny underground table Lakstingala set out a cheese, three sausages, a brick of heavy black bread, a jar filled with soup that was still a little warm, and a small bottle of liqueur. And then, from his knapsack, he took a small portable typewriter and a stack of carbon paper, as well as twenty sheets of typing paper.

"You still can't move around much," he said, "so at least we can put you to work in your old profession, writing the newspaper. The typewriter has no ribbon, but if you strike the keys hard enough you can get four carbon copies."

"And have you brought me news as well?" asked Lukas.

He had. Lozorius would meet him in the bunker in a week. In the meantime Rimantas had found some paper and wanted to see Lukas again.

This time they met in a granary, a small building with barely enough room for the two of them to fit inside. Lakstingala stood outside on the porch as Rimantas and Lukas huddled inside on a bench, their knees almost touching.

"I brought a little of my poetry," said Rimantas. "Can I read it to you?"

The building had a small window and Lukas could see the out-line of Lakstingala as he surveyed the farmyard.

"By all means."

And so Rimantas began to read as Lukas listened with a growing sense of unreality. He liked Rimantas and remembered him fondly from their student days, but this poetry of his was terrible. How dark it all was, as dark as plowed earth in the rain.

Rimantas read at great length about inner anguish, about pain and fear. Intellectually, Lukas could see that everything Rimantas wrote was true, a reflection of the lives of the people in the country, but emotionally he could barely stand to hear it. Lukas himself had not been feeling all that hopeful, but there was nothing like seeing someone in a darker mood still to make him realize he had always been better off than he knew.

"Well," said Rimantas after an interminable reading, "what do you think of my poetry?"

"I think you handle the language very well. I think that your themes are very dark, though."

"Yes, exactly. I'm the only writer who's telling the truth. Nobody is writing about the interior lives of the people in this country. It's as if we became prepsychological or something. Dostoevsky would never get into print today."

"So there you have it—another reason to fight for freedom, in order to be able to print this kind of poetry."

"I brought along the *Lighthouse* magazine too. I'm involved a little bit there."

"You're an editor?"

"Not exactly. I'm the informal correspondent from the Byelorussian marches."

"That's the place where you're going to teach in the fall, right?"

"It will be more bearable if I'm assigned to write from there."

"And how are your typing skills?"

"I am an excellent typist. When I was a student before the war I worked in the theatre office. I'm fast and my accuracy is brilliant."

"Good. I have some handwritten articles about life in the West. Do you think you could type those up?"

"I could, but I don't have a typewriter."

"We have a typewriter."

"But I couldn't very well type at home. Someone would hear the machine and get suspicious, and I don't have a permit for a typewriter."

"If we found a place for you to type up these articles, would you do it?"

"Of course I would. I want to make myself useful to the cause."

Lukas left him where he was and walked out to talk to Lakstin-gala. Resources were few, but Lakstingala agreed that Rimantas could use the fallback bunker to type. It was dangerous to give up the place, but they had to find somewhere for Rimantas to work, and it would lift the spirits of the partisans and the people if Rimantas wrote out one-page articles that could be circulated.

"Congratulations," said Lukas when he went back to see Riman-tas, "you'll be writing notes from the underground. You'll be our partisan Dostoevsky."

"Let's not get carried away with our admiration for Dostoevsky," said Rimantas. "He had his shortcomings."

SPRING 1950

*T*HE MUD of a Lithuanian spring was legendary, marooning farmers at their homes because the roads were impassable, leaving children barefoot when their boots became stuck in the mud on the way home from school, sinking the horses of reckless riders to the stirrups. No cars ventured into the country. It was a very boring time of year for those who were tired of the winter, but on the other hand it promised weary farmers a little relief from the visitations of government officials, who were well on their way to eliminating the last of the private farms.

Lukas's hideaway was near a forest, and once the snow was off the ground he could walk there without fear because the bed of needles both supported his weight and then sprang back to wipe out any sign of his passage. Even the barren woods and fields of early spring were fascinating to eyes accustomed to the gloom of a bunker or the single view available from the bunker's passageway.

Some little movement was happening in the animal kingdom: rats ran above the earth and moles dug a series of tunnels, their underground paths now visible on the earth as humps on the grass, and the magpies and ravens called their harsh warnings in the air.

In one place, his eye attracted by a slight reflection, Lukas came upon a tiny spider spinning an optimistic web for insects that were barely awake yet.

By moving from copse to copse, by following overgrown fencelines where the bushes were high, as he ranged a little farther each day Lukas began to understand better where Lakstingala had hidden him, especially when he came upon the farmstead of the American farmer, the traitor who had attempted to drug the partisan Anupras. Lukas watched this place from a distance, and when he moved cautiously forward it became clear that the house was abandoned. No animals moved about the yard and the barn door hung open. The windows at the back of the house were broken and inside he could see smashed bottles and loose papers scattered about.

Nearby was the place where he and his brother had first started their underground lives, and like a man returning to childhood haunts he found the places he remembered much diminished by time. This wreck of a house was the place where he had sat with Flint and the drunken forger to plan his trip to meet Elena.

Twice during his rambling, Lukas caught sight of Rimantas in the distance. The poet had not been shown Lukas's bunker, but he must have divined it was not far from the place where he was typing the newspaper in his own tiny burrow. Just as soon as the earth dried out a little, Lukas and Lakstingala would need to decamp and dig new bunkers somewhere else. Old bunkers attracted bad luck—sooner or later the Cheka dogs sniffed them out no matter how much lamp oil was sprinkled around.

Upon his cautious return from one such walk, Lukas saw movement near his bunker, and he hung back in the trees to see who was there. From a distance one of the men looked like Lakstingala, but he was not alone. There were some people whom Lukas could trust, and Lakstingala was one of them, but it was good to be cautious just in case Lakstingala himself was being duped. Lukas drew closer with his assault rifle at the ready, but when he was within thirty yards he recognized the unmistakably turned-out ears of the second man and he went to them.

"I was afraid I wouldn't find you alive," said Lukas.

"I told you once before, they can't kill me. They've tried again and again. Besides, what kind of a host would I be if I weren't around to welcome you after I invited you? So you made it into the country all right?"

Lozorius's colour was very poor. He was like a frog coming out of hibernation, pale, almost translucent. But for all his bad colour, by virtue of being alive, Lozorius was still on a winning streak.

They went inside the bunker and closed the lid behind them. The upper bunk was hopelessly wet, but they could lay their jackets and arms on the lower one and sit around the small table with their feet in a shallow puddle of water.

"Lozorius was almost impossible to get here," said Lakstingala. "When I finally found him, he grilled me up and down about you. Then he didn't want to come here, and he wouldn't let me bring you to his own bunker."

"What's this all about?"

"I transmit from my bunker. I run the radio antenna up at night and I send out messages. I also receive. As far as I know I'm the only free radio sending information out of this country, and if the Cheka gets me, the last bit of light will stop escaping from here. No one comes to my bunker."

There was a flash of the spirit that Lukas remembered, the confidence that made Lozorius so attractive.

"Don't you give yourself away if you keep transmitting from the same place?" asked Lukas.

"Not if I'm very brief and infrequent. Did you bring a radio?"

"Not me personally. The others I came with might still have theirs, but I don't know what happened to them."

"I do. At least one of them is working for the Cheka, but I don't know if he was always with them or if he was forced into this only after you landed."

"How can you know that?"

"Because he's sending information to Stockholm that contradicts mine," said Lozorius. "He's trying to undermine my credibility."

"The Cheka know about you?"

"Of course they do. They're looking for me so hard I'm afraid to breathe. I'm the last free transmitter in this country—they need to close me down. And here is the irony: I know your compatriot is compromised, and so is Stockholm, for all the good it does me. The villains know I'm here and I know about the villains, but those who might still be honest back in Stockholm can't tell us apart."

"What are you saying?"

"I'm saying there is a hole in security somewhere. I had a farmer up in Palanga freelancing for me personally. The forest was full of Cheka troops before you landed, so you were expected. They set a trap for you, but you still managed to slip out. I'm amazed you got away."

"I was lucky," said Lukas.

"I hope that's true." Lukas looked at him, not quite understanding what he meant at first. "Don't look so shocked, my friend. You can't trust anyone anymore, unless it's someone you've known for a long time, and even then you can't be sure. But Lakstingala is not only lucky, he has a good nose. I knew he'd sniff you out if you were a smiter. I've known for a year that there were leaks on the other side."

"What kind of leaks?"

"The Reds have penetrated either the British or the Swedish secret services. I don't know which one and I don't know who betrayed us. It might be Zoly himself, but I don't think so. He's too much the diplomat and he doesn't like to risk himself, so he probably wouldn't take the chance of playing a double game."

"Just a moment. If you knew your communications were compromised, why did you ask for me in particular? You were calling me into a trap."

"Because I knew if anyone could get in, it was you."

"You're saying you lured me back in?"

"In a way, yes."

"And maybe you lied about Elena just to get me in?"

The bunker was so small that they were pressed in close to one another in a huddle, the candle shedding the only light. Lakstingala and Lozorius were both smoking. Lukas would have liked to smoke too, but the bunker felt airless enough as it was.

"No, that part's true. Elena *is* alive and I knew you'd want to know it. A miracle, eh? I had to tell you, but I did compromise her a little by naming her. If all our communications are being read by the traitors in Stockholm, the Reds know she's alive too."

"You used her code name?"

"Our code names haven't been secret for years. They know us all by our real names. There are files on each of us in Vilnius. There are investigators assigned to each of us and there's money on our heads. Either you or I would bring enough to make a man rich. Even Elena has a price on her head."

"Where is she?"

"In Merkine. She's living with false documents."

"How is it possible? Flint saw her die in an explosion."

"We've all seen people die. Sometimes they die and sometimes they don't. She was wounded and taken to a hospital. When she was almost well, she was sprung out with a few other women."

"How can you know this?"

"I know this and I know a hundred other loose ends of information, but none of them is any good to me. Yours is the only thread that will take us anywhere."

"I can't understand all this. Why did you give away her secret through your transmission? And why did you call on me?"

"Because I knew if I told you she was alive, you would come. And I knew that you were the only one who had a chance of survival even if a trap was set for you."

"But why did you need me in particular?"

"Because I need someone like you to help me get out of this country."

"You gave an oath," said Lakstingala. He had been smoking and listening to them in silence although he was very close to them, his face no more than an arm's length away. His eyes had gone cold.

"What good are our oaths now? The movement is broken. I've seen that. The only ones left are the lucky ones like us. The whole structure has crumbled and what hasn't vanished is shot through with betrayal. Most of the farms have been collectivized—we have no base of support anymore. I was ready to die for my cause when there was hope that someone from our side might win, even if it wasn't me, but I don't see hope anymore. The best we can do is get back out and take what news we have with us. I'd give anything to be sitting in a restaurant in Stockholm right now."

"What are the spy agencies going to say about that?" asked Lukas.

"To hell with them. They were just using us anyway. The British or Swedes have been penetrated, and for all we know, the Americans too. I'm terrified of being taken alive. I know too much. I don't think I could withstand the torture."

"Then you should shoot yourself," said Lakstingala.

Lozorius looked away from Lakstingala and would not look back again. "Do you have anything to drink?" he asked.

Lukas did. He had been saving some cassis Lakstingala had brought. He opened the bottle and poured each of them four fingers.

Lozorius drank half the liqueur and then rested his glass on the table. "I don't think I want to die anymore. That's the problem."

"I'll kill you if you don't have the courage to do it yourself," said Lakstingala.

"Don't be so harsh," said Lukas.

"You think he'd be the first one? We've had partisans that were bad to begin with or went bad later, and others became cowards like this one. We had field courts when there was still an organization, and I took part in a couple of executions."

"I've been in dangerous spots before," said Lozorius, "but something has broken in me. You can't blame me for that."

"I don't blame a horse for breaking its leg. And the cure is the same," said Lakstingala.

"Stop it," said Lukas, and Lakstingala closed his mouth and hunkered down. "Lakstingala, come outside with me. Lozorius, you stay here."

They walked out a distance to the nearest copse.

"The man makes me furious," said Lakstingala. "He knew what the dangers were when he came back here. Now he's lured you in for no good reason and he's put all of us at risk."

"There's still the matter of my wife, though."

Lakstingala nodded. "That's true, but you'll do her no good. Leave her alone. If she's living with false papers, she's built some kind of structure for herself, but it will be very fragile. If you go looking for her, you could destroy all that."

"But I haven't come here to ruin her life—I've come here to save her and get her out again. She should be dead. For all I know she was dead, but she's risen from it somehow. You don't look indifferently at that kind of miracle. I'll get her out somehow."

"What you say will be hard enough for two. Do you want to risk it with Lozorius?"

"I don't know. I wouldn't want to leave him behind. He has a bad look to him."

"I'll execute him. He's a traitor, in a way, for endangering you."

"Don't be so hard. We all have to find a way to survive, even you."

"Don't worry about me."

"Why not? You worry about me."

"Honestly, you have to stop talking like that. If sentimentality is what you lived off in the West, I'm glad I'm not going there."

Lukas smiled but hid it from him. "Would you come with me if I went looking for Elena in Merkine?"

"I'd lead you to the edge of town. In the meantime, let's take this one back where he came from—or rather, let me do it."

"Go easy. When I knew him before, he wasn't like this."

When they stepped back into the bunker, they found that Lozorius had finished the blackcurrant liqueur in each of their glasses. "I'm sorry," he said, "but I thought you might shoot me when you returned." He looked at them sheepishly.

It seemed for a moment as if the furious Lakstingala might do just that, but he got over it. Lukas and Lakstingala both went part of the way back with Lozorius, but Lukas left them to return to his bunker. He invited Lozorius to visit whenever he felt the pressure grow too great. The man needed bucking up.

Upon his return to his bunker, Lukas saw the three glasses still on the table. He put his finger into the bottom of one and tasted the tip of it.

He heard a noise outside. He reached for his assault rifle and put a hand grenade in his pocket as well.

"It's just me," a familiar voice called.

"Rimantas, what are you doing here?"

"You're supposed to call me *Poe*. I'm sorry, but I just wrote a new poem and I knew you'd want to hear it."

Lukas should have been angry, but he could never stay that way with Rimantas. The man was too outrageously amusing for his breaches of security to be taken seriously.

---

TWENTY-FIVE

*L*AKSTINGALA AND LUKAS surveyed the town of Merkine
from the same position where they had stood when they first
attacked the town, five years earlier. The woods were behind
them and a hundred metres of field before them, and beyond that
the backs of the wooden houses on the edge of town. Then, there
had been half a dozen men in their unit and dozens more in other
positions. Of these men, only Lukas and Lakstingala were still alive.
It was hard to look at the town without a sense of bitterness for all
that had happened since they had been there, for the futility of all
the deaths that had left the sleepy town unchanged.

Merkine had two and a half thousand inhabitants by 1950, not
so few that a stranger would be remarked upon but not so many
that Lukas would go unnoticed. He needed to wait until evening in
order to enter the town.

"I'll stay here for a while after you go in," said Lakstingala. "If
you're in trouble, try to make it this way and I can cover you from
the forest if you need to run across the bare field."

"The earth is still wet. If I have to run across the bare field, I'll
be a dead man. Once I disappear from your view into the town,

go back and make yourself safe. And if I don't come back, don't go looking for me."

"All right."

Lukas studied the house on the other side of the field. He had once shot a sniper who was inside that window.

"If anything happens to me," he said, "do what you can for Elena."

"All right."

Lukas looked at Lakstingala, but the partisan would not meet his eyes. "Not that I expect to outlive you, but did you want to tell me anything about *your* wife in case something happens to *you*?" asked Lukas.

"I think I'd rather you didn't know anything about her at all."

"There's a chance we could all make it out together. I could take Lozorius and Elena, and you could take your wife. Five of us might be able to do it."

"It's not just my wife. We have a daughter, and I wouldn't want to leave her behind. Besides, there are still a few partisans around, and I'm the oldest one among them. They make jokes about me all the time, and it would be bad for morale if I suddenly disappeared. I think I'm not going anywhere, unless it's northeast, and I'll put that off as long as I can."

It was hard to separate this time, and they lingered by the edge of the forest.

"There's one more thing. I wouldn't mind getting word out to the West whether I make it or not," said Lukas. "I've written a letter. Do you think you could try to get it out if anything happens to me?"

"I thought Lozorius said the British and the Swedes were infiltrated."

"That may be so, but it's not them I'm worried about. There are people who helped me out there—I had a whole other life . . ."

Lakstingala held up his hand. "I don't want to know. Do you have the letter?"

"Yes."

"Hand it over."

Lakstingala did not even look at the address. Lukas glanced up at the evening sky. It was still a little too early to go into the town, but he couldn't wait.

"Do you think this country will ever be free?" Lukas asked.

"Maybe. I don't know. One thing is sure: we won't live to see it." He said it so readily that he must have said it before and it must have been what the other partisans believed.

"One more thing," said Lukas.

"Are you never going to leave?"

"About Lozorius."

"What about him?"

"If something happens to me, he'll lose his last hope for getting out of the country."

"My heart is bleeding."

"Why are you so hard on him?"

"He's too dramatic for me. He played the hero—a kind of Robin Hood. The pose was too good not to be false."

"Didn't you once call me Robin Hood as well?"

"You're different. I watched you grow up with the partisans. I tell you, when we went out on that first mission, you were pitiful. But later, what you did with Elena at that engagement party, that was astonishing."

"I'm not so sure I'm proud of that anymore. We killed so many, and what good did it do us?"

"It stung the bastards a bit. But as for your regret, that's what makes you different from Lozorius. Don't worry about him. If something happens to you, I'll change his diaper for him. Anyway, listen, I'm sick of this 'end of days' talk. I have another bottle of liquor waiting for us on the table back at the bunker—homebrew, but not too bad. Go find Elena now. See how things are. Then, when you come back, we'll drink and talk it all through."

There was nothing more to say. They embraced. Lukas had an assault rifle under his long coat, a revolver in one pocket and a hand grenade in the other. It was still too bright, but he had to leave now. He picked his way carefully across the wet field to the edge of town, stood beside a house and waved to Lakstingala, who waved back and then stepped into the forest and disappeared.

Lukas stood at the side of a house and cleaned the mud off his boots before he went into the town proper.

Bearing a sheaf of poems, Rimantas had come looking for Lukas a while earlier. He went to the bunker where Lukas lived and called out his name but didn't hear any response. He listened by the lid and heard snoring, so he tapped lightly on the door and then opened it to see Lozorius stretched out on the lower bunk, sleeping. There was an empty bottle on the small table and the bunker smelled of liquor.

Rimantas knew who Lozorius was, remembered him from their school days. He knew a great deal more than people gave him credit for.

Rimantas opened his briefcase and set his poems down on the small table. He had intended to read them to Lukas; maybe Lozorius would like to hear them instead. Rimantas sat down on a chair, intending to wake him up gently, but he hesitated. If he felt the least threat, a man like Lozorius would start shooting as soon as he opened his eyes.

Rimantas had a hand grenade and a pistol in his briefcase beneath the place where his poems had lain. He closed the briefcase.

Rimantas sat for a while and studied Lozorius's face. Like Lukas, Lozorius had been abroad and chose to return. What a fool. He should have stayed away while he could. Rimantas himself wished he had chosen to emigrate, but he was a poet and one could not pick up a new language so easily as to be able to write verses in it. What a shame that poetry was not valued very much under the present circumstances, when collectivization and industrialization were all the newspapers talked about.

Rimantas looked at the sleeping Lozorius, the man who had killed dozens of Chekists and slayers if the legends were true. He did not look all that powerful while he was asleep. He looked rather vulnerable.

But that was probably an illusion. Lozorius was a wild man, and the more Rimantas thought about his reputation, the less comfortable he felt sitting in the same bunker with the sleeping man. Maybe Lozorius was only feigning sleep. The more Rimantas thought these thoughts, the more nervous he became. He could not stay there.

Rimantas collected his poems, crept out of the bunker, closed the door and stepped in among the trees to consider his options. His heart was beating madly and he needed to calm down.

He was irritated by the situation he found himself in. These men, Lukas and likely Lozorius, were the only ones who might understand his poetry. They were exactly the kind of intellectual audience he wanted. Not Lakstingala, of course. He was a peasant through and through, sturdy but with practically no subconscious to speak of.

Things were not going according to plan. His instructions were to go with Lukas and Lakstingala to find out where Lozorius was hiding. The authorities wanted to take the radio as well as the three men. The second-best plan was to discover when Lozorius came to this bunker. Rimantas was to inform the authorities so all three could be taken. Now Lozorius was here, but Rimantas did not feel inclined to inform the authorities of anything. Something was up in Merkine. There was a suppressed buzz in the town.

The Cheka workers were of very low calibre. Most of them did not even have a high school education, and half of them were alcoholics. If Rimantas had had any ambition in that way, he could have made quite a career in the Cheka. But the Cheka men were idiots and, worse, boring, and he had no interest in spending his life with boring men and drunks. He had a higher calling. In a better world he would have been left alone to work on his poetry. In the Middle Ages he might have been a monk of some kind.

Rimantas wanted to write and to publish, but the authorities would not let him do that unless he paid for his sins. They knew all about him and his anti-Stalinist poetry during the German occupation. Therefore, he was doomed to work for them for a while. But he still might be redeemed, and he wanted to shake off his obligations as soon as possible.

Now that the Reds had been in power for six years, they were building their ideological infrastructure. There was a new children's publishing house opening up soon. He could be the publisher there and still have time to do his own writing. He had imagined a more illustrious life for himself, something a little more bohemian. Rimantas hated the world he lived in. But what could he do?

He had intended to buy his freedom with Lukas, but they had not been content to take only Lukas. No, they wanted him and Lozorius together, and so gave Rimantas an impossible task. How was he to get both of them?

The odds were very poor, but perhaps he had stumbled upon a solution to all of his problems by finding the sleeping Lozorius. If he gave Lozorius to the Cheka, they would be grateful to him. He would have fulfilled his part of the bargain. And if he gave them Lozorius in a way that blew his own cover, he would be out of a job with the Cheka and permitted to get back to work on his writing. In a way, this plan saved Lukas; Rimantas would be doing him a favour.

Rimantas's plan, such as it was, was risky. But everything was risky now. In a world of many bad options, he had to take the one that seemed the least bad. He looked inside his briefcase. The grenade and the pistol were at the bottom.

He studied the landscape thoroughly. No one seemed to be around, but one could never tell. Worst of all would be to be caught by Lakstingala and Lukas. Neither would show mercy.

Rimantas walked over to the bunker and listened. The snoring was still very loud. He looked about one more time, pulled the pin of the grenade, waited a few seconds, wrenched open the lid, and threw the grenade inside. Then he closed the lid again and ran, pistol in one hand, briefcase in the other.

The grenade seemed to take a very long time to explode, blowing the hatch off the bunker. Rimantas waited a little, looked around, and then saw to his horror that Lozorius was crawling out of the bunker.

"You can't kill me!" Lozorius shouted. "I swore that nobody could kill me!"

Whether the grenade had rolled under a table or gone into a corner or been deflected, Rimantas did not know. All he knew was the dreadfulness of a dead man rising to chase him. Rimantas had never been so frightened in his life. He fired off a few ineffectual shots from his pistol and began to flee across the fields. But the earth was muddy and the going impossibly slow. The faster he tried to run, the faster the mud adhered to his shoes. He heard Lozorius fire behind him and fell to the earth, trembling with terror, afraid he might have been shot.

Lozorius had awoken to the explosion, ears ringing, brain rattling, with a pain all down his left side where wood splinters had driven into his skin. But through the smoke and confusion and the ringing in his ears, he could see the square of light of the blown-out doorway. Freedom lay where the light was, so he took his pistol and charged out, firing.

Once outside, Lozorius had stood there, dazed. He shouted that he could not be killed, and then heard a few shots. He could not see properly—blood was running in his left eye—but there was a figure in the field, a figure that fell to the earth when he fired at it.

But where there had been one figure, soon there would be many. The Chekists did not go out alone. Lozorius looked to his left arm, all bloody through his shirt sleeve. He stood swaying, and considered his position for a moment, and decided it was hopeless. He felt a surge of relief.

"No one can kill me!" he roared. "No one but me!"
He put the pistol in his mouth and fired.

Lakstingala heard the explosion and the firing in the distance, but
he was hampered by the wet fields and his need for stealth, as well as
the darkening sky. He made his way as close as he dared and hid in a
ditch. After a time a number of cars pulled up and slayers stepped
out. A very tall man came to them. The man was finding it hard to
make progress because his boots were encumbered with mud. He
carried a briefcase in one hand.

*I*N THE FADING LIGHT, Lukas began to walk into the town of Merkine, to the house where Elena was living. Hardly anything seemed to move in the streets except for a dog at some distance, a hungry creature that slunk around the corner of a building.

The church bell rang at nine o'clock, causing him to jump a little. This must be the only town in the whole Soviet Union where the church bells were still permitted to ring. Somewhere a Red official would pay for this oversight when an inspector general came to town and discovered this bourgeois remnant.

In the dimness, Lukas thought of the machine gunner who had been up in the bell tower, and of the partisan who had fallen at the very crossroads Lukas was walking past. He went on. The brick house that they had blown up with the panzerfaust had been rebuilt, although he could not see the details in the twilight. Everything the partisans did in the town had been erased, as if they had done nothing at all.

A small Russian Orthodox church with a tiny onion dome stood in a square, a remnant of the czarist times, but boarded up now. He had no memory of such a church in the town. How was this possible? He had studied the place before the attack and kept watch on it during the fight, but if anyone had asked him, he would have said there was no such thing there.

They had gathered the bodies of their fallen comrades in the town square, but the body of his brother, Vincentas, was never found. That body must have been buried close by, and so Lukas felt as if his brother's spirit hovered somewhere in the night, looking over him.

At the high school, once a Jewish school but now used by others, the light in the principal's flat was burning. She was a very young principal, one who had graduated from this same high school herself not all that long ago. She had been the first to join the Komsomol, and was almost killed in those days for daring to do it. She had done better than any of her classmates, some of whom were shipped to the camps before they graduated. The others who still lived in the town were not in the least friendly with her, but she did not mind. They respected her position and that was enough.

Although Merkine was a small town, it was very old and it had once been a provincial capital, so it had a few houses that would not have been out of place in any old town. It was in this quarter that Lukas found the steps down to the half cellar, and knocked lightly four times on a door and then repeated the knock.

It was getting dark now; light came from a lamp on a distant street corner.

"Who's there?" a woman's voice asked from inside.

"An old friend," he replied, as he had been told to.

She unlocked the door and opened it and he stepped inside.

She wore a head scarf to hide something wrong around her ear and down to her cheek on the left side of her face. There were two teardrop-sized scars on her left cheek, and her left hand was sheathed in a cotton glove with an empty finger. She took two steps back, and he could see she limped. She looked at him noncommittally, waiting for him to declare himself so she could begin to parse out who he was: a partisan or a Chekist, a slayer or a smiter, or one of the many types of men who worked for any of a variety of conflicting interests.

"Don't you know me?" he asked.

"My eyesight is not very good."

"Listen to the sound of my voice."

"You do sound a little familiar, but it's a voice I haven't heard for a very long time."

"Elena," he said. "It's me, Lukas."

She turned away at the sound of her name. "Many people show up here. They confuse me with other people and they tell all kinds of stories, trying to turn the head of a poor invalid. I don't know why they should be so interested in someone like me. I was in a terrible accident and I'm afraid I don't remember very much from before that time. If you can leave a ruble or two on the table I'll be grateful, but if you want to ask me anything, I'm afraid there's nothing I know."

This was what remained of the woman who had joked with him, the woman who had bucked up his courage the night he had to kill those people in Marijampole.

The room where they were standing had a low ceiling and a narrow window up by the sidewalk outside. Even now they were still underground, half buried. The room had a table, two chairs and a cot. There was a door to another room.

"Elena, we were married in a church by moonlight. We drank French brandy on our honeymoon. I've come to take you away from this place. I've come to take you to America."

Even at this, she kept away from him and laughed. "You must be thinking of someone else. Why would you want to take me to America? It's dangerous there, with gangsters. I'm much better off where I am. But if you want, you can go yourself. First, though, let me make you a cup of tea."

"I don't need tea. I want to talk to you."

"Tea will help us talk."

She put a kettle on a gas ring, set out a pot and heaped in two spoonfuls of tea, put out a bowl of sugar and two cups.

"You have both sugar and real tea," he said.

"I'm very lucky. I also have a radio. Let me turn it on. There is often music from Warsaw at this hour."

She turned on the radio and indeed a foxtrot was playing. When the water boiled, she put a little in the small teapot to make *esensia*, a very strong, concentrated tea. She let this brew for a couple of minutes and then added hot water to the cups and topped them up with *esensia*.

"Please sit down," she said.

He did as she asked and she passed him a cup. Then she sat down across from him, took her cup in both hands and leaned forward.

"Why did you come back?" she whispered.

"Who is listening?"

"I don't know. I can't be sure. But I'm fairly certain I'm being watched, and maybe I'm being listened to as well. You haven't answered my question."

"I came back for you."

"Why?"

"I never would have left you if I'd known you were alive."

"You're a fool to do this. If you'd loved me, you would have stayed away and saved yourself."

"I'm going to get you out of here. I've fought my way across the border before—we can do it again. There are others who will help me."

"Or lose their lives trying."

"Yes, that's right. All of us are ready to lose our lives, but we don't give them up cheaply." He made to reach for her hand, but she pulled it back.

"Don't appear too familiar with me. Someone may be watching." He felt her foot against the side of his leg under the table. This was all the touch she could give him.

"Couldn't I hold your hand under the table?"

"They might see it."

He longed to touch her, but he could not. She looked down at the table, avoiding his eyes, ashamed, he guessed, by her looks. He didn't care.

"Did they take you?" Lukas asked. "Did they hurt you?"

"You can see the scars well enough, but Flint got me out before I'd healed so much that they could begin to torture me. But how long can I last in hiding? Look at me. I'm disfigured, and the authorities know it—my wounds were thoroughly described on my hospital chart. This little paradise won't last."

"All the more reason to come with me. We've escaped before. Maybe we can do it again."

"It's no good. It's over."

"Don't give up hope. I can help you."

"You can, but not in the way you think. They're outside, waiting for you."

"Now? Are you sure?"

"I don't know anything for sure. There's been a strange atmosphere in this town over the last few days. More cars pass through than usual. They may have found me already, or they may have found you and followed you here. And if neither is true, it will be soon."

"Why didn't you run?"

"I couldn't. They have me where they want me."

"This talk is all confusing. Why won't you go with me?"

"Wait here."

She rose and went into the other room but did not illuminate a lamp there. Lukas heard the wail of a child being awoken. She came back with a very small boy on her hip, not much more than a toddler, a cranky child with curly brown hair very much like hers. She no sooner sat down than the boy snuggled into her shoulder and fell back to sleep.

A hand seized his throat. "He's ours?"

She nodded.

"How is that possible?"

"Small miracles happen. Not often, but sometimes they do."

He wished he could see the child a little better, but he was so tightly tucked into his mother's side that Lukas did not want to tear him away.

"If you had stayed away," said Elena, "you might have been able to do him some good. One day maybe they will permit people to send packages from America. But what good are you to him here and now?"

"I didn't know."

"No. There'll be no fighting our way out of this place, and there'll be no flight to America. Everything has changed now."

Everything had changed. She was right. He looked at the boy and was overcome with the wonder of him.

Elena let him look at the boy a long time.

"Is there anything I can do for you both?" asked Lukas.

"There is something. But it's very terrible. I'm afraid to ask it."

"What?"

"If you go outside and they are there, and if they try to seize you, let them take you alive."

Lukas had not touched his tea. He looked at the cup and drank it all down. He considered what she said. If he did as she asked, they would torture him and might make him tell what he knew. He was not sure he could withstand torture.

"What good would it do?"

"They will have their prize. You are it. I'm not so foolish as to think I'll get off. But if I'm lucky they'll give me ten years for collusion if you don't tell them about me, our past."

What she asked was very hard. To give himself up to torture would be bad enough; to try to hold something back under torture would make the pain go on longer.

"What's the boy's name?" Lukas asked.

"Jonas. I wanted a simple name, with no history, no subtexts. I couldn't call him after you."

"No."

Lukas looked at the child. He had never had quite this experience before, the sense of being able to look for a long time and feeling unflagging delight.

"What if there is no one waiting for me outside? Couldn't I just walk away?"

"Yes, of course. You might be able to survive for a while and so might I, but I need to keep the child. It's the first thing they'll use against me. If I confess to being a courier, they'll send both the child and me to Siberia. Maybe things will not be so bad in the camps for mothers and children. They don't separate mothers and children anymore. Maybe we could stay alive. But if they really do discover all I've done, they'll torture me too. And they'll put him in an orphanage. You have to do whatever is right. I'm not sure what that is, but I do know he'd be better off with me in Siberia than in an orphanage here."

It was unbearable to speak of these things, and so they whispered about other things, of people they had known and what had happened to them. They whispered under the sound of the radio. Time and again Lukas would stop to look at the boy. Time and again Elena reminded him that he could do as he chose.

Lukas sat with Elena through most of the night. He wanted to drink up the sight of the boy and the sight of her as well. He wanted to wait until there was a little light on the street, and when he saw the window begin to brighten, he looked long at the boy again and then returned to what would happen next.

"What should I tell them about you?" he asked.

"You must hold out for a while. You can't tell them everything immediately or they won't believe you. I was a courier once, you can say that. Say you came here hoping for a letter from your parents."

He was afraid to kiss her because he was afraid of waking Jonas, but he had been afraid to kiss her before, years earlier, and he had found a way. Now he found a way again. She let him, heedless of who might be watching. He kissed the boy too, who awoke and cried out, pushing him away before settling back into his mother's shoulder.

"I'm going to tell you an address," said Lukas, "of a place in America. If you could get a letter out there somehow, I'd be very grateful."

"I don't know what I can do."

"It wouldn't have to be right now. Whenever you can. Even if it's years from now. But you mustn't write down the address, so you'll have to memorize it."

"All right."

He gave her an address in America, the address of Monika's uncle. He also told her what to say to Lakstingala if she had a chance to speak to him. They talked about the people they knew who had died. After the music from Warsaw ended for the night, she left the radio on and it gave off a sound of static that she did not turn down.

"I understand you were out of the country, in the West," said Elena.

"Yes. I was in Sweden and Germany and France."

"Tell me about those places."

He described Stockholm and Paris and the towns he had visited in Germany. She asked him questions for a long time.

"It's good to know life goes on somewhere," she said.

Then much too soon it was full dawn. Lukas looked at the brightening window and then at Elena.

"Please don't cry," said Lukas.

"Why not?"

"Because if you do, I will too, and I don't want to be taken with my eyes full of tears." He paused. "Will you tell Jonas about me? Not for a while, but later, when he's old enough to understand. Tell him I saw him and admired him and I knew he would be all right." He could not say more for a moment.

"I will, I will."

"And if you can, tell him about my parents' farm by Rumsiskes. When this is all over, maybe someone will be left alive, my mother or my sister. It would be good for him to know there is family somewhere."

"I will."

It was all so hard. He had been willing to suffer, but he did not know it would be like this.

He wanted to stay longer, but it was time to go. He touched her hand and kissed her wet cheeks. Elena could not help herself after all. Neither could he.

Lukas went to the door and opened it. He wasn't sure, but he thought there was a little movement at the periphery of his vision. He kept his hands visible but turned back to face the two of them at the table before he closed the door.

"I always loved you, Elena," he said. Then he stepped out from the underground and turned to face the street.

TWENTY-SEVEN

CANADA–LITHUANIA

AUGUST 1989

*T*HE OLD STORIES stayed underground in Lithuania, and others like them in Estonia and Latvia, in Poland and Ukraine and other places. As for knowledge of them in the West, they were forgotten in the malls, suburbs and high-rises of America. A generation of immigrant children grew up and joined the mainstream, forgetting their sources, the springs and rivulets they had come from, except for a few who were caught in the eddies, turning endlessly, in neither the present nor the past, mulling over the unknowability of history and the banality of the present.

By 1989 the Soviet Union was collapsing, although no one guessed it at the time. As the restrictions eased, every trembling mole was digging its way out of the underground and brushing itself off. Seeds long dormant began to sprout and reach out for the light. Messages began to travel again. Many went to addresses where no one lived any longer, but some found their way to the proper destinations.

In early spring of that year, a letter arrived in the mailbox of Luke Zolynas, a high school French teacher who lived in Toronto, Canada. He was a tall, gentle man with eyeglasses that slipped down his nose when he was in a rush, to the amusement of his students, and he was always in a rush because he had three children between the ages of two and eight and his wife worked in a bank and he ran both the drama club and the chamber quartet after school. His father had died young of lung cancer and his mother in a car accident a few years after that. Luke would have liked to know more about his past, but his parents were dead, his one aunt lived far away, and anyway, he was busy with everyday life.

The letter came from Jonas Petronis in Lithuania, and it explained that the Lithuanian basketball coach had discovered they were half-brothers. Could Luke come for a visit?

Luke was startled, then curious, and eventually ambivalent about this alleged half-brother, who appeared to disrupt the busy flow of his life. Everyone came from somewhere, and memory was a mixed blessing. Look what happened to immigrant kids who didn't forget: they became enthusiastic ethnics, slightly comical figures in folk costumes, objects of derision. Or else they nurtured ancient hatreds and let them fester.

Luke Zolynas loved Canada, in a way, not that he would ever put it in those words. But to him it never felt altogether like home. Sometimes he wondered if he'd landed in the wrong country, and now this letter confirmed some complications about his origins.

Luke's father had been a very discreet man. His one weakness was cigarettes, which he sometimes held, maddeningly to Luke, between his thumb and forefinger, as if he were a villain in a European movie. He smoked a pack and a half each day, never leaving home without a spare pack in his briefcase. He'd worked for a couple of decades as a clerk at city hall. He didn't talk a lot about his own origins.

Luke's mother was a nurse who was often out, working shifts. His mother and father had always had a cordial if slightly cool relationship, unlike the relationships of most of his parents' friends, who bickered passionately. His parents had had separate bedrooms for as long as Luke could remember. They even took their vacations separately.

It had never occurred to Luke that the man who helped raise him, whom his mother had always called Zoly, was not his biological father. But after he received the letter from Lithuania, when Luke phoned his French aunt in Lyon, she confirmed that Zoly was his stepfather, and told him a whole series of stories about his mother's first husband. In a second letter from Jonas Petronis, Luke learned the outlines of another part of his father's life.

In late June of that year, after school was out, Luke flew to Vilnius, where an athletic man with curly brown hair and thick eyeglasses as well as an atrocious plaid suit met him at the airport intending to drive him by car to the town of Merkine, where he lived.

Jonas Petronis was not exactly warm but not exactly hostile either. He was ambivalent too. He seemed to study Luke's good shoes and luggage too long, to resent him a little. On the drive to his hometown he explained that any such visit would have been against the law a year earlier, when the old travel restrictions were being enforced and tourists were not permitted to leave the capital. It was still against the law technically, but no one was really paying attention anymore.

The countryside they drove through was made up primarily of pine forests that had been planted because the Soviet planners decided the sandy soil was too poor, and so the old farms had been liquidated, the fences dismantled, the houses bulldozed and the people resettled; geography was a slate that could be wiped clean, within limits. The rivers still flowed in their courses, but the farms that had once hugged their banks were gone, their people scattered. History, like geography, could be wiped away within reason as well, but like shards of pottery from ancient settlements it had a way of working up to the surface. A determined man or woman could piece some of it back together.

Jonas Petronis wanted to get to Merkine before dark. His eyes were poor because he'd suffered malnutrition as a boy in a Siberian work camp. But they were unavoidably delayed by road construction, and so they drove slowly down the empty country roads by night, where the darkness of the forest beside them was greater than the slightly less dark night sky above them.

They talked awkwardly about the past, two strangers trying to reassemble the stories of their parallel lives. Jonas Petronis had not known a great deal about the past either until, after the funeral of the aunt who raised him, his uncle Povilas had taken him aside at a place far out in the country, in order to fill him in on a little family history. Povilas was not really an uncle, just a family friend who had started hanging around with his aunt in the sixties.

Povilas had a half-acre garden plot in the country and a storage shed that he had enlarged until it was more like a small cottage. There, over shashlik cooked on an open fire and a few glasses of Armenian cognac, he'd told Jonas some surprising things. Povilas told him that his aunt was not really his aunt, but his mother.

The information was all a bit much for Jonas. He only half believed what he was told. He remembered Siberia from his childhood—the fleas the children played with, the potatoes that were sweet because they'd been left in a heap in the fields to freeze. Jonas had half thought Povilas was beginning to lose his mind. But some renegade historian, calling himself an "underground" historian, had looked up Jonas Petronis and asked him questions about his father, about whom Jonas knew nothing yet others seemed to know something.

It was all very unsettling, and it all became more unsettling. Jonas found out that his story had layers, and one of them lay in Canada.

For his part, Luke would have doubted the story even now if not for a pair of letters on the dashboard, which he read by the overhead light. They were from his mother, Monika, to Jonas's mother, Elena, and they had been written in the late sixties.

Jonas had ferreted out a few more details from his uncle Povilas, once known by his code name, Lakstingala, stories about their father, who had been executed some months after his capture in 1950.

Down through the tunnel of darkness the two half-brothers drove, on the road to Merkine, Jonas's home, where soon monuments to the Lithuanian partisans would join the monuments to the Red partisans and the Red Army. There was no shortage of cemeteries, for the Polish partisans who had fought in the region at various times, for German soldiers in the First World War and Napoleonic soldiers before them.

First there had been no more Jews in the Jewish Pine Forest, and then there was no longer a pine forest at all. In 1959 the Soviet engineers and the bulldozers came, and the hill, the forest and the south of old Rumsiskes were drowned to form the Kaunas Reservoir.

If the pressure were great enough and the time long enough, the sand of the dune forest would form into shale, and the stories that lay there would be pried apart by the archaeologists and geologists of the future.

Acknowledgements

This novel could not have been written if not for the collapse of the Soviet Union and the independence of Lithuania in 1991. These events opened up various archives and personal memoirs that led to the publication of a large number of histories about the partisan resistance to the second Soviet occupation in 1944. The story of partisan resistance not only in Lithuania but also in Estonia, Latvia, Ukraine and Poland remains largely unknown in the West. The partisan resistance in Lithuania was strongest in the early years, with as many as thirty thousand active participants and many more supporters. By the early fifties, numbers were down to a couple of thousand, and these were being slowly exterminated. Curiously, First Deputy Prime Minister Laverentiy Beria had one of them, Jonas Zemaitis (code-named Vytautas), brought to Moscow for talks about accommodation, but Beria was executed and Zemaitis as well, leaving one to wonder how things might have turned out if both had survived.

There has been speculation, unsubstantiated, that the British attempts to land agents on the Baltic coast were compromised by the infamous turncoat Kim Philby. One thing is certain: the

Soviets infiltrated the British operations quite thoroughly, and many agents dropped inside were double agents and those who went with them were doomed. One of these agents, however, survived prison and lived to see independent Lithuania. He apparently asked for thirty-five years of back pay from the British. I don't know if he received it.

Before 1991, few of the details of the partisan resistance were known beyond the stories told in Juozas Luksa's *Partizanai*, published in 1950 when Luksa came out to the West, fell in love and married, and then returned to Lithuania, where he was betrayed and shot in an ambush. I used the outlines of the Luksa story for this novel, but what you find here is in no way meant to tell Luksa's story. His love story was entirely different and even more romantic than the one I have told. Notwithstanding the many differences, I couldn't resist using a simple anagram of "Luksa" to create the name of the protagonist of this novel.

Those familiar with the partisan literature will see that I have drawn not only from Luksa's book but from several other classics of the genre that came to light after 1991, most of them available only in Lithuanian. These include, but are not limited to, the following: *Daugel Krito Sunu* by Adolfas Ramanauskas (code-named Vanagas), *Sita Paimkite Gyva* by Povilas Peciulaitis (code-named Lakstingala), *Pavarges Herojus* by Liutas Mockunas, and *Partizano Dzuko Dienorastis* by Lionginas Baliukevicius (code-named Dzukas). Another valuable resource was Roger D. Petersen's *Resistance and Rebellion*, an excellent study of partisan support structures in a typical Lithuanian village. There are now many, many other books about the partisans. An excellent new study of the partisans in Eastern Europe appeared just as I was proofreading this novel, too late to have an impact but too important to leave unmentioned: *The Soviet Counterinsurgency in the Western Borderlands* by Alexander Statiev. Another important background history to the partisan movement is Timothy Snyder's *Bloodlands*.

I should add that a certain number of accusations against the partisans do exist, holding that they were all simply bandits or fascist criminals, but I have found no documented evidence of large-scale crimes. However, there is no doubt there were partisans who went bad. Some were executed after court martial. As far as I can tell, the broad accusations against the partisans as a whole are based on a Soviet piece of disinformation called *Vanagai is Anapus* [Hawks from the Other Side], published in 1960. This novel depicts all the historical partisans and their supporters as criminals, cynics or fools. Although no one who reads this mass market–style novel could take it seriously, some of the accusations in it seem to have lingered right up to the present, demonstrating that any story, even a bad one, can have an afterlife.

Thanks: above all to Snaige, who was a supportive and intelligent reader during the tumultuous period of a few highs and numerous lows during which this novel was being written; and to my sons, Dainius and Gint, who were valuable sounding boards. Thanks as well to Anne McDermid, my agent, who continued to believe in this project; to Patrick Crean of Thomas Allen, whose enthusiasm for the novel was exhilarating; to Janice Zawerbny, whose insight into its structure was critical to its successful completion; to my first readers and critics, Joe Kertes, Wayson Choy, Madeleine Matte, Charlotte Empey and Nathan Whitlock; to the Canada Council, whose funding helped cover my research trips; and to two surviving partisans who told me the details of their lives as well as their sufferings in prison—Juozas Jakavonis (code-named Tigras, who should have been there for the seizure of Merkine but narrowly missed the event) and Tekle Kalvinskiene, on whose father's farm on the Polish side of the border many partisans, including Juozas Luksa, took refuge.

Thanks to in-country helpers and advisers Dr. Arvydas Anusauskas and Darius Ross; and to all the following, in no particular order, though with great love and appreciation for their kindness: Saulius and Silva Sondeckis, Antanas and Danule Sipaila, Jonas Jurasas and Ausra Marija Sluckaite-Jurasiene, Giedrius Subacius, Neringa Klumbyt, Leonidas Donskis, Violeta Kelertiene, Darius Kuolys, Paulius Sondeckis, Justinas Sajauskas, Stasys Stacevicius, Aldona Raugalaite, Grazina Siauciunas, Egle Jurkeviciene and Habib Massoud (of the office of the Canadian embassy in Lithuania), Genius Procuta, Richard Handler, John Bentley Mays, Wodek Szemberg, Monica Pacheco, Laimonas Briedis, Milda Danyte, Ruta Slapkauskaite, Daiva Mikalonyte, Egidijus Aleksandravicius, Algis Mickunas, Jurate Visockaite, Birute Garbaravicius, Arturas Petronis, Algis Ruksenas, Vilis Normanas and Gitana Judvytyte.